PRAISE FOR *Tears of*

"*Tears of the Trufflepig* is the most engagingly original novel I've read in years. So phantasmagoric, fearlessly out there, and yet it feels like a revelation, piercingly true to gritty human experience and as wild as anything you might sense lurking in the borderland night. It's the borderland speaking to you, a tale told from the future by the wiliest, funniest, most battle-scarred *cabrón* in the cantina."

—FRANCISCO GOLDMAN, author of *The Interior Circuit: A Mexico City Chronicle*

"*Tears of the Trufflepig* is one of the most thrilling novels I've read in ages, a true wild original. By turns a surreal page-turner, a send-up of the consolidation of wealth, and an excavation of life on the border, this novel doesn't bend genre: it explodes the precedents and creates something completely new. Fernando A. Flores is the kind of writer who will reinvigorate your faith in the power of literature."

—LAURA VAN DEN BERG, author of *The Third Hotel*

"Fernando A. Flores has created a world that looks a lot like ours, but without the fat, without the self-complacency, and without the shadows that impede us from seeing the universal drama happening before our eyes. *Tears of the Trufflepig* is a beautiful story about the struggle between the profane and the sacred and what we can do about it."

—YURI HERRERA, author of *Signs Preceding the End of the World*

"Dear reader, do you want to experience something wonderfully new, something dizzyingly wild, something utterly strange? Do you want to discover an imagination of beauty and humor and horror and majesty? Do you want to see the world afresh? If so, then Fernando A. Flores is for you. I know, for I have met the Trufflepig and I shall never be the same again."

—EDWARD CAREY, author of *Little*

"I started to think this book was Juan Rulfo meets Philip K. Dick. But Fernando A. Flores smacked me in the head. He sidesteps clichés and expectations. We expect magical realism in a Latino novel as we have come to expect dystopian stories in a sci-fi novel, but his audacity is to ignore all expectations and shoot the moon in any way he chooses. *Tears of the Trufflepig* is thrilling. Flores has created his own genre."

—LUIS ALBERTO URREA, author of *The House of Broken Angels*

"Fernando A. Flores's wonderfully weird, myth-making *Tears of the Trufflepig* brings us to that hot land of absurdity—the U.S.-Mexico border—all the while stretching ideas of family, fantasy, and the fictions that create us. Flores is funny and fierce and not to be forgotten."

—SAMANTHA HUNT, author of *The Dark Dark*

"With his striking debut novel, Fernando A. Flores has refashioned a world I thought I knew—the Valley, Texas, the strange alchemy of life on a border—into a grotesque yet familiar fever dream. His imagined future captures the truth of our uncanny now with frightening accuracy. Funny and tragic and ultimately compelling, *Tears of the Trufflepig* is a gorgeous and unsettling read."

—MANUEL GONZALES, author of *The Regional Office Is Under Attack!*

"In *Tears of the Trufflepig*, the metaphor and actuality of the borderlands shimmer together into a vision of haptic, granular, and superbly controlled, convincing reality. A deep dream. A clear-eyed hallucination. Studded with the sweet delayed snap of the nonchalant reveal, cunning details of new worlds—demimondes, hellscapes, mythic lands—bloom naturally from scene to scene. Fernando A. Flores writes like a hard-boiled psychotropic angel."

—EUGENE LIM, author of *Dear Cyborgs*

"Funny, futuristic, phenomenal, Fernando A. Flores is from another galaxy. Fasten your seat belt. You are in for a stupendous ride."

—SANDRA CISNEROS, author of *The House on Mango Street*

ERIC MORALES

Fernando A. Flores

TEARS OF THE TRUFFLEPIG

Fernando A. Flores was born in Reynosa, Tamaulipas, Mexico, and grew up in South Texas.

ALSO BY FERNANDO A. FLORES

Death to the Bullshit Artists of South Texas

TEARS OF THE TRUFFLEPIG

FERNANDO A. FLORES

TEARS OF THE TRUFFLE-PIG

MCD × FSG ORIGINALS
FARRAR, STRAUS AND GIROUX NEW YORK

MCD × FSG Originals
Farrar, Straus and Giroux
175 Varick Street, New York 10014

Printed in the United States of America
First edition, 2019

Library of Congress Cataloging-in-Publication Data
Names: Flores, Fernando A., 1982– author.
Title: Tears of the trufflepig / Fernando A. Flores.
Description: First edition. | New York : Farrar, Straus and Giroux, MCD × FSG Originals, 2019.
Identifiers: LCCN 2018044001 | ISBN 9780374538330 (pbk.)
Subjects: GSAFD: Fantasy fiction.
Classification: LCC PS3606.L5886 T43 2019 | DDC 813/.6—dc23
LC record available at https://lccn.loc.gov/2018044001

Designed by Abby Kagan

1 3 5 7 9 10 8 6 4 2

This work was made possible with a 2014 literary grant from the Alfredo Cisneros Del Moral Foundation.

For all the disappeared

What will you do, Don Nicanor,
In a heaven where no horses run,
Where there is no debt, no stake, no score?

—JORGE LUIS BORGES

PART 1

ONE

BELLACOSA WALKED CAREFULLY OVER THE ROTTING planks, unsure if this was the shack where he was born. Its roof was missing, and he looked up at the aluminum sky. It hadn't caved in, so he figured some South Texas zephyr galloped away with it. He stomped down hard and fine orange dust lifted and formed a ghost in his own image, eager to dance or play cards, then sank back down into the cracks. He lit a Herzegovina Flor cigarette and murmured, "Somebody out there isn't doing their job," noticing he'd dirtied his authentic, ostrich-knee Wingham dress shoes. He tried to imagine what the place could've looked like all those decades ago—where his mother gave birth, what the hustling midwife looked like, where his father stood wringing his hat. The shack was small, as he'd expected. He didn't know why, but he thought there'd be no floor. The planks surprised him.

He walked out of the threshold as if emerging from quicksand and smoked the rest of the Herzegovina Flor by his old Jeep, admiring the cavity structure on the dry, barren farmland. The sky was different than it appeared from inside, giving the impression time had never changed in the shack, and the rooms where we are born keep giving birth to us forever. The sun was rising. It was a roosterless dawn, in the part of South Texas where no beast yawned.

The old Jeep sped down the even older military surplus road. It had one of those stereos with the knobs and the needle, and quietly a *corrido* sang to Bellacosa, *"Y llegaron Noviembre, y Diciembre, y Enero, Febrero, Marzo, y Abril."*

He was doubtful now that that had been the shack, and as the pavement ended and the old Jeep hit the powdery road Bellacosa slowed down, feeling strangely relieved that his birthplace was still a mystery to him.

A few days prior, when he learned he'd have to make the drive to Calantula County, Bellacosa stopped by the records office for a copy of his birth certificate. His parents had been migrant workers and Bellacosa was the only of their two sons to be born in America, for which he felt grateful. Though he'd always been poorer than his brother, Oswaldo, down in Mexico, he could still cross back and forth without too many problems, and in his line of work this came in handy. Bellacosa was a widower trying to pull himself out of debt, but he never felt that he lacked for anything. He'd learned, unlike many people in South Texas, not to curse God for his problems, for his deep losses. *All my grievances and disgraces have been my own,* he'd say, *and it's the divine spirit that throws me bones now and then.*

Bellacosa arrived at the McMasters property on time, 7:30 a.m. He parked by the doghouse-sized mailbox on the edge of the property, turned off the old Jeep, and waited for the cloud of dust from the road to pass by. Bellacosa knew he'd have to talk to the Aranaña Indian farmer who cared for the land, and he was ready. He had no problem talking to these working Aranaña Indians. A lot of people now did, because of the stigma from the syndicates and shrunken heads, the filtering of animals. But it was all an accident. *It wasn't these people's faults, these fucking Indians,* he thought. *After all, I'm a fucking Indian, we are all fucking Indians in the Valley. That's why we're here. And what the hell is a Mexican Indian, a mistake. Columbus thought he landed in India somewhere, so that's what he called all these Mexicans. Fuck Columbus. Fuck the Indians. I'm an Indian, too. Fuck me.*

Bellacosa got out of the old Jeep and climbed an embankment of dry ferns onto the property. There were moaning whirlwind pillars and tufts of raisin-eyed, pockmarked chickens clucking around. Before even saying a word to anybody, Bellacosa was already exhausted from the encounter he was about to have. He looked around for the 7900 Rig—what construction people call *La Mano de Chango,* and what the Americans call "the Claw," a machine used to dig up large holes in the ground. He spotted the giant yellow bastard out back, moping, wanting to hug the ground like a friendless drunk with its one mechanical claw. It was nearby a tiny green trailer, where the farmer presumably lived, and about fifty feet to its left was a carpet of grain and feathers, boards nailed together like small bleachers, and a short, dry trough. It was the chicken coop, apparently, but the chicken wire that kept it together was missing. Markings on the thirsty ground outlined the coop about twenty-five by twelve feet, and standing on the feathers and grain, waving a denim hat around, was the farmer.

"You're the one about the machine?" the man yelled at Bellacosa, in his high, singsong, campesino Spanish.

"I am. You Tranquilino?"

"Here to serve you. It's just that this wind in the middle of the night, it took away the roof and the fences of my chickens. *Mire nomás.*" Tranquilino sighed. "The ground here is so dry the posts in every corner came off like toothpicks. My wife woke me, she thought the wind would take our little trailer, too. I'm a heavy sleeper since I don't get much sleep, and when I woke everything was shaking, and the chickens were making a racket like they're being attacked by coyotes like when I was a boy, *y ayayay.*"

Tranquilino pointed with his hat to an old black van propped on cinder blocks at the other side of the property, with chicken wire mounted where the doors ought to be, under a mesquite tree hunched like the Hermit in the tarot. Installing the chicken wire was a boy no older than seven dressed like a barefoot basketball player, with taut and rugged features brown like the sun, his small hands pinching and twisting the wire using needle-nose pliers.

"I have my son Matador making a temporary coop out of my old van, where I lived as a bachelor. That *pinche* van gave me nothing but trouble. Maybe the chickens will have something else to say about it, we are giving it a chance with them." Tranquilino squinted his eyes as if Bellacosa refracted light, then put his denim hat back on his balding head.

"So you just here for *La Mano de Chango*? Still runs well. I turn it on once a week and move it so it won't expire. Just like everything else here expired. After the land expired first. You know, right before you got here I was standing there thinking the chicken coop flying away serves me right. It reminded me that it was me who let this land expire. Doesn't look like much now, but that is my fault. I let it get this way." Bellacosa looked around at the bones of the land as he listened to the farmer, and for a moment wondered if it still had running water underground.

"The *jefe* McMasters instructed me to let the crop die some time back. It was fine by me. To this day he still pays me to look after this land. Mr. McMasters no longer wanted to farm and distribute naturally grown onions since his company makes them now the filtering way much faster. But I could have continued maintaining the land myself without a problem. After all, I'm still living here. I could have found buyers for the onions, because people always want food that is grown organically. But I didn't bother in those days, and everything died. Now the land has gone bad and nothing will grow. So after my son finishes, and all these chickens are put away, and you get what you came for, I'm gassing the tractor. My family and me will bring this land back to life. It's what needs to happen."

Tranquilino motioned Bellacosa to follow him. Bellacosa checked the time. It hadn't been two hours since his last smoke, but he was on an empty stomach. He plucked out a Herzegovina Flor, offered one to Tranquilino.

"*No, gracias,*" Tranquilino said, pointing at a pile of bloody, pale leaves on the ground. Thick blood appeared to be slowly trickling away from its center, like organized army ants leaving their nest. Pinching the cigarette with his lips, Bellacosa took a good look: They were bright red ants, yes, the size of sunflower seeds, crawling all over a dead, twisted chicken. The ants were slowly carrying the chicken away.

"They are dragging the dead away like the *calaveras del diablo*. It is because of these ants my coop flew away, you see. Listen," Tranquilino said, looking around. "Can you hear all that racket? That's the company working for McMasters now drilling for something way over beyond that field of mesquite. They are in business with the government, I think. They must be drilling for gases or petroleum for the economy. We have been getting a lot of big ants here, because with the drilling they are driving them away. Now here they are all over this property. You think there is nothing under us but a world of ants now, with all the drilling?"

Bellacosa held the cigarette between two fingers like a pen and carefully surveyed the property. Everywhere he looked, there were veins of army ants draining the land itself of blood from right under them. The dried field where the onions had once grown was cracked, pallid, and tubercular. Through his peripheral vision Bellacosa thought he saw the earth shifting, felt like it was being encircled by an invisible army. It bothered him how confidently the ants carried that dead chicken, and whereas earlier he was confused as to why the farmer hadn't stopped them, now he understood. Death was the order of the day.

Bellacosa was impatient to talk business and said, "I don't know anything about the habits of army ants. So, the machine works?"

"It works. You want me to start it for you?"

Tranquilino mounted the lonely yellow beast and started it up, moved the claw on the hydraulic up and down and side to side, then tilted the claw as if about to take a bite of the ground. Bellacosa was thankful and, satisfied, clapped his hands. As Tranquilino climbed down the rig muttering to himself, Bellacosa saw that the man barely had any teeth. He was dirty and everything about him should have smelled like sweat and squalor, but Bellacosa admired Tranquilino's composure, bordering on nonchalance.

"I'm calling a company to pick up this machine tomorrow and I'll call your *jefe* Mr. McMasters at his office to get the transaction rolling," Bellacosa announced. "The people picking it up for me will ask for a signature."

"Oh, no, I never sign anything," Tranquilino said, waving with his hands.

"Okay, then I'll figure something out."

"Do what you need. McMasters and his men just came and left that thing anyway. Nobody uses it."

The chickens around the land looked brain-dead and hobbled about, pecking at pebbles and clumps of dirt off the ground. They looked as if they'd already been fried and digested, imitating the people who would consume them. Occasionally a gust of wind would frighten them and their wings fluttered; feathers would dart out like the nine of clubs or five of hearts in a card game gone bad.

Bellacosa noticed his left thumbnail was longer than the other fingernails on that hand, like he was a guitar picker. In his mounting anxiety he dug his index finger under the nail, then lit another Herzegovina Flor. Tranquilino suddenly looked very familiar to Bellacosa, as if he'd been a friend in a distant dream.

"All of this on this wacko day," Tranquilino said. "Have you listened to the news already? The police in Mexico found El Gordo Pacheco, dead. His ostriches ate him up. They killed him and his entire family. Can you believe that?" He laughed. "El Gordo Pacheco, he was a bad man to the end, you know. He had all the birds he could ever want, only to be killed by real ostriches. They ate him and his entire family. This powerful, rich person, the king of Sindicato Casablanca. Look at that now, you know, with the ants and the chickens, and the ostriches of El Gordo Pacheco. It's the earth finding ways to fight back. That's why I need to continue cultivating this land, to please the laws of nature so the ants don't come for my family next. I need to tell the *jefe* McMasters this." Tranquilino removed his hat. He held it in his hand like a large compass, or a magic eight ball. "Doesn't matter if natural onions are no longer a moneymaking business, it is still good land, and we need to continue working it."

As Bellacosa processed this news about the untouchable Pacheco, Tranquilino's son had finished turning the van into a chicken coop and was going around grabbing each pockmarked chicken to crowd it inside.

Bellacosa found this a bit bleak, and he mentioned to the man and his son that it'd be better to let the chickens run free. Tranquilino protested, telling him that he couldn't lose the rest of the chickens.

"But there's nothing around for miles," replied Bellacosa. "Where would they go?"

"Still," Tranquilino said. "I can't lose the rest of the chickens. As a human being, I can't lose the rest of them."

Bellacosa, slightly dismayed, shook Tranquilino's calloused hand and as he walked away watched him and his barefoot son in the basketball jersey pluck chickens from the ground and stuff them into the van. He thought he saw a plump purple one sitting on the steering wheel.

From inside the old Jeep he heard the horn of the van honk and saw a flutter of feathers fly upward like hats at a graduation ceremony. But Bellacosa was thinking about the red army ants now. *What are they doing down there? How many can there possibly be?*

TWO

AS LONG AS IT'S ONLY MEN THAT ARE OUR PROBLEM, NOT diseases, Bellacosa thought. *As long as it's only men who are the diseases. Men we can get rid of. With diseases you're in the doctor's hands and it's over. A doctor is just a different kind of killer. Hospitals and me, never again. Had enough hospitals when they took my daughter, then when they took Lupita,* que en paz descansen mis mujeres. *Me, when it's my time, I will go standing up. Walking in the middle of the street in the sunlight, the divine switch will be flipped, and that will be that.*

Rodrigo Esparza, a great friend of Bellacosa's for many years, was only forty-six when he suffered a heart attack. Nothing brought him back; he died instantly. *Young guy, what a shame; but lucky bastard, too,* Bellacosa thought. *His kids were still in school, though, and his wife didn't work.*

Pobre señora. *Varo Sanchez, he's gone, died in an expressway car wreck on the way back from the beach with his wife, they both died when the paramedics arrived. The ones still around are either limping, diseased, or missing their teeth. Me,* gracias a Dios, *I'm not limping, am healthy, and have almost all my teeth, though at times they've given me trouble and Oswaldo's checked them out.*

Bellacosa phoned his client Don Villaseñor, who was visiting his offices in Piedras Negras, Mexico, and gave him the good news, that he'd found the 7900 Rig faster than he'd anticipated. Don Villaseñor expressed his gratitude and reminded Bellacosa he was his favorite freelance scout for his construction company, even told him he was the best in all of Texas. Don Villaseñor was in a hurry, so he gave Bellacosa a seventeen-digit transfer code, which he sloppily jotted down, to pick up fifteen thousand dollars in cash at the small bank built into Tin Can Spur Truck Stop in order to purchase the rig from McMasters.

Relieved now that he'd advanced to the next step of the deal, with money coming his way, Bellacosa told himself it was time for breakfast. He drove downtown, found a good spot to park around the corner from Baby Grand Central.

It was a calm hour of day, and Bellacosa jaywalked across Broadway along with *el elotero,* the man who sold roasted corn out of his shoddily painted purple pushcart. In the barrow of the cart, covered with many thick blankets, the man kept the plastic ice chest filled with the piping hot roasted corn, next to the skewers and homemade hot sauce in tin containers.

"*Qué fue, señor,*" the *elotero* said to Bellacosa, "you hear the news about El Comisario?"

"Who?"

"*Pues nuestro señor* Pacheco. He can rest in peace now, no longer living his life evading the law. Who knows why we do the things we do on this earth. Now that he's no longer with us nobody will know the real truth of his story."

A couple of young businessmen in shades approached the *elotero*, each signaling with dollar bills for roasted corn. The *elotero* parked his pushcart along the curb and began peeling away the layers of blankets in the ice chest as Bellacosa walked toward Baby Grand Central.

In its early days Baby Grand Central was Centro Bautista, the first open-air market you encountered after crossing the Rio Grande from Mexico into the United States. It was a place to trade grains and buy produce, tobacco, European snuff, and thick comforters with imprints of exotic animals, like lions and panda bears. Since then, the largest city in South Texas—MacArthur—sprouted around, the land got taken over, sold, buildings started shooting to the sky, and Baby Grand Central got its Americanized name, along with a concrete floor covered by a roof. Its tall arches on both sides of the city block each faced a different street downtown and inside it was filled with little shops. By night Baby Grand Central was a questionable hangout, but during the day Bellacosa's favorite place to grab a bite was always open: Marselita's, a small restaurant with furniture in the style of an old diner out of an Edward Hopper painting.

He walked through the arches facing Broadway and passed the magazine pushers and fruit-cup vendors, passed the lady who sold stockings and handmade change purses, passed El Rey de los Churros, La Reyna del Taco, and finally sat along the yellow counter at Marselita's. It was already past lunch, a slow hour, the way he liked it. A young woman whom he'd joked with before was the server, and Bellacosa saluted the Poblano, Julio, working the kitchen alone in the back. He liked both these people.

"Can the cook score me some good fish soup? That's spicy, and however else he wants to make it?"

The young woman walked to the back and handed the cook a guest check scribbled with purple ink and whispered the special instructions, gesturing with her smoky-quartz eyes in Bellacosa's direction.

She brought him water, a cup of coffee, and an ashtray. Though the rule was No Smoking at Baby Grand Central, Bellacosa was there often enough that they made an exception.

Sitting at the other end of the yellow counter he saw the man he called Tcheco. The past couple of weeks, more often than not, he ran into him at Marselita's. Bellacosa didn't know if the man was really Czech, but he carried a strange dialect, and Bellacosa had never caught his real name. He guessed the man wasn't older than thirty-five, but the dark circles around his eyes revealed he'd seen his share of long nights. Suspicious to make new acquaintances, especially at Baby Grand Central, Bellacosa was reluctant to speak to him at first, but in time got sucked into the ridiculous—usually political—things Tcheco always said. Bellacosa fancied Tcheco to be some kind of writer or pimp or pusher of filtered fur.

Tcheco waved the day's edition of *The Bugle of Plenty* in the air. Bellacosa signaled him over, remembering the improbable story of El Gordo Pacheco's death from the old farmer Tranquilino. Tcheco wore wrinkled trousers and a short-sleeved blue shirt, tucked in, with a brown aviator jacket, and sat on the stool by Bellacosa as the server refilled his coffee.

Bellacosa took the paper and skimmed through the article about the kingpin of Sindicato Casablanca for the basic facts. It was true. What the paper said was more or less what Tranquilino had described.

Tcheco said, "He brought back the dodo bird, and for what? To find out it was just a stupid bird. Remember reading the book *The Island of Doctor Moreau*, when you were a boy? They had it around way back then, too, right? By . . . how do you say? A-che, Heh, Wells? The machine that Moreau invented, that operated on you and turned beasts into men? Gave beasts human characteristics and way deeper tragedies?" Tcheco tapped on the table in a manner that didn't make any sound.

"Well, here now, we no longer need machines, vivisection, or whatever it's called. Here, we watch men just naturally become beasts. It's no miracle of science, either. Maybe a miracle of nature. We see people every day just turn into beasts. Exceptions get more and more rare by the day, exceptions like you and me, Bellacosa." He stared at Bellacosa and for a moment was silent.

"I can tell you'd never hurt a fly. How can I tell? Because you're constantly being dicked over by these so-called Valley businessmen. But it's okay, it's not your business, it's theirs. Their only business is fucking anybody over for a dime or a pig's fine fuck. Money is just a game to them. But this is the world we're in, where men don't need machines to turn into savages, into beasts. You know what the conquistadors from the 1500s would call us, if they walked in here right now and saw all of us, you and me included, here in Baby Grand? If it was Pizarro, or Cabeza de Vaca, who walked in? Bare-asses. They'd call us bare-asses, and they'd be right. Maybe the machine that needs to be invented now is a machine that lets all men and women keep being humans, and not become beasts. That would be quite a scientific achievement. A machine that would let people maintain their human dignities, that won't let them succumb to barbarism." Tcheco looked up at a mossy cloud of grease smoke that shot up from the grill at La Reyna del Taco, followed it with his eyes until it dissolved.

"Do I sound pessimistic, Bellacosa? I don't mean to be. I'm an optimist, facing the facts head-on. I'll let you eat in peace. Keep the paper. I'm on my way out, anyway."

Tcheco knocked twice on the counter, got up, and waited for the waitress to notice him leaving. He waved to her as he walked away, almost bumping into a stout old woman carrying a bucket of corn tortillas wrapped by the kilo.

Bellacosa looked down at his bowl of soup like it was a steaming tortoise on its back.

Halfway through the meal, and having thoroughly read the article, Bellacosa lifted the paper so the waitress could wipe the spot where Tcheco had sat. "You think that was really El Gordo Pacheco that was killed?" she said. "It wasn't. It was a double he paid to look like him. They said he had not only one, but several doubles, to pose as him and members of his family, so people could think they are dead and they can escape all that crime to just live normal lives."

"You believe that?"

"Why not?"

"Who said all this?" Bellacosa asked, then sipped his water.

"Everybody that's passed through here today, pretty much. It's the only thing people want to talk about."

"What about you? What do you want to talk about?"

She finished wiping the counter and smiled, but not in a flirtatious manner.

"How's the soup? Is it spicy like you wanted?"

"Served me just fine, thank you. Here's my money. Keep

the change. Don't listen to every cologned, shaved face that stops in here flashing his belt buckle, *jovencita.*"

Outside, the woman who sold white roses and sang as her husband played the accordion winked at Bellacosa. He dropped a couple of crisp dollars into a hollowed-out Bible on the ground and declined a white rose from her. A purple lowrider then parked along the curb blasting a West Coast rap number, the speakers thumping:

> *Goodbye drones*
> *Rainin' down*
> *Lemme teach ya a thing*
> *Or two about flyin'.*

AMONG THE LIES and exaggerations, these were some of the facts Bellacosa had picked up over the years concerning Galdino "El Gordo" Pacheco, alias Motita, alias El Turco, alias El Mochadedos:

Born in the mountains of Michoacán to a poor farmer and Cuna Indian mother, Pacheco never attends school nor learns to read or write. When he is nine, Pacheco's eldest sister is raped and sent home naked, bruised, and bleeding, by the rapist. The following year, Pacheco guns down the accused, Pablo Molina, at a party, then flees to the northern border, and nobody in his family hears from him for many years. While living in Tijuana, Pacheco works as a window washer and runs errands for local pimps and dealers. As he gets older he climbs the ladder of command, after many bodies, many shifts in gangland power. Shortly after the year of the world food shortage, which killed off a fifth of the world's population, and the legalization of drugs in the west, with the old kingpins either dead, in jail, or in cahoots with the feds, Pacheco is informed of the 4th Annual Filtering Sciences Summit being held in Guatemala.

In the wake of the food shortage, "filtering"—the artificial production of an organic substance—had been explored to speed up the growth not only of fruits and vegetables but also of animals for corporate farming. In a moment of imagination, the way some people have mystical visions, or feel the echoes of imminent doom, he sees the entire future of a new trade unfold in a matter of seconds. Pacheco rents a plane, hires a pilot, and cuts in a couple of men he trusts to fly to Guatemala City. On the third day of the conference, Pacheco and his hired muscle kidnap the scientists Dr. Henrik Rosokhovatsky, Dr. Anatoly Parnov, and the renowned American Dr. Ian Barraclough, all of whom speak fluent Spanish. They are taken as hostages to the rural mountains of Nuevo León, where in a matter of months, through extortion, kidnapping, and infiltrating the underground art market, selling indigenous artifacts and relics to collectors at top dollar, Pacheco finances a lab featuring the most advanced filtering equipment in the Western Hemisphere to perfect their science.

He gains the reputation of treating his scientists humanely, even making sure their families are taken care of financially. The first non-farm animal the scientists are able to filter using "the method" is the ivory-billed parakeet, to compensate for the crackdown on elephant poaching. The parakeets reach full maturation in the third week after their gestation period, hit old age by the seventh week, and meet their death by the eighth. The scientists are able to produce two parakeets a day, then five, then seven, and as more and more student scientists are kidnapped and trained, the filtering of ivory-billed parakeets grows up to thirty a day. They are maintained in several indoor aviaries adjoined to the filtering facility, separated according to developmental stage, and in their fourth week of artificial life, when their ivory bills are tested to be at their richest, Pacheco has his goons slice the beaks off and collect them. Accounts of how this was accomplished vary, with some saying the goons shot down the screeching birds first, or that they were gassed, all while wearing earplugs because the shrieks led some men to temporary fits of madness. The ivory then is polished at a separate facility and sold on the Turkish black market, used mostly to create bombshells for terrorists or molded into high-end dentures and fillings.

Pacheco sees a quick profit, and his team of scientist-hostages, under the duress of being held against their will, inevitably discard the humanitarian aspect of their endeavor. Secluded from the world and watched by Pacheco's private army of unstable renegades, the scientists go on to duplicate and filter a variety of animals classified as extinct, all smuggled out of the country and sold to rich collectors and enthusiasts, bored and eager to show off their wealth. Now into his thirties, Pacheco marries a young beauty queen who gives birth to twin boys. Then his dark partnership with the scientists goes south. Some say Pacheco grows distrustful and paranoid, overly self-conscious of his lack of education in the face of the scientists. He has his renegades cut the thumbs and big toes off every scientist in his fortress facility and mails the severed appendages to each of their families. When twenty-three of the greatest young scientific minds according to *Harvard Medical Journal* are found in a mass grave in Culiacán, the Mexican military, with the assistance of the United States, locates and busts into Pacheco's compound in the middle of the night.

He gives himself up without a fight, asks that his wife and boys be taken safely. He is sentenced to Gallegos Penitentiary in Tabasco, where it is rumored that within a year Pacheco has every prisoner, guard, even the warden paid off and under his control. It is also no secret Pacheco still has a clandestine filtering lab running out of somewhere, making him richer by the day. Men in prison later enjoy telling anecdotes of Pacheco boasting of his ability to handle Kolokkan dragons, that he is the only living Mexican to have felt resting on his arm a mature Guadalupe caracara bird, and stroked the feathers of a rainbow macaw. After his escape from prison, in a truck supposedly delivering food for the inmates, Pacheco becomes a living legend, and the subject of many *corridos*, groups singing of the filtered animals attributed to him, sometimes satirically, but always with respect. A popular one goes:

Come frijoles de panda
Y huevos de di-no-saurio
Se traga el água del mar
Y le dicen el co-mi-sario.

Pacheco becomes a ghost. He makes the FBI's Ten Most Wanted list, and is the thirty-ninth-richest man in the world according to *Forbes* magazine. Defending himself, in his only recorded public statement, given via speakerphone in the editor's office of the newspaper *La Jornada*, Galdino Pacheco claims, "I am a man who deals in commodities. Given the right price, I'll let you have whatever dead animal you'd like, and keep it for as long as it lives. This is a luxury. It doesn't matter how long the animals are alive, when they are here they are perfect. Like you and me. Now, you say that I don't have a heart, that I don't care if the animals die very quickly. But if not for me, you could never have it. There in your hands. Now that is a luxury. And above all, I am a provider for my family and for others. I give well-paying jobs to men, something this country has promised and never delivered.

I have the biggest heart. As far as the government, they're all hypocrites. And anybody thinking that because the government legalized drugs that they have all become saints is dreaming."

He never admits to resurrecting the silver-coated moonfox and killing the species in large numbers for its fur, to be sold to unscrupulous clothing designers, or the onyx mountain bear for the same purpose. To this day, mass graves of their furless, decomposed carcasses are found.

Meanwhile, dedicating one's life to ending world hunger through the filtering sciences starts coming with a hazard factor. The Pacheco factor. Students and professors from all over go missing, presumably taken by Pacheco's men or the steadily growing rival syndicates. Changes in harvesting and trade laws go into effect; the filtering of any animal for profit becomes a big case for lobbyists and inspires worldwide activism. The filtering summits are discontinued after their seventh year. Perceptions on what defines a living being shift, definitions change, and it is agreed by world leaders through international laws that the filtering sciences can only be used to harvest vegetables and fruit, and no human has the right to play God.

Pacheco's myth gets out of hand throughout his years on the lam. One famous account has him dining in an expensive restaurant called El Pariente Norteño, in the Mexican state of Durango. Thirty of his men, armed with shotguns and automatic weapons, burst in and announce that nobody can leave or enter the restaurant, that phone devices will be confiscated, and that El Comisario Pacheco will have dinner among them. He will also feed everyone with his preferred meal, a glass of the most expensive wine in the house will be provided, and the tabs will be taken care of afterward.

Pacheco walks table to table, introducing himself to everybody like a rich distant relative, then secludes himself in the back corner of El Pariente Norteño. His own cooks take over the kitchen and in no time prepare a dish called Galapagos Gumbo, which includes the extinct king conch tortoise, healer greasefish, and rainbow trout, served in the actual tortoise shell, which everybody is free to take as a souvenir. Later, it is reluctantly described by many as a divine dish, an elixir that opens pores and mental faculties. Around the same time, in the Yucatán Peninsula, patrons at El Cielo Marino are treated to a similar experience, where they are served sautéed Vietnamese panda chops with steamed vegetables and fried heath hen gizzards with peach vinaigrette as an appetizer. Pacheco's contribution to the dark sciences matches only his contribution to the black-market culinary world.

But the dog-eat-dog rivalries he's perpetuated his entire life start closing in on him. He knows it, feels trapped, and can't get out of this self-induced whirlpool. The underground market of exotic furs and animal commodities that has built his empire, and opened new levels of violence in northern Mexico and the United States, turns over drastically. Rival syndicates that once specialized as head-hunters for the European art market start leaning toward the filtering sciences, growing more and more ruthless in their treatment of the scientists, their disposed animals, and anybody who gets in their way. The three contending syndicates—Los Mil Condes, Sindicato Unidos, Los Pacificos—cut limbs, sever heads and skin, maim, torture, pimp, rape, burn, pillage, steal, and counterfeit all to gain control over the filtering empire Pacheco and Sindicato Casablanca ruled over.

If there is a savage in all of this, however, Pacheco comes to accept that it is himself. Toward the end of his life, he develops into a collector of real, exotic animals, almost as a way to remind himself that creatures are meant to live long, happy lives. He buys elephants native to Indonesia and tigers from Thailand, and owns the last flock of the same hyacinth ostriches that go on to kill and consume Pacheco himself, his twin boys, and his loyal, remaining men. Pacheco's island gets discovered accidentally by a private vessel, as if the dead are calling, yearning to be found. Some hyacinth ostriches are found bullet-ridden, and the remaining flock have taken over the secluded compound, along with other wild animals and birds. It is a mystery to the officials how everything occurred. Through DNA testing, Pacheco's body is identified. His boys were picked to the marrow; the only rotting skin left of their remains hangs from their eyes and mouths. His young beauty-queen wife had locked herself in a closet and her naturally decomposed body was the last to be found and identified, the autopsy inconclusive thus far. The end came tragically, melting like a cheap Milky Way galaxy, for Galdino "El Gordo" Pacheco, alias Motita, alias El Turco, alias El Mochadedos.

THREE

BELLACOSA ALWAYS TRAVELED WITH HIS SHOESHINE KIT—*el cajón de bolear*—containing a horsehair brush, Martinique sponge, and the Nightflight polish that matched the two pairs of shoes he wore most. Though he showered every morning, he could be sweating and stinking and having a hell-ride, but as long as his shoes were polished and shiny, he felt he could accomplish anything. He combed his hair and maintained its length, but Bellacosa's only vanity was for his shoes. He tucked in the laces below the tongues, and grew ashamed for humanity when he saw a grown man with shoelaces flopping around. Downtown, on Yuca Street, where he parked the old Jeep, Bellacosa stood under the awning of the taqueria Tacon Ganas leaning against a pole, polishing his ostrich-knee Wingham shoes. He waved at the teenage waitress who stared at him with annoyance through the window, finished up, and drove away.

Bellacosa fiddled with the needle in the stereo, trying to rig up a station, until he found talk radio. The anchor was saying, ". . . we're talking about a syndicate unlike anything a Western nation had encountered before, a growing empire of evil that Pacheco, after the days of the great drug cartels, spawned, not masterminded. To say 'mastermind' would be to compliment him, but Pacheco spawned this evil on humanity and Mother Earth. Fact: twelve years ago, when Pacheco, at gunpoint with his men, kidnapped Rosokhovatsky, Barraclough, and the other Ukrainian biologist, the year their first filtering experiment lived past the fetal stage and matured the twenty-year life span in a time frame of weeks, the meaning of trafficking, something that is not drugs or bootlegging moonshine, or the hideous branch of pornography, but the—"

Bellacosa turned the needle again and found a station airing a live Glenn Gould concert in Salzburg, a recording he knew well and was fond of. He drove out to Pharr, pulled into Tin Can Spur, and in the parking lot full of eighteen-wheelers he parked next to a yellow bug by the office. A suspicious, hunched man, who looked at once old and young, was working behind the bulletproof glass of the small bank. His name tag read "Edgar." Bellacosa always felt this man rub him the wrong way. He legibly rewrote the seventeen-digit transfer code Don Villaseñor had dictated and slipped it under the glass to the scowling, hunched, boyish old man.

Bellacosa, not meaning to stick it to him, asked, "How are you doing today?"

Edgar ignored this and stared into the green phosphorescent screen of a computer, clicking on things, and on a separate, bulging keypad Bellacosa watched him plug in the numbers.

Shortly after, a whirring machine was eagerly printing, which meant the check was printing, and that the money had come through. "What a miracle it is, when the money comes through," Bellacosa whispered.

He thanked Edgar after reading the sum of fifteen thousand dollars on the check and tapping it twice on the counter. From the old Jeep, Bellacosa called the office of Mr. McMasters, the owner of the 7900 Rig in Calantula County, and told him the deal was set on his end, that the twelve thousand dollars would be in his bank account by the following morning. Bellacosa then arranged to get a driver with a flatbed at Tío Primo's Towing to haul the rig to the border, then finally dialed his client Don Villaseñor's border office so his secretary could schedule one of their own drivers to take it down the rest of the way into Piedras Negras, Mexico. The deal was rolling, and Bellacosa was excited to be making the rounds.

DEPOSITING THE CHECK, Bellacosa knew the funds would clear by nightfall, and the people at his bank assured him he had access to 30 percent of the sum immediately.

Bellacosa waited until he entered Edinburgh City to

fill the old Jeep with premium gas, and got himself a bottle of high-end drinking water, from the underground river of the volcanic island Hsi, which was also the name of the brand.

Hsi, he thought to himself, driving in the old Jeep, *like "Yes," in Spanish, because the "H" is silent. Yes.* Si. *"Yes"* en ingles, *just what the body needs, original and real water from Mother Nature. It's funny now, the biblical phrase "He turned the water into wine." You hear it a lot in those old songs from the South, too. The Bible Belt, is that what it used to be called? Either way, it makes me laugh now if I really think about it. Turning water into wine no longer impresses anybody. Any teenager with a chemistry set now can turn even gas into wine, so if the Lord were to come back he'd have to brew up a new trick to keep the party going.*

"But I know you'll say, Lupita," Bellacosa said out loud to himself, "that whereas anybody can turn water or gas into wine, it'll have to be through science, and the Lord can do anything science can but better, simply with his divine touch. I guess that is true, you got me there. The Lord, they say, had a hell of a divine touch."

On the edge of Edinburgh City and the small town Vela, Bellacosa saw another branch of his bank, walked in, and withdrew thirteen hundred sixty dollars in hundreds and twenties, which the teller gave him in a sealed bank slip after counting it out for him and the cameras.

At LuAnn's Cafeteria a few blocks down from the bank, Bellacosa ordered a cup of coffee and a slice of chocolate pecan pie called the Lloyd Sherman, and nursed all of it until 6:30 p.m., reading the copy of *The Bugle of Plenty* that Tcheco had let him keep. He tipped a fiver and thanked the server for making the coffee dark and strong.

Bellacosa left the paper on the table, though he'd circled two ads in the classifieds; one for a man in Donna who welded and sold his own grappling hooks, and another for a Thai lady who gave affordable massages specializing in bad backs.

FIFTY FEET FROM THE BORDER, Bellacosa paid for parking at the privately owned Nevarez Lot, where the keg-shaped man working the booth recognized him.

"How are things along the border today?" Bellacosa asked the man.

"It's an orange alert day, but there's no shootings and no commotion, so I would say things are pretty okay."

Bellacosa slipped him a few extra dollars and said, "Keep an eye on my Jeep, okay?"

"You got it, *hermano*."

Bellacosa parked and walked to the pedestrian side of the international bridge. The Border Protectors didn't have any tanks set up, and as Bellacosa walked to the toll booth the armed officer handed him an illustrated pamphlet warning of the current dangers in Mexico. Bellacosa paid the toll with a crisp bill and crossed the bridge that took him into Reinahermosa, the first Mexican city directly across.

Bellacosa threw the pamphlet away when he passed the

first trash bin. He noticed that the lines of cars and pedestrians crossing back into MacArthur weren't very long as he ascended the arch of the bridge to make the leap over the river and the two border walls. Halfway over the Rio Grande the fabric of the bridge changed—the Mexican half was built out of cobblestones and was slightly more vandalized. Bellacosa stopped at the bolted plaque commemorating the spot as the official divider of the two countries, and looked through the ten-foot chain-link fence along the railing, down at the river. He knew the Rio Grande naturally flowed eastward toward the gulf, but Bellacosa swore it was running the opposite way.

He watched as two children climbed the railing as high as his waist level to take a look. They were both pointing and smiling with a look of wonder Bellacosa hadn't seen in a child in so long that the sight nearly touched him, until he noticed the source of their amazement. It wasn't the water, but the two border walls, one built along the south side of the Rio Grande, the other along the north, and like two scheming sentinels they escorted the river, their dying queen, as far as the eye could see into the horizon. The look of pleasure on the children's faces made his blood harden like lava in his veins. Suddenly, against the northern border wall a few hundred yards away, a howling, tall flame sprung to life. The children clapped. Bellacosa knew it was a controlled fire for the great cane, which threatened the structural integrity of the border walls, and he continued his walk.

As he approached Mexican customs, there it was: one of the ancient giant Olmec head monuments for border crossers to see, carved to depict a long dead Olmec king. It had been a gift from a previous Mexican president to the old mayor in Reinahermosa. Its presence on the international bridge was initially a huge controversy, critics demanding its return to the south, where the Olmec people had lived.

Bellacosa laughed when he had first seen it, but now he no longer saw the humor. The wonder the border walls failed to inspire came over him like a blue shadow as he stared at the giant Olmec head. It reminded him of the shrunken heads of Indians and the syndicates that lopped heads, shrank them, and sold them to sick collectors for exorbitant prices. Bellacosa was convinced the Olmecs predicted Mexico's present reality long ago, predicted the museums and private collectors abroad paying in gold for made-to-order shrunken heads from down south, with Indians now killing other Indians for their heads, because they are left out on the margins of the modern world and have few recourses to feed their families. A price tag is now placed on every Indian's head to be mounted and encased, turned into conversation pieces at fancy cocktail parties thrown by rich, trendy circles, calling themselves aficionados of the arts and of ancient cultures.

Bellacosa got in line behind about eight people to pass through Mexican customs. He was perfectly composed, though he'd decided not to declare the American cash he was crossing over. When his turn came, the dark-skinned Mexican officers scanned Bellacosa's left palm, he got a green light, and they didn't search him. Bellacosa thanked the officers, and let out a chuckle of relief.

At 7:15, right on time, he saw a taxi painted green and red like a giant sliced watermelon. The driver was inside and the car's motor was running.

When the driver saw him approach he leaned out the open window and said, "Bellacosa? Come on," in Spanish.

Inside, as the taxi zoomed along La Zona Rosa, Bellacosa asked, "Are you Manolo Segura's friend Videncio?"

"Nah, I'm just a *taxista*. I was hired only to pick you up."

Bellacosa was confused by this reply, but somehow trusted it. They sped over potholes and a long section of unpaved, muddy road. He saw a mustard-colored two-story house with the second floor missing a big portion of the exterior walls—inside was a living room setup, and a woman breastfeeding a baby while watching a telenovela on a black-and-white replica. They passed a pharmacy with a pile of gravel next to the entrance and an old man dressed in a western shirt and trousers shoveling some of it onto a wooden wagon hitched to a station wagon vehicle. Curiously, at the soccer field, nobody was playing a game, but a group of boys ran around with bows and arrows made of sticks and strings, and Bellacosa wondered if there were others dressed like cowboys hiding in the brush. He took a good look at the driver's Japanese-style hat, his Hawaiian shirt, and listened to the voices and static from the CB radio, turned down low.

The taxi passed the abandoned San Efrén de Edessa Cathedral and Bellacosa crossed himself, telling the taxi driver, "Not a single dove on the steps of the church."

When the driver didn't reply Bellacosa felt slightly ashamed at having crossed himself. It was a subconscious Catholic gesture he'd renounced after his daughter's death, and picked back up years later when it was his wife who'd passed away.

Bellacosa then recalled what El Gordo Pacheco had said in his famous recorded statement, how he considered himself to be a man who dealt in commodities. The statement had surprised him. As a freelance buyer for these Mexican contractors and being Don Villaseñor's confidence man—the one he called when he needed a rare piece of machinery, fast—this was the way Bellacosa also described his trade. He was a man who dealt in commodities.

"Me and Pacheco," Bellacosa whispered. "We both think highly of our damned selves."

At a light he saw a newspaper vendor waving a copy of *Hoy Mismo* in the air, which documented the latest atrocities in the filtering syndicate wars. A mass grave had been found outside Reinahermosa by the mountains, and the authorities believed it contained the headless bodies of the first-year biology students from Universidad la Reforma who had gone missing the previous semester. Though DNA tests were pending, the people of Reinahermosa were at a loss as to how to react to this iniquitous, unfathomable revelation. Looking at the gruesome front-page photograph as the vendor waved it around and hollered, Bellacosa could no longer feel shocked. However, there was always a sadness in him that could unroll like a carpet of damp autumn leaves if he let his emotions wander too far into sentimentality.

Though Bellacosa had been raised in Reinahermosa, too much had changed in the decades since he'd moved away. It was the city where he learned to make a peso, where he first saw what a blue-eyed girl and an American dollar looked like. But he no longer felt the town was a part of him, more of a reflection at the bad end of a cursed looking glass, and he romanticized the old image of the city in which doves and pigeons still flapped their wings. He chewed on an energy booster pill with papaya enzymes as the driver sadistically scratched the back of his own neck and the taxi hurled over railroad tracks.

Recently, Bellacosa had discovered something slightly unsettling about himself: that he neither liked nor disliked all these Mexicans and Americans living along both sides of the border. He saw them now as one and the same people, both stale imitations of the cultures they were meant to be a part of. This revelation neither disappointed nor astonished him; it was simply how he felt. The border walls, the filtering syndicates, headless bodies of scientists, shrunken Indian heads—he felt these things were always around even before they'd materialized. It was all the continuous overflow of the tension that had been boiling for over a century along the border.

Bellacosa didn't recognize the neighborhood the taxi driver was driving him through and it was starting to get late, so he said, "*Oye*, how far out are you taking me?"

Just then the driver pulled over in a paved, abandoned parking lot under a bridge and said, "Get in the car that's on the other side."

"How much is the fare?"

"Twenty-two thousand cubic pesos, not counting the tip."

Bellacosa gave him thirty American dollars, got out. The cloudy sky grimaced like an old retiree counting change. The overhead bridge, like the parking lot below it, also appeared unused and abandoned. He climbed the cement embankment to reach the road and saw a dark sedan with Manolo Segura wearing crocodile-skin boots, leaning on the open driver's door. Manolo was smiling and looked like he'd had something greasy and covered in cheese for lunch.

They shook hands and Bellacosa, taking out his cigarettes, said, "So many theatrics. You worried someone's following us, Manolo?"

Manolo cackled, patted Bellacosa on the back a few times, and said, "What do you think we're doing here, compadre? Everybody in the police department and the syndicates could have me killed for no reason if they wanted to. What is that, the shit the Russians smoke? I'll try one, if you're offering." He took one from Bellacosa. "Come on over here, walk a little with me. I want to show you something."

Manolo led him over the abandoned bridge as he lit the cigarette with Milenio de Oro matches and soured his face upon tasting it.

Bellacosa saw broken beer bottles, crushed cans, cigarette butts, and gun shells on the empty two-lane bridge, which led to a swamp on the other side. Manolo remained silent. As they made it a fourth of the way over Manolo pointed to the ground up ahead. There were about three scores of some duck species lying motionless over the middle of the bridge. The ducks had long orange bills and dark green and gray feathers, and were dead. Their feathers hadn't been plucked, the bills weren't sawed off, nor had anybody taken their feet to make the expensive salve rich ladies paid high prices for.

Bellacosa said, "Did they just dump these birds here without taking anything?"

"They aren't decomposing either, you notice?"

"That's right. How long you think they have been dead?"

"Not sure. I discovered them here last week. So I don't know. They didn't take anything because I presume these ducks have to be real, God-made ducks. They must have been flying and something in the air or the clouds killed them."

"It doesn't stink. Even if they died a while ago it would

still have that death stink, right? That's how it is with dead things. Don't you think so?"

Manolo shrugged. "I don't know what to think. The last time I saw any birds flying through Reinahermosa must have been over five years ago. Before the filtering got bad. This means there are five-year-old kids now that have never even seen a real bird. Forget it." He turned to Bellacosa. "You brought the money with you? All thirteen hundred, in American dollars?"

Bellacosa handed him a carefully folded wad of money.

"I'll count it later, I'm not worried about it. I want you to understand that this money you're handing me here is not all for me. To score information things need to be set up, to pay off dinners and drinks and people."

"I understand. But it took a lot of looking around and hustling to get this money, Manolo. It may not be a lot of money to some people, but it's a lot to me."

"Hey," Manolo said, "I don't want you to think I'm a dishonest or greedy man. We've known each other since we were boys. I'm playing this the way it is, and that's it. Though of course a little of this money is for me, yes. It's our business, Esteban. I have good news for you, *de todos modos*. I talked to two of my guys who are deep in the syndicate network here in the city. Both of them were able to confirm that your brother, Oswaldo, is still alive. They're keeping him in a cell somewhere. I'm not sure where. Possibly I can find out. But I can't guarantee anything right now. I'm sure you've heard what happened with Pacheco? With him gone, there's this big scramble for power down here. My guys are very reliable but anything can change. You and I know how this whole network thing works: Whatever anyone says, the complete opposite is sometimes the reality."

Bellacosa was unconvinced. "And what do you think, Manolo? Seriously? As far as this being only a case for you, and not this whole money thing, with nothing of me or my brother involved. Just your professional opinion, as a detective."

"I think I would trust this lead. It's the only thing we have. These two guys, they have nothing to do with each other, and told me almost identical stories."

"What else did they say? Was there any harm brought to him?"

"They said he was badly beaten. Not terrible, but in a bad way. Everywhere except on his face. They consider him dark-complected enough to cut his head and sell it as an Aranaña shrunken head. It's the trend with Sindicato Unidos and the headhunting syndicates now, to scope out non-Indian people and kidnap them. The only reason they haven't cut his head off is because they're waiting. They've taken a special interest in your brother, almost like he's a filtering scientist. Do you have any idea why?"

"I don't know. He's just a damn dentist. He checks people's teeth for a living, has two grown boys, he's not into all this syndicate stuff. I haven't even been close to my brother in years, but I'd do anything to get him out of this. What do I do, Manolo?"

Manolo slightly kicked a dead duck using the tip of his right crocodile boot. "That's a difficult call. They're not asking for a ransom or anything. Just holding him for the moment. I'm telling you this, though, Esteban, not just because you're from the old barrio and we grew up practically neighbors, but also because I am personally interested in all this as well, as an enforcer of the law. I will try very hard to find out what is happening, and I'll keep you informed. If they do ask for a ransom, or if I hear anything else, we will arrange another meeting. But not here, maybe on the American side. I have a little business to attend to over there soon. A little job. Hopefully. A big, little job."

Manolo cracked his knuckles against his own thighs and yawned, revealing silver- and gold-capped molars in the back of his mouth.

"Sorry for all the driving, too. I had been wanting to come and see if the ducks were still out here. Saw our meeting as a good opportunity for it. What do the Americans say, kill two birds with one stone? Plus, this whole area is secluded, a perfect place to talk. The last mayor laundered city funds for the roads and left connections like these half-finished all over. Get in the car, I have another cab waiting for you at the nearby Super Siete."

Manolo drove Bellacosa to a white cab shaped like an egg, which took him close to the border, and he asked to be dropped off at La Zona Rosa in downtown Reinahermosa. The streets were drunk with rumbling motor vehicles and loud pedestrians, made even more vertiginous by the pulsating neon lights of different businesses, which faced the sidewalks of the old buildings. The air-conditioning units sticking out of the windows up above dripped water like hanging lambs after a bloodletting. Bellacosa walked between these drops and American border crossers, Mexican working-class men and women, and people who made their living in the streets.

He passed a young family closing the fruit stand El Tropical, as a little girl accosted him, holding a basket of chicharrones, chocolates, and mint-flavored Chiclets.

"*Oiga, señor,* chicharrones and candy here for your children."

Bellacosa politely declined with a wave of his hand, and the little girl moved along.

He reached La Calle del Taco as nighttime crawled out of the sewers and tailpipes of zooming automobiles, walked through a babel of cheap portable radios playing Norteño classics in different busy taco stands, until he found his preferred spot, Don Ecuador's Tacos. Bellacosa took a seat on the empty stool under the tiny green awning. To his right sat three men dressed like charro musicians without their big, round hats, chatting casually and slurping their tacos. The grill hissed like a beast's open mouth, and Don Ecuador nodded at his new customer.

"Y *usted?*" Don Ecuador asked Bellacosa as he quickly cooked diced fajitas, prepared a plate of tacos *al pastor,* popped a bottled soda, and took another order from a young boy all at once.

"I'll have an order of *bistec* tacos and a *papa asada* with everything on it, *por favor.*"

"*Sale y vale,*" Don Ecuador said, and slapped eight tiny corn tortillas on the grill while whistling at an approaching mangy dog in an attempt to scare it.

FOUR

THE PEDESTRIAN LINE TO CROSS BACK INTO THE U.S. WAS relatively short. Bellacosa stood in line for only fifteen minutes until he approached the Inspection and Declaration of Goods Station. He watched as two officers hassled an empty-handed elderly man ahead of him. The Border Protectors scanned the elderly man's hands and held the facial recognition scanner in front of his face as they asked him over and over where he was born, where he lived, where he'd attended school, where his children and grandchildren attended school, even asked him who the previous and current presidents of the United States were. Bellacosa got aggravated for the old man, but knew better than to interfere in any way. The Border Protectors let the old man pass; one of them cracked open a candy bar as the other took a big chug of water and signaled Bellacosa to approach. They eyed him up and down, scanned his face, and let him cross without any questions.

Back on the American side, as Bellacosa drove the old Jeep away from the Nevarez Lot, the phosphorus blue night was young and smelled like a dry water fountain. Bellacosa hardly drank, but the idea of a drink wasn't so bad at the moment. He couldn't help overthinking this situation with his brother. Knowing that harm was inflicted upon Oswaldo hurt Bellacosa deep down to his pickled bones, a pain that shot outward and then clawed at his entire body. It was the same pain he'd felt when his daughter died, and in those long months when Lupita was slipping away, months it took him even longer to stop reliving in his mind, insisting on how it could have gone differently if this or that had happened. But the Creator had it planned another way, whatever that may mean, he thought now, and was lucky to leave it at that with no remorse.

Bellacosa phoned Tío Primo's Towing Service and confirmed the flatbed would be at the property in Calantula County the following day before noon to haul away the 7900 Rig. He pulled over at a Casa de Cambio and with his bank card had twelve thousand dollars wired to Mr. McMasters's business account, which Bellacosa counted on clearing the following morning as per the agreement.

After that, Bellacosa admitted to himself he was rocking-chair tired. He pointed his old Jeep to MacArthur, the city where he lived, and drove to the shack he rented on the north side.

He parked in his usual spot along the curb and walked inside his place. Bellacosa chugged a bottle of water that was on the kitchen counter. Then, across the dark living room by his small altar, he saw the flare of a cigarette and the purple silhouette of a smoker. Bellacosa didn't panic, didn't wish he still owned a gun, and walked slowly to the altar he kept for all the dead in his life. He saw it was only the two votive candles he'd bought the previous day and had kept lit, the flames biting the bottom of the glass, burning the last of the wax. One candle was for St. Martha, and she was depicted holding a bouquet of burning branches: the artist had drawn a winged reptile behind her, but it wasn't clear if St. Martha was fending off the beast or if it was on her side. Bellacosa knew his wife, Lupita, would have appreciated this touch.

The other candle was for La Santa Muerte, hooded and holding a scythe like a landlord coming for the rent. He watched the last of the wax in both candles be consumed, the flames fizzed out and turned to powdery, stringy ribbons of smoke. Bellacosa admired his altar, the photos between the candles; one of his wife as a young woman, another of the two of them together when she was older; a small sonogram photo of his daughter, Yadira, and a Polaroid of her in purple pajamas, surrounded by presents in a hospital bed on her fourth and last birthday; a photograph of his teenage parents in the old neighborhood in Reinahermosa. He ran his fingers over the Bengali quartz crystal; the palo santo from Cuzco; an old brass pocket watch with the engraving of a tank engine; the tooth of a Panhandle coyote; a wax seal with his family's supposed coat of arms, stained with red paint; a petrified piece of turquoise coral; and a tiny chunk of meteorite he and his wife once hid from the authorities when they went yard to yard looking for remains.

From his breast pocket Bellacosa pulled out an old black-and-white photograph of his brother, Oswaldo, taken when they were boys. He'd found it sitting on a pile of suitcases earlier in the week, to his surprise and wonder, at the storage space he rented monthly. In the photograph Oswaldo was speaking into a telephone in the alley of an old building—the telephone had been discarded, and Oswaldo was having a good time pretending to be using it. Bellacosa couldn't remember who had taken the photograph, or how it was he'd had it in storage for it to just randomly appear. He added it to the altar and lit the edge of the palo santo, waving the smoke around.

Bellacosa felt emotionally exhausted, took his clothes off, and fell asleep in his underwear on the living room couch.

EARLIER THAT EVENING, a couple of blocks east of downtown MacArthur, the man Bellacosa referred to as Tcheco walked on the sidewalk down Neches Street carrying a brown paper bag of groceries. He had learned from a waitress at Marselita's of a long alley named Nogales Row—a location deemed by the city as free game to graffiti, after studies showed it helped lower vandalism if there was a designated place for it. The city also gave away prizes for the best art throughout the year, and a lot of low-level vandals developed into popular muralists and community organizers.

The man who was Tcheco in Bellacosa's eyes was actually a journalist named Paco Herbert, and when he arrived in a new city he was always more interested in the street art than his story assignment and would go out of his way to find it. It was his belief that every city was trying to tell its own story. The obsession of big galleries is always with the past, and the only way Paco Herbert could read the story of a city's present reality was through the street art—beyond the artists simply tagging their name, like SHERRYZ, or LAUTRÉMONTALVO, which actually Paco Herbert admired. But among the mediocre was always something visually admirable, poetic with its slogans or lyrics, which told him something about the current social climate.

Paco Herbert found Nogales Row and went in with the curiosity and caution of walking into a forest. He'd been told there were usually kids hanging out getting stoned and banging on trash cans, but this evening the alley was vacant. The first piece he saw—which ended up being a phrase he'd have stuck in his head all day—read MASTICATED OSTRICHES & PARROTS MAKE ME HUNGRY, in a Paraíso-style font.

He walked straight to the far end, and on the left building

saw the mural of a nightingale flying out of a ripe grapefruit, the juice from the fruit gushing like blood; on the right building was a mural of the actor Mimoso Kline dancing a tango with the first lady of Mexico—slightly to their right were paparazzi snapping photographs, and slightly to their left and in the background was an elaborate, iridescent mushroom cloud. He saw another mural, wheat-pasted to the brick wall at the far end of the alley in lifelike scale, of a young immigrant girl holding the hand of a drowned older woman Paco Herbert assumed to be her mother—the mother lay on the shore of a beach, which was propped up on a stage, as theatergoers looked on. At the bottom right of the mural the word ALDEA was written, which Paco Herbert knew to be the Spanish word for "hamlet."

Emerging from the alley as if he'd had a mystical vision, Paco Herbert spotted a cab and took it a few blocks south to the empty apartment he'd subleased for six more weeks.

He opened the refrigerator and took his blue one-subject notebook out of the brown bag, then stuffed the groceries inside and shut the door. Paco Herbert moved toward the living room. Along one of the beige walls were various yellowing newspaper clippings pinned in every direction like a giant crossword puzzle. Some of the headlines read: "Great Apes Die Off at Gladys Porter Zoo"; "Fifth Filtering Warehouse Raid in Weslaco, Phantom Recruits Credited"; "Phantom Recruits: Real or Urban Myth?"; "Third Border Wall Quickly Becoming Reality"; "Five Border Protectors

Indicted for Corruption"; "The Vanished Nightingales of San Juan"; "Australian Man Scales Border Walls as Protest, Deported."

Using thumbtacks, Paco Herbert pinned up El Gordo Pacheco's obituary from the *Times*, along with an article about the Food Shortage Truther Movement, both below a clipping on Galapagos Gumbo, the most coveted black-market culinary dish.

Paco Herbert had left the phone cable unplugged in the empty living room. He knelt on the floor by the old-fashioned touchtone phone and a dusty blue boom box. Immediately after he plugged the phone cable into the wall it rang, crying like a calf getting slaughtered.

He picked up the phone, and instead of saying anything he whistled into the receiver.

"Francisco," he heard—a voice not from a human, but from a mossy boulder resting between two frosty, gloomy mountains.

"How can I direct your call?" Paco Herbert answered.

"Very funny, Paco, you should've been a sideshow clown. Not the main act, the one supporting the star, playing the slide whistle. I've been dancing around my office all day trying to get ahold of you, what've you been doing?"

"I'm getting to know this city again, Cecilia. I haven't been here in a long time, remember? I've gotta get a feel for it, you know. But to what do I owe this call? Did you find out anything for me about the Phantom Recruits?"

The moment this conversation began Paco Herbert

remembered the CD—carrying the telephone, and dragging its cable around like a tail, he opened the refrigerator, reached into the grocery bag to fish it out. It was a burned copy in a plastic case devoid of artwork. He unplugged the dusty boom box in the living room and placed it on the ground in the empty bedroom, plugged it in. He inserted the CD, pressed play, and picked up the volume all the way, left the bedroom door open only a crack. The boom box blasted with drums and distorted guitars as if from deep inside a well.

Paco Herbert walked to the far end of the living room and sat on the floor looking up at the newspaper clippings as the conversation continued:

"That's something I'm still working on," Cecilia said. "We have the relations lined up, it all just needs time to cook. Francisco, you're on a landline, right? We are safe to be talking?"

Paco Herbert pictured Cecilia's office, saw her holding the phone and looking out the window past the empty soccer field and toward the monastery, while the newsroom on the other side of her door was a madhouse.

"Yes, Cecilia, of course."

"I assume so, but I always have to ask. You heard about Pacheco's death already, huh? What a tragedy, boo-hoo. You're in a great spot right now, Paco, at the border. I hear things are going to get out of control there with the syndicates fighting to usurp Sindicato Casablanca's power. Keep an eye out. Be safe. When the kingpin dies he's only replaced.

The filtering facilities, equipment, and people are still around. Anyway. Great news. The angel investor and our dinner connection came through."

"For the dinner-dinner?"

"Yes, the dinner-dinner. Paco, we've pushed this as far as you and I possibly can with the budget we have to work with. Without this angel investor we'd have nothing, so it's all in your hands now to produce a story that's worth breaking. Didn't you receive the package already? It should contain two tickets."

Just then Paco Herbert saw there was a white envelope with a brown string tied around it on the floor by the front door. Moving toward it and opening the envelope, Paco Herbert was slightly disappointed in his cognitive and journalistic senses for not having spotted it upon entering.

Inside was a blank business card. When he turned it over there were two words typed out in lowercase: "*pollo asado*."

"I didn't get the tickets," Paco Herbert said into the phone.

"If you didn't, I'm sure you will at any moment."

"No, I mean I did. But they're not tickets, it's just a card that says '*pollo asado*' on it."

"*Pollo asado*?"

"Uh-huh."

"Well. You got me. I don't know how the actual ticket part is done, you figure it out. Those words might be the tickets. All right, I'll call and confirm and will let you know.

Don't leave the phone again today. Remember the tickets are for two people. You're the only one we have in that region, Paco, so I need to confirm that you are fine with finding a reliable person to take with you. I also have to tell you the rules. Please write them down."

Paco Herbert thought he heard Cecilia bite into an apple.

"What's that sound going on, are you at the club? No, you can't be at a club, this is a landline, right?" Cecilia said.

As Paco Herbert fumbled with a pen and shuffled through his blue one-subject notebook for a blank page he said, "It's punk rock. A local all-girl punk band. It helps me concentrate when I have local music blaring in another room. Cecilia, what about a rental car, I need one bad, did you work it out?"

"I did, I did, but hold on a second and write what I'm about to tell you. This is important."

THE FOLLOWING MORNING Bellacosa woke up, showered, and gave his ostrich-knee Wingham shoes a good polish, all before sunup. He bought a cup of coffee at La Gloria Panaderia, and drove the old Jeep to Calantula County once again, ready to finalize the deal with the farmer, Mr. McMasters, and the 7900 Rig.

"What trigger, what napalm?" a man with a French accent on the radio was preaching. "These things are reflections of ourselves, we are the triggers, we are the napalm.

The syndicates, El Gordo Pacheco, the filtering of exotic species, and the counterfeit dinners that've been thriving with the rich and privileged: these excesses are inside all of us, and we in a sense encourage this type of criminal activity simply by projecting it. I am guilty of this, we are all guilty of this. But if we begin to try shifting our way of thinking then maybe our collective mind will also shift and push away all these negative projections that have produced so many dead bodies. Not only dead human bodies, but the bodies of species being filtered and smuggled, and at the cost of our selves, of our inherent humanity and the planet that is our duty to protect. After all, these creatures, these animals created in underground laboratories, aren't completely manufactured, because souls can't be manufactured. But they can be replaced. In order for artificial life to be created, souls, the fabric of our existence, have to be taken from one animal, to be given to another. Humans cannot keep playing God, because we don't know the cost, which one day will be collected . . ."

Bellacosa couldn't help himself and drove again past the shack where he suspected he was born, but this time didn't stop. He recalled the time shortly after his daughter, Yadira, was diagnosed with Wittinger's, the degenerative blood disease, and required round-the-clock supervision. The medical expenses had gotten out of hand for Bellacosa and Lupita—a debt he was paying off to the present day. Bellacosa had walked into his brother Oswaldo's practice after many failed attempts at reaching him by phone. There were no scheduled patients at that hour, and the two brothers had lunch together at a burger joint a couple of blocks away. Bellacosa explained to Oswaldo he'd found a part-time job changing tires at a corporate mechanic shop after working full days at the screen-printing spot, and was still barely making it. Lupita had devotedly become their daughter's full-time caretaker. With nobody else to turn to, and aware of the improbability of actually getting it, Bellacosa asked Oswaldo for a loan. Not a lot, just what his family needed to float by. This was before Mexico's economic collapse, which broke down the peso into a cubic denomination equaling a tenth of its original worth. Oswaldo owned several properties around the Reinahermosa conservatory and his two dental practices were doing well. Even then, he declined Bellacosa the loan, citing his own son's music and English lessons, car payments, and personal debts.

Bellacosa had never known the cruelty and frustration he experienced in the drive back to South Texas after that fateful lunch. Less than two months later Yadira died, and Oswaldo's condolences and statements on how he had no idea it was so serious came pouring in. Then the economic collapse happened, Oswaldo was forced to sell his properties, and his practice lost many clients who could now only afford government care. The syndicate wars escalated and restoration along the border declined dramatically, turning the southern tip of Texas into a dark spot on the map.

Look what's happened, hermano mio, Bellacosa said to himself. Oswaldo kidnapped, without his wife, who divorced him, and his two boys, who have no respect for their father. Though initially Bellacosa hesitated doing anything when he caught news of the kidnapping, thinking Oswaldo deserved to die for deserting his own blood, he was able to put these feelings aside and remember their suffering mother, and that despite everything, blood was still blood, and they were still brothers. Bellacosa was making moves now that Oswaldo would never have made for him. Bellacosa meditated again and again over what there was to be learned out of all these regrettable experiences, and he came to the conclusion it was this: the more innocent you are, the closer you are in line toward death.

BELLACOSA'S OLD JEEP was suddenly surrounded by thick black smoke as he parked at the edge of the McMasters property in Calantula County. He was there to supervise the handling and mounting of the rig, in case it was mishandled or dropped, and didn't want to take any risks. Something was on fire, and he immediately thought the worst: that the van Tranquilino and his son had stuffed the chickens in had exploded. As he stepped out of the old Jeep and got closer, Bellacosa saw a pile of burning branches and trash in the middle of the property, and half expected to see flaming chickens running around. The 7900 Rig wasn't anywhere in sight. Bellacosa's timepiece read ten till nine. He thought maybe the Tío Primo Towing boys were shockingly ahead of schedule and had already hauled it to the border.

Bellacosa heard chickens clucking like loud typewriters coming from the black van and looked at it indifferently, since it wasn't on fire and nothing appeared to have exploded.

Tranquilino was at the spot where the ants had carried the chicken the previous morning. He had an opaque beige tank with a sloshing liquid strapped to his back, rigged with a piece of garden hose and spray that shot out a green mist toward the ground. Tranquilino saw Bellacosa approaching and stopped what he was doing.

"*Buenos días, oiga*, did they take the 7900 Rig already? Did you end up signing for it?"

"*Si, se lo llevaron*," Tranquilino replied, in an agitated, rude manner, which surprised Bellacosa. "They came last night. Look what they did to me. In front of my son and my wife, too. They threatened to kill us, and challenged me to do something about it."

Tranquilino had a black eye, blotches of dark bruises around his neck, and cuts and scrapes along his face.

Bellacosa didn't understand. "*Señor*," he said, "what happened, again? Who took the machine?"

"Who do you think? They did. *Los hombres malos*."

"What *hombres malos*?"

"The only *hombres malos*. The ones without honor who have no shame, who go around torturing and killing and nobody puts them in jail or does a thing about it. Say what you want about the kingpin Pacheco, at least he had a code and didn't go around torturing poor farmers like me, the poorest workers in the world."

Bellacosa felt his heart trying to crawl out of his throat. He took a deep breath, swallowed it back down, and held it there as he felt this deal coming undone. It occurred to him that Tranquilino was poisoning all the ants that had taken refuge on the property. His son had the same clothes on as the previous day, only filthier. The boy was gathering several piles of dead ants using a rake and with a shovel scooped them up and hurled them onto the burning heap of trash, where they crackled like bamboo, or fireworks.

"My son, *pobre niño*, he saw everything," Tranquilino stammered. "His mother was crying, and three men held her by the hair and abused her. And look at me, I'm an old man. I worked hard but got started late in life. I didn't marry Paulita until I was sixty-one. I'm not the young man I used to be. But now after this what does it matter? If they come back I'm going to give them a good run. I was a brave young man once. I'm from where people settle things with machetes. A *machetazos*. I have to do it, to teach my son, *señor*. What else could I have done? First the storm in the middle of the night, then these men. After a long day of hard work, you saw how we were yesterday. Now, look. We took care of the chickens and the ants, but now what do I do about the men? I won't be scared anymore. Let them come again so they can see I'm not scared."

Tranquilino kept mumbling and trembling and continued to spray the land with the sour-smelling chemical. Bellacosa stepped away and breathed deeply as he smoked a cigarette, trying to see the bigger picture and calm down.

He got a signal and dialed Tío Primo headquarters, to see where the flatbed he ordered was, if by chance it had shown up early and taken the rig, but the nervous, apologetic operator told him it had just now left MacArthur and should arrive in the next fifty minutes. Bellacosa thanked her, hung up, then called her again to cancel the whole thing, to which she apologized further.

Bellacosa walked to the spot where the 7900 Rig was set, looked at the heavy indentations on the ground, and followed the tracks, which vanished and led nowhere. Not knowing what else to do or what the hell was even going on, he walked to take a look at the chickens in the black van–turned–chicken coop. There were plastic milk crates stacked around and it actually looked quite spacious in there; the chickens were now peaceful, their clucking like soft schoolhouse gossip in the air.

He shuffled back to Tranquilino and said, "*Señor*, forgive me. This is terrible. Let me ask, did you call Mr. McMasters about this, and let him know his property was stolen? I already wired him the money for it; the machine actually belongs to my client now."

"I called, but nobody answers, like always. I've been dialing his office all morning, and I'll keep trying. I could call the police, but they'll deport me and my family, and then what? You know what I think? Listen to those machines, all the way over there. The ones all the ants are running from. I think that is them, the same men who were here last night. I've seen them going up and down the road in their big trucks, sometimes at night, too, and I've heard them shoot guns in the air."

Tranquilino walked up the steps of his little trailer, opened the screen door, and slammed it behind him. Through the screen, Bellacosa saw for the first time Tranquilino's wife. She wore a yellow dress and had indigenous features. She was very young, probably not even thirty, and eyed him with animosity and suspicion. Bellacosa felt she suspected he was also one of the *hombres malos* and with slight shame he walked away.

He climbed in the old Jeep, cursing in a balled-up torrent of border Spanglish, and drove down that unpaved, rural road. He rolled his window down, and the passenger one as well, clicked off the radio, and let in the high-tide autumn breeze, gunning the gas with a death wish. Bellacosa got to a marked farm road and stopped in the middle of a powdery intersection. He jumped out of the old Jeep and listened for the clanking and whistles of construction equipment. He couldn't hear a damned thing and continued to drive, turned after a dried apple orchard, where the road narrowed and seemed to slope and slide off the earth into some kind of tunnel, or poorly executed labyrinth.

Bellacosa put his Herzegovina Flor out in the ashtray with a feeling like he'd walled himself in and was now awaiting death.

The road suddenly ended at a locked gate that led down a throaty driveway, covered by thick foliage of mesquite. Bellacosa could distinctly make out the cacophony of construction equipment, and he was sure it echoed from the other side of the hill through this driveway. He stepped off the old Jeep cautiously, and as he walked toward the gate his tongue dried up and he smelled a sour, acrid smell, like ammonia mixed with gasoline, or a statue covered with bird shit in the heat, or five generations of hobo piss in an alley, only worse. It made his eyes water, reminded him of riot police, and mustard gas stories from the First World War; it had a yellow, unctuous fiber about it.

Turning around and driving away, Bellacosa was starting to panic and relit that Herzegovina Flor from the ashtray. He tried to picture every step he'd hit on the way down, having been given money from a client for a product, having spent a chunk of it on a personal matter, then the product not coming through.

He remembered to breathe deeply and calmed down, cracked his knuckles on the dashboard.

Mr. McMasters, he hoped, was a reasonable businessman. He was sure he'd be able to understand the situation and wire the money back.

Bellacosa pulled sharply into the sandy shoulder and

almost hit Tranquilino's big mailbox. The flaming pile on the property had grown bigger, and as he watched it burn, he couldn't accept that the 7900 Rig had simply been taken by these *hombres malos*. These evil men. Bellacosa told himself he'd be back, reversed the old Jeep, and drove away.

FIVE

THERE'S A WAY TO INVITE ONESELF TO ANY SITUATION without being intrusive. Bellacosa had become a master of this. Leaving Calantula County, and desperate for a human encounter that had nothing to do with business, he decided to drop in on Ximena, very conscious that it was close to lunchtime and he needed food in his hollow belly. Bellacosa had met her shortly after the death of Lupita, his wife, when he was at a loss with how to deal with his grief and started attending counseling for people directly affected by the years of the food shortage and the subsequent filtering syndicate wars. Ximena's husband had been a truck driver who one day disappeared delivering a shipment of natural cantaloupe to Camargo, Mexico. Not having his body to properly mourn, and never having had children, Ximena developed a kinship with the only man of her age in the counseling group, Bellacosa. After the funding for the group meetings at the Y fell through, the two of them continued to meet whenever possible and were very encouraging toward each other's lives.

Ximena was sitting on her blue porch and humming a tune that she said an apparition of her godmother taught her a few years prior in a dream. On a small wooden table next to her was an empty cup of Moroccan tea, a ramekin with a teabag, a glass pipe, and a Japanese geisha fan, which she grabbed and snapped open like a switchblade.

"*Vaya, vaya,*" she said teasingly, upon the approach of Bellacosa. "*Que cosa tan fea tengo aquí, mira nada más. Santos cielos.* And this miracle? Come, give me a hug, I'm only teasing, of course. I knew you were coming. I heard a coyote in the middle of the night last night. I know they say there aren't any more coyotes or wolves living freely in these parts. They know to stay away from humans, but they come close sometimes, taking stuff that's food for them in the trash. You look good, Esteban. How are you?"

"Well, you know. I'm not bad. Better, now, being here."

"Have you been cutting down on the sugar, and the smoking, like you told me last time? Did you start exercising? Or was that a joke? Let me make you a cup of tea and read your leaves. Or do you prefer a cup of coffee? I think that works better for you, I can read your grounds instead."

Ximena brewed a cup of Limoncillo-blend coffee from the Santa Josefina Estate out of Panama, with the coarse grounds directly in the cup. She brought out her deck of tarot cards designed by the late-nineteenth-century artist Anselma Pontecorvo, which she considered sacred and let nobody else handle.

Ximena's movements were archaic, yet had an air of a hidden choreography, in the way she opened doors, pulled chairs, poured drinks, and shuffled the tarot deck. She brewed herself a whole pot of chamomile from Yucatán and was going on about her favorite subject, the Ancient Egyptians, saying, "So in this dream, this cosmic dream, the entire planet was an ocean, just covered in water with no land anywhere. And in the bottom of the ocean there were volcanoes erupting, while all these animals and species lived in the water, of course. But if you imagine hundreds of years of this erupting, these explosions, all that molten lava eventually hardens and builds and builds. And one day it accumulates into a piece of land that finally peeks up from the ocean surface like a fish for a breath of air. And guess what?" With her hands she made a shape that resembled a pointed roof.

"It is in the shape of a pyramid. The first bit of land that ever came up from this ocean planet was in the shape of a pyramid. The Ancient Egyptians knew this, Esteban. The pyramid is an image embedded into our collective dream for a reason, it drove civilizations mad, so mad that they worshipped the pyramid, worshipped its shape, so mad they built temples in its image, like we keep building statues of Jesus and images that represent something deep and sinister about who we are and why we exist."

Bellacosa shifted in his seat. "Yes," he said. "That is interesting."

"Do you understand, then? How that involves us?"

"Us?"

"The people here in South Texas."

"I don't. But. Please. Tell me."

"Well, you know what the Aranaña people believed, right? In the Ballí Cave, deep in the Ballí Desert, over fifty years ago, when the Aranaña people began to return, they found those cave paintings of pyramids that once stood here in South Texas. The Aranaña themselves built those pyramids that were possibly destroyed, or buried by nature. Interestingly enough, various civilizations in different parts of the world that seemingly had nothing to do with each other built and worshipped pyramids, too. They all believed pyramids were a method of communication and transportation. Have you heard about this? Because I have been reading and meditating on this subject, Esteban, and I want you to at least listen to me, even if you disagree, or don't believe. The Ancient Egyptians and Aranaña believed that if they built a pyramid, and if the people in the tribe would all at once worship around it, then those people would be transported to another corner of the world with other tribes, worshipping around another pyramid, and vice versa. Pyramids were, in a sense, like phones to communicate with other tribes, which linked them to other people from the original diaspora of the very first people on the planet. Can you picture it?"

She gestured toward Bellacosa's hands. "Are you almost

done with your cup? Hurry up. Here, let me see, don't stir the grounds. Have you been eating well? I have *chiles rellenos* left over from last night, *de carne y de queso*."

Ximena heated up some *chiles* for Bellacosa along with white rice in the special way she made it, with peas, finely chopped carrots, paprika and other spices. As he ate, Ximena read the coffee grounds in the brick-red ceramic cup and said, "You see this trail of grounds in your cup? It's a thick swirl, but look at those spirals that formed, in the pattern of a braid. It starts at the center of the bottom and swirls upward, toward the lip where you drank out of. Now, look at these," she said, holding up four unique ceramic mugs.

"I've saved these four other cups you used, from previous visits. Look at this first one, it's only a stringy, straight line from the center to the lip again, with no swirls, no braids. In this other cup you see the line start to ripple, start wanting to take form. Look at these others, the line gets more and more out of control, and now look at the one you drank today. You're attracting something. A powerful energy, Esteban. Like the vanished Arananña pyramids sending us signals, something resting inside you wants to break out. Knowing about it, perhaps you could wield this energy and use it positively, don't you think?"

IT TOOK BELLACOSA a good amount of fortitude to not be spooked by the events of the day thus far. He chewed three tablets for a tingling of heartburn the *chiles* stirred up, and to make himself think of pleasant things thought about archery, how elegant being an archer in the old days seemed. Under the overpass on Tenth Street, waiting for the light to turn, Bellacosa saw purple graffiti that read *NO TE APURES PARA QUE DURES*, under a colorful border-disarmament symbol.

He decided against telling his client Don Villaseñor down in Piedras Negras, Mexico, the bad news about the 7900 Rig—at least for the moment. He dialed the office of Leone McMasters and let it ring over ten times, but nobody picked up. The tingling heartburn in his chest quickly expanded into a melting sensation over his vital organs. Bellacosa pounded on his rib cage, then on the steering wheel, and like a balloon gradually loosing wind the heartburn receded. Bellacosa gasped for air and said, "*Ay, Dios*," wiping sweat from his brow, then dialed Leone McMasters one more time. He let it ring too long, hung up, and pulled over by the side of Buddy Owens Boulevard and Lavaca Street.

He lit a Herzegovina Flor and stared at a water tower the size of a small building about a hundred yards off the southwestern intersection. It'd recently been painted dark blue and yellow, but somebody had already vandalized it with the shoddy drawing of an odd purple farm animal.

Taking one more drag, Bellacosa puffed out his chest, then flicked the lit Herzegovina Flor as far as he could. He was about to drive away; then, like a person changing his mind about abandoning a dog, he got out of the Jeep and walked toward the burning cigarette. He put it out on the heel of his shoe, which he never did, and packed it into the old Jeep's ashtray as he drove away.

He breathed in deeply with the radio shut off and hoped there'd only been a misunderstanding. That nobody was trying to purposely pull a fast one on him and things would get sorted out.

As he pulled into a warehouse building with a sign reading "McM Imports" off Sugarland Road in Hidalgo, Bellacosa immediately noticed that the metal screens were all shut and no eighteen-wheelers were backed up along the dock. A white Suburban was parked against the air-conditioned section of the building and in the small parking lot there was an array of brown and black Lobo pickup trucks with smoky windows, and a dark sedan that resembled Manolo Segura's. Bellacosa circled around the sedan but it had South Texas plates and couldn't have belonged to a Mexican detective. When Bellacosa parked and walked toward the office entrance he thought it out of the ordinary that all the parked trucks had been left running.

He walked into a plain lobby with an unpainted cement floor under fluorescent white lights that made Bellacosa squint. There were two vending machines—one emitted a buzzing sound and sold chips; the other sold canned sodas and whirred—and four unmarked beige doors.

Taking a chance, Bellacosa opened the third door to his right. A brown-faced man wearing a greasy blue jumpsuit and headphones was eating tacos wrapped in foil over a tiny table next to a counter with a microwave. Bellacosa was about to ask him a question when the man vigorously signaled with his thumb to the next room.

"*Buen provecho*," Bellacosa said to him, closed the door, and entered through the fourth door.

There was a carpeted, bright hallway with three doorless rooms to Bellacosa's right, and at the far end was a shiny wooden door incongruous to the entire building. Out of the three rooms, only the middle one had its lights on. Inside were four men in jeans, cowboy boots, and snazzy shirts, playing cards over a low table, while a man in a brown suit held a CB radio and sat on a tall counter watching them.

None of the men directed their attention to Bellacosa.

"*Buenas tardes*. Is Leone McMasters in today?"

After a brief silence the man in the brown suit responded, "Yes. He's waiting for you in his office. We know who you are. Just go in, we told him you're here."

Bellacosa hesitated thanking him and walked toward the wooden door, stared at the brass knob for a moment, then knocked once. When he was sure he'd heard no response Bellacosa walked in, wiggling his toes in his ostrich Wingham shoes.

"Mr. Esteban Bellacosa."

The room was long and wide. Bellacosa closed the door behind him and walked toward Leone McMasters. He was standing behind a rectangular desk with a smooth ivory top like a giant piano key that had no paperwork or office supplies. Between the door and the desk, three separate games of billiards could have easily been going. There were no paintings along the walls, the lights were dim, and as far as Bellacosa could tell there was nobody else in the room.

As they shook hands McMasters said, "Finally, I get the pleasure of meeting the man I've been doing business with. Please sit down."

Bellacosa sat on one of the two chairs in front of the desk.

McMasters had a silver mustache, and parted hair graying at the temples. He wore a navy-blue button-down shirt with brown trousers. Behind McMasters's desk was a brown coat with an Astrakhan collar hanging from a rack built into the wall.

After the formalities McMasters said, "You've come for your money back, I suppose. My apologies. I have the sum here in cash, all twelve thousand, Mr. Bellacosa. I hope you don't mind doing it this way, to avoid wire transfers, banks, and all those distractions."

Relieved to see the pile of money laid out on the ivory table, Bellacosa was about to take it and excuse himself, when he said, "*Señor,* is everything okay around here? Why is the warehouse closed? Where is your secretary?"

"My staff is on leave while things are in transition here. Times are changing. I am looking at ways to expand my business."

"The man," Bellacosa said, "who takes care of your land

out in Calantula. Tranquilino. You should know he was attacked and robbed. They took the rig you had out there last night, the one I was interested in purchasing."

"Yes. He's the cause of this whole misunderstanding between you and me, sir. See, Mr. Bellacosa, I wasn't trying to stiff you. As you can see, it is me who is getting stiffed, and it was by none other than that man, Tranquilino."

Bellacosa tossed these words around in his mind then said, "How do you mean?"

"This ex-employee of mine. The Indian that you met, sir, Tranquilino. He's abandoned his post, betrayed my trust and my property. He took his little trailer and left. The conclusion we've come to is that Tranquilino sold the equipment himself for his own gain, packed up his family in the trailer, and ran. Probably up north, where it's easier to buy immigration papers from a forger."

Staring at the pile of money in front of him, Bellacosa found this story pretty incredible.

"I don't know," Bellacosa said slowly, thinking of his words. "I saw the man this morning. Thinking back on it, he looked bad. Pretty beat up."

"And did you do anything about it?"

"Do anything?"

"Did you notify anybody, Mr. Bellacosa? Like the authorities?"

"Just you. Right now. I mean, I couldn't. The man doesn't have papers. They'd just send him and his family to a deportation camp without even hearing them out."

"Well," Leone McMasters said, looking bereaved, "unfortunately that's the reality of the situation. It's better we don't implicate the law. Between us, Esteban, I am a believer in people. And though a lot of crooked politicians don't want us to hire illegal immigrants, I like to invest in these people and give them opportunities. Unfortunately, you often get stiffed. Maybe I believe in people too much. Here is your money, Esteban, and thanks for understanding. As a businessman yourself, you are familiar with the X factors in this trade. Especially along the border."

McMasters got up, grabbed the coat with the Astrakhan collar, and put it on hastily to walk Bellacosa out. When they reached the door Leone McMasters extended the sleeve of his coat and said, "Feel the texture of this leather here, Mr. Bellacosa. Do you feel that? It's the skin of an African lion. Isn't that interesting to you?"

Not knowing how to respond, Bellacosa nodded, and made it out the door with the twelve thousand in cash, his fingers barely having touched the leather of the coat.

AS HE DROVE AWAY from McM Imports, Bellacosa felt slightly put off by what he'd heard, but grateful to have the money.

He deposited the cash at his bank. Holding the transaction receipt, he sighed a hosanna of relief and drove to one of the only places he considered sacred in South Texas, the cherry orchards in the town Colinaroja. Surrounded by the blossoming, marble-like fruit, he shined his ostrich-knee

Wingham shoes. When he finished, Bellacosa came to the conclusion that Tranquilino stealing the machine and running away didn't add up. One look at that Indian, he thought, and you'd know him incapable of committing any crime, especially against a powerful American citizen like McMasters. Tranquilino and his wife were both considered illegals and would have nowhere to go if they ran off. Plus, aside from the freak problems Bellacosa had witnessed on the land, it didn't look like Tranquilino led too bad a life there. He was able to support his family and live on the property rent-free. If he ran, where would he go? It's not like he could just park that rig or trailer anywhere. And his chickens, where would he park his chickens?

Paranoid that the cash had turned to sand, Bellacosa checked his account balances in three different cash machines—because one could never be too sure, especially when it came to businessmen in South Texas, especially after the events of this day and what Ximena saw of his future in the grounds, along with everything she said about the Ancient Egyptians and the pyramids, but in the printed bank statements everything came out solid.

SIX

ACROSS THE RIO GRANDE, SHORTLY AFTER MIDNIGHT OFF the shoulder of the road to Linares, a dark Explorer that belonged to the Reinahermosa police department had wrecked and flipped upside down, covered in mangled and butchered meat. Half a cow's bleeding body crushed the driver of the vehicle; the other half remained on the road as cars sped by, some of them honking and nobody stopping to help. The back windows of the Explorer were shattered and the men remaining inside were unconscious or dead and covered with pieces of cow innards and glass.

A kilometer and a half away, a disheveled, barefoot man limped low to the ground like a lame coyote through a shantytown, where completely destitute people lived in small huts made of cardboard, scavenged wood, car parts, and old furniture. As he crept through, various dry, scaly hands reached out to touch him, one of them refusing to let go of his ankle until he stomped hard on its wrist. The barefoot man's bloodied clothes were in tatters, and the thinning hair from his balding head was a mess. He moved like a spider with two missing legs, and his mouth was sewn shut in the traditional headhunting manner, with the *huarango* thorns stitched in the cicatrix pattern.

He reached the Rio Bravo, where the half-moon reflected like an ingrown toenail, and waded quietly into the water, unaware he was so close to the Rio Grande and the first border wall on the Mexican side. He reached the deep end and grunted heavily as he was rushed away by a current, his nose gushing with the polluted water and struggling to breathe. His emaciated body managed to push through a crack in the underwater spillway along the border wall, where the Rio Bravo merged with the Rio Grande.

A Border Protector truck sped by along the edge of the American side, flashing its blinding white beam at the figure in the river. The officers could be heard laughing as they fired a few rounds at him and he plunged deep into the brown and stone-gray turbid waters. An underwater current pushed him along and the collar of his shirt got hooked on a floating log, which spun around, and he was suddenly on his back, facing the phantom moon.

He lost consciousness and saw a river of charcoal, and from it floundered a gust of powdered bones, the sainthood of hunger turned inside out into a giant fish, *fish, what are you,* the man thought in a deep well that may have been a dream, a dream or death itself, which is also a dream, inside of which we die, and suddenly there are panthers again and it is easier when the sky is made of thorns, the ground is made of thorns, he spotted a cave dweller and grabbed a stone, heard a language resembling Latin, saw shadows on a dark wall like an intravenous puppet show, the light emerging from the throat of that great, cosmic laugh, another universe sucked away and recycled, never has the dirt illuminated like it did in the beginning, never have horns emerged from the ground like when all the animals started dying, blood all around the mouth as if the Creator had forgotten to add one, and with a fine razor pierced a slit with an indifferent expression, bloody teeth, brown water, flesh blue not from frostbite but from the piercings of the *huarango* thorns, the man heard chants, prayers, and his sons running around like when they were children, felt the worms already biting his intestines underwater, that polluted water dripping like a cascade down his face, he was a drowned man, never remembered leaving the river.

DOWNSTREAM, driving carefully along a poorly lit section of the American side, a Border Protector truck was making the rounds at the tail end of a night owl shift. The officer was alone, thinking about a documentary he'd seen on Arctic wolves, when he noticed by the drop of the river embankment something like a whirlpool opening up in the mud. The smoky, muddy water in the whirlpool slithered and reflected the gray twilight in a perfect circle that dazzled the Border Protector officer. He pulled the truck over and left the motor running as the river groaned like a sleeping animal having an unsettling dream.

Cautiously, suspecting part of the embankment was breaking off into the Rio Grande, the officer approached the whirlpool and clicked on his flashlight. The light revealed a puddle of hundreds of earthworms squirming in a frenzy, like a rotting wound in the ground. The officer got in closer. The sight was fascinating and repulsive to him. Then he let his flashlight wander toward the clustering giant cane, the trash and sediment buildup, and clearly saw the paleness of cold flesh, a torso, one human arm pulling itself out of the water.

The Border Protector officer's first instinct was to draw his gun, but pressing his thumb against the holster's buckle he decided against it. He looked toward the river's western darkness and didn't see signs of the other Border Protector truck monitoring this sector.

Caring little about muddying himself up, the Border Protector officer worked hard to help the man out of the river embankment. The officer then sprawled the man out on the ground and made sure he was still breathing. Under the moonlight the officer studied his face. For a moment he thought there was a tarantula trying to crawl out of the man's mouth. When he looked closer with his flashlight the officer recognized the *huarango* thorns sewn in the cicatrix pattern, clasping the man's mouth shut.

THE BORDER PROTECTOR OFFICER drove the truck along the river toward the monitored opening on the second border wall. The officer stationed there noticed his dirty uniform and said, "What happened here?"

"I slipped in the mud."

The officer working the gate shook his head and laughed. He hit the buzzer, a section of the border wall opened lethargically, and the truck drove through.

AT THE STATION the Border Protector officer told his supervisor, "I'm driving the truck home tonight. Had a little accident out there and don't wanna dirty my car up again, like last time."

"That's okay, Angelo. Just don't drive it out of uniform."

"Of course. See you tomorrow."

IT WAS A COUPLE OF HOURS until dawn in a ghost town named Los Alfaros. Angelo, the Border Patrol officer, turned off the truck's headlights as he pulled into an unmarked, badly paved road. He'd hacked the truck's receiver, which tracked the movements of the truck, but made sure it was really disconnected one more time. Before he knew it Angelo spotted the brick house by the side of the road, slowly pulled in through a clearing in the brush.

Angelo turned the truck off but left the ventilators running, got out, walked a jagged caliche path to the brick house. It had a narrow chimney and the place was small, no more than twenty by twenty feet, but standing in front of the door Angelo felt himself the wanderer at the steps of a great cathedral. He knocked three times, and shortly afterward an old man with a bald head dotted with liver spots answered the door. Both of them stood in silence, then the old man opened the door a little wider. Angelo saw there was a lantern and two cups of coffee on a small table inside. A shadow above the lantern billowed, shrank, then an old woman was under the threshold with the old man, staring at this Border Protector in a muddied uniform—both of them knew it could only be bad news.

The old man helped Angelo carry the cold, disheveled, emaciated man with the stitched mouth inside the small house. They set him faceup in front of the kindling in the fireplace, where the old woman prayed beside his body eight times. Angelo and the old man stood by the door watching this. In a mortar made out of volcanic rock the old woman mixed herbs along with lemongrass, melaleuca clay, native kapok, and tickweed, and using a pestle mashed them to create a gray paste. She knelt with the mortar and an empty bowl next to the sprawled man. The old woman covered her brown, calloused fingers with the gray paste, then rubbed the muddy concoction over the man's sealed mouth and the *huarango* thorns. Then, as if plucking fleshy flowers from the ground, the old woman began unstitching the *huarango* from the man's lips. Dark blood oozed from the wounds and, mixed with the gray paste, covered half the man's face, his pale neck. The old woman's fingers dripped with blood before the growing, heckling fire.

BELLACOSA AWOKE at dawn but stayed in bed for a few hours staring at the wooden ceiling, trying to read the knots and grain patterns on the wood like an ancient Sanskrit text. After showering, Bellacosa opened a can of ethically grown tuna, drained its juice into the sink, and with a fork ate it right out of the can. He inserted a cassette in the tape deck of Rubinstein playing his nineteen favorite Chopin nocturnes. Most recently, he'd been revisiting a boyhood memory that took place in Reinahermosa. Bellacosa's father passed away early in his childhood, and left him living, along with his mother and Oswaldo, in a room without plumbing near the city's center. Bellacosa was sent out to work at seven years old, and he remembered clearly now Don Jaimito, the old, good-hearted carpenter who made him his first shoeshine box out of leftover scraps of wood from his shop. He remembered the mint-colored houses in Calle Zenaida, La Rotonda Michoacan, where the unemployed bolero musicians would gather in the evenings to smoke their cigarettes and play standard folk songs from their youth. Sometimes an anonymous lady would bake them *polvorones* or *empanadas* that the children ran by and snatched from the trays when they were busy belting out songs like “Caballo Azul,” “Amorcito Corazón,” and “Tu Rostro en la Madrugada.”

One of those musicians (Bellacosa couldn't remember his name, Jonathan, Jacobo?) was paying for his daughter to take piano lessons at the conservatory. This was a regular topic of conversation, and the other musicians would inquire, “How are your daughter's lessons? What tunes does she practice? Who can she play?” One day in a chance encounter the carpenter Don Jaimito sent word with Oswaldo to call on his older brother, that he could use some help at the shop, and when Bellacosa arrived the old man amiably gifted him the shoeshine box, along with a brush and a rag. He said it belonged now to Bellacosa to go around the town square and earn some pesos to give his mother and contribute to the household. Remembering the details of this moment made Bellacosa laugh, because though these memories were among the cruelest in his heart, they had somehow become his most precious, the ones that revisited him like ghosts, taking him for a stroll in the graveyard, reading aloud the names on the headstones.

On the run back home to show his mother that day, after cutting through an alley, he saw that an upright piano had been set up at the *rotunda*. A girl in a yellow dress sat playing. She had freckles on her light brown skin and her hair was in braids. The unemployed musicians, smoking Hombre cigarettes, were gathered around her, along with Oswaldo and strays from the neighborhood, listening attentively to the young girl's impromptu recital. Oswaldo, lulled by the music, didn't even turn when Bellacosa called his name to show off the shoeshine box. Bellacosa was too young and excited about the shoeshine box to appreciate that musical moment, but many years later he remembered this encounter, upon hearing a piano tune on the radio written by Chopin and played by Hauke Hottinger, which transported him to that time in his boyhood.

After this experience, he found two cassettes at the Tejano music shop Voy y Vengo, in a tiny cubicle they had labeled as the Classical/R&B section, and filed under "El Chopin." One as played by Hottinger, another by Rubinstein, and after a few weeks of listening to both Bellacosa came to the conclusion that Germans have no business playing Chopin. Nobody did, in fact, except Jewish pianists. Only Jewish pianists could capture the elegant despair in the nocturnes, the Jewish pianists and this young girl from the old neighborhood. She couldn't have been Jewish, but the quiet magic of those old streets in the Reinahermosa of his boyhood helped her capture the right mood of that nocturne. And Oswaldo standing there, seduced by this tune. Bellacosa remembered all this again as he sat on the living room easy chair by his altar, and Rubinstein played Chopin like he was the Great Dane Hamlet himself, wandering the hallways dressed in black and plotting his revenge.

LESS THAN A WEEK LATER, the new atrocities buried all talk of the death of El Gordo Pacheco. With demand for exotic feathers, king conch tortoises, and angel hair llamas growing in Australia, Helsinki, Tangier, New Hampshire, and all Asia Minor, syndicates were now at full-blown war for complete control over the filtering market. Sindicato Unidos and Los Pacificos, which dealt primarily in the shrunken heads market, were now competing to become the only real filtering syndicate to rival Los Mil Condes, who were rumored to be the heirs of Pacheco's market.

Every morning the headlines sought to outdo the tragedies of yesterday. Along the border, the Mexican reporter Melinda Gaitán, on her way home from picking her kids up from their drama class, was sprayed with ivory bullets along with her eight- and eleven-year-olds. News anchor Zacharias Zamarripa was confirmed poisoned by the venom of a pinstripe rattlesnake, known to be filtered for such purposes by Los Mil Condes. The famous tenor Eduardo Guillermoprieto, during his set in the Camargo State Opera, denounced the fur of filtered animals in the fashion world and the popular black-market dish of yspiri birds, cooked a variety of ways, but meant to be swallowed whole. The next day he and his entourage were found hacked to pieces in an ice cream truck looping the tune "Swipesy," at a Soriana parking lot. The bodies found in an unmarked grave earlier in the month were confirmed officially through DNA tests to be those of the missing biology students from Universidad la Reforma, and the nation declared twenty-one days of mourning, a day for every student. There wasn't a science lab in the world that didn't extend its solidarity to its martyred colleagues. The Mexican president made a televised statement scolding the cowardly guilty parties, demanding they come forward to face their heinous crimes before the law, or else live in fear for the rest of their lives. He vowed to come after them and called on all Mexicans with any information to report it immediately to a twenty-four-hour hotline established specifically for this case.

Off the coast of San Diego, California, a Soviet-era submarine shoddily rigged with satellite control emerged on the private Feneon Beach unmanned, filled with seventy-eight rotting bodies of eleven-inch-tall iringiré Amazon new world monkeys. Presumably, the vehicle was destined to some underground port for a private zoo and the smugglers had lost satellite control. Judging by the stage of decomposition, they'd been dead no less than five days. The monkeys were incinerated to prevent the outbreak of disease, the American government hauled the submarine away for further investigation, and the private beach was put on the market at a discount, by its record-mogul owner.

The new trend with the filtering syndicates was to cease spending on building labs at hard-to-access locations like mountains, hidden valleys, or private islands; instead, old warehouses left over from the drug wars were taken over and converted to laboratories in plain sight. These filtering labs were now ubiquitous but not being reported by citizens out of fear for their own and their families' safety. Three governors in the southern states of Mexico fled the country after they'd been linked in various ways to El Gordo Pacheco, and were rumored to be hiding out in Switzerland. Fingers were pointed at many officials who aided in their escape and who also did their best to look the other way. One afternoon in broad daylight, members of Sindicato Unidos and Los Pacificos crossed paths near an elementary school and stray ivory bullets shot through the walls of the building, killing fifteen children and wounding twenty-three, along with an elderly janitor from the state of Guerrero.

—

IT WAS THE WEEKEND AGAIN, and the grocery/retail store Hatfield's Supercenter that operated throughout the south was having a Valley-wide 20 to 40 percent off two-day sale on all its products, which varied from groceries to hardware, horticulture needs, children's toys, electronics, clothes, cosmetics, medicine, and home improvement. People traveled like an exodus from Mexico to attend these first-come-first-serve yearly sales, often waiting for hours to cross the congested international bridges. The pedestrian toll-crossing line in Reinahermosa was eight kilometers long by six in the morning, and old, repainted school buses provided transportation from the border to the nearest Hatfield's and back, with people returning carrying bulging, heavy bags, ready to pay the taxes to cross American products into Mexico.

Bellacosa, not counting the money meant for the 7900 Rig that needed to be paid back in full to his client Don Villaseñor for failing to provide his service, was low in funds. Without a doubt, he needed to return the fifteen grand in full, and felt a little bad he hadn't kept Don Villaseñor abreast on anything that had happened. The fact was, Don Villaseñor had been his primary client for going on three years now. Every piece of machinery the man needed to fulfill contracts in his construction company, from a horizontal MLE to a dirt-sifting tractor, Bellacosa had found in less than a week, and at a discount. More important, both of them had always been honest and straight with each other. So Bellacosa wasn't too worried. Including the money he gave Manolo for the situation with Oswaldo, he'd spent just over a grand and a half of it, which was less than his fee would have been had the deal gone through. He was starting to wonder what the odds were he'd find another 7900 Rig so he wouldn't have to explain a thing to Don Villaseñor.

He thought about the connection he had with the Oswaldo situation in Reinahermosa, the head police detective Manolo Segura. Bellacosa didn't quite trust him. Manolo's father had been a Bible salesman and former horse swindler from southern Mexico. Bellacosa tried to picture him in the days of the old neighborhood, and could see even then he'd felt uneasy about Manolo and his kin. Bellacosa had given him a lot of money, racking his brain to come up with it fast, to possibly negotiate his brother's release. It was a shame Manolo was the only person he knew who could help. Whereas before Bellacosa felt desperate to get the money to Manolo's hands, he now felt ripples of a mysterious distrust and cold anger, anger for his brother getting kidnapped, anger for Manolo, anger because he definitely could have used those twelve hundred dollars. Bellacosa cursed Manolo, wished all sorts of evil inflicted upon him.

Though he rarely let it happen, Bellacosa was feeling glum, very untaken-care-of by the universe. He took out the black-and-white replica he kept in his closet and balanced it on his kitchen table, adjusted its ears to find the recording he wanted. Bellacosa found it difficult to watch the replica, could rarely sit through a picture, but there were a few older pictures he kept recorded specifically for when his spirits were down and there wasn't much business action out in the world. He poured himself a bowl of bran cereal with clusters of oats and 2 percent milk. With the replica on the table, Bellacosa watched a picture with his wife's favorite actress, Tallulah Bankhead, titled *Guinevere in Manhattan*.

The picture opens in Arthurian times, with Tallulah in the titular role. It's a time-travel plot device, where, after denying Lancelot a parting kiss, while being carried by the good nuns back to her chamber, and hearing Lancelot wail like a stormed beast, Guinevere falls into a glowing crack in the crumbling earth. She pierces space and time in a sequence filled with double exposures and camera tricks, and appears in Manhattan to an eerie score by Bernstein.

Guinevere befriends a community of homeless folks, and ends up falling in love with a failed long-distance runner in Central Park after inadvertently saving his life in an armed mugging. In the end, the long-distance runner goes off to war, and Guinevere falls into an open sewer and appears back in Arthurian times just in time to die and be buried royally by her husband, whose name is never mentioned in the picture.

The recording had already started, so Tallulah was already in Manhattan, and having her first emotional connection with the long-distance runner. Bellacosa ate his cereal and paid attention with the volume up high, until the credits faded out and the ones for *Lifeboat* began to roll.

Bellacosa put the replica back in the closet and drove his old Jeep into downtown MacArthur to check his bank account, just to make sure his figures lined up again. When he saw there were twenty-five dollars more than he estimated Bellacosa walked a few blocks to Baby Grand Central and sat at the yellow counter. It was a slow news day; no atrocities had been reported yet.

At the opposite end of Marselita's yellow counter sat the man Bellacosa called Tcheco. He was the only other customer and was chatting up the young waitress, Colleen Rae, who was laughing and enjoying every bit of the interaction. The right half of Colleen Rae's head was buzzed closed to her skull, revealing auburn roots, while the left half was dyed dark blue and tied in a pigtail. She wore red prescription glasses and drank out of a plastic cup filled with iced tea as Tcheco gulped his warm coffee. They both said hello to Bellacosa as he sat down.

Tcheco said, "Check it, *hombre*," and handed Bellacosa a small pink flyer that read: THURSDAY THE 24TH @ CANTINA PRADO ON THE RIVER: HORSE DRAWN MARRIAGE, THE NAHUALETTES, UNCLE SAM BOTTOMS, AND STAMPEDE FORENSICS, with an image of what appeared to be a creature put together with magazine cut-ups of other creatures.

Bellacosa didn't even pretend to understand what it meant; he simply admired the many-hooved creature with many mouths, many eyes, and many wings, then politely handed it back.

"Guess which one is her band," Tcheco challenged him.

"Ah, okay. This is an advertisement for a concert? One of these is your band? You're joking with me."

"Why, you see a young woman working as a waitress and you assume she's a single-mother high school dropout?" Collen Rae said, teasing.

"To be honest I don't think about your life outside this place at all. That goes for everyone else here. To me, all of you belong only to this place and never leave. I have a feeling I'm not the only one. I hope I'm not being offensive."

"Jesus, when you say something derogatory all nice and pretty like that, how could I take offense?"

Bellacosa remembered the article he'd read about today's youth rediscovering sarcasm, and though he rarely had contact with young people, he believed it.

"The Nahualettes," Bellacosa said. "That one's got the

most character. People can remember it. That one is your band."

Colleen Rae busted out her guest checks and asked, "You want your usual soup? Made hot? We don't have fish, he'd have to use the cauliflower, is that okay?" and wrote the ticket without looking.

Tcheco scooted over to the stool next to Bellacosa as Colleen Rae handed the order to the cook in the back. Though Bellacosa planned to read the day's edition of *The Bugle of Plenty* and felt slightly intruded upon, he really didn't mind Tcheco today.

Tcheco, on the other hand, had already read the paper. He'd read the third of a series of anonymous reports on the Calle Veinte Boys, an organized crime network in the city of Tixtla, Guerrero, of boys no older than seventeen wanting to build their own headhunting syndicate. They'd taken over the entire Calle Veinte in the span of eight brutal months, only to be shot and bombed down by Sindicato Unidos, using outdated equipment left over from the first Gulf War and acquired illegally from the American military. Members of Sindicato Unidos were hopped up on the synthetic drug crystal-kind and zoomed up and down Calle Veinte in MV-1300s, shooting down the kids and bombing homes and buildings using grenade launchers and assault rifles. By the end no two bodies were recognizable.

Tcheco picked his teeth with a splinter and while pointing his middle finger at the kitchen in Marselita's said quietly to Bellacosa, "That vertical stick of meat they got back there, what is that? Shawarma? *Al pastor*? Look at this guy lighting it. Unmistakably native, short and brown, hustling his ass off back there for minimum wage to feed us our tacos and fries. It's crazy, how the shrunken heads market has steadily grown, right? People pay good money for those little heads. And if you, as a dealer, can prove a shrunken head is of indigenous descent, made by another person of indigenous descent, you got it made."

Bellacosa watched as Tcheco wadded a napkin into a ball with his fist. "And I don't have to tell you how much those fuckers make. In Switzerland and Venice, rich people who are far away from this culture have convinced themselves it's an art. They even have a rating system, like they used to have to determine how mixed your blood was. I bet those people look at a shrunken head and can't even imagine that it was once a living, breathing human, with desires and loves. That poor cook back there knows he's worth more with his head cut off and sold on the black market, with a plaque of authenticity and everything, than being a slave here, working in kitchens, sending money back home to his mother and father, and probably wife and kids, too. Hoping it makes a difference. Meanwhile, in his village, all the young people keep vanishing. Either to be slaves up here, or slaves for the syndicates, or killed by the syndicates, or lost as shrunken heads, with their souls trapped forever in that tiny ball of skin and skull. Sick. Revolting, Bellacosa. We're lucky, people like us. Our heads aren't worth a thing.

Our indigenous blood has all but washed away. With what? With America, *compadre*."

When Colleen Rae brought Bellacosa his meal, Tcheco moved back to his original stool and smoked his own brand of cigarettes, ashing in a fish-shaped brass ashtray. Tcheco had his blue one-subject notebook and he scribbled notes to himself. He seemed to regress into an inward state, deep in thought and detached from his surroundings. When Bellacosa was almost finished Tcheco slid the open notebook his way. Without giving it any thought, he read what it said: "Don't look now but those two guys eating at the taqueria, sort of facing us? A few times I've noticed that when you arrive they arrive. When you leave they leave, too. Do you know them??"

The spiciness of the soup got to Bellacosa; he blew his nose on a napkin and placed it on his lap. Then he sneaked a look at the men as he drank water. Tcheco took the notebook and quietly tore the page up, wadded it into a ball, and put it in his bomber jacket pocket. At the Frutería Feliz, the short owner with the comb-over and squinty eyes balanced a small color replica on a chair and turned it to a Croatian soccer match, the mono speaker piping an excited commentator's voice low and clear.

Tcheco paid Colleen Rae his ticket and she said, "Don't forget to come to the show."

"I won't," he said, and took the flyer from the counter. He stood next to Bellacosa and looked over at the soccer game, then leaned in and said, "There's probably a soccer match to allegorize every great battle and war. Well, *amigo*, I have to be off. But I have something to say. I have an assignment tonight and need somebody I can trust. Doesn't pay much, I can probably give you a hundred in American. It comes with a free, classy meal, too. What do you say? Interested? Let's talk about it."

SEVEN

MOMENTS LATER BELLACOSA AND TCHECO EXITED BABY Grand Central and walked along Broadway together.

Tcheco said, "Let's keep an eye out for those *cuates*, okay?"

"Sure. Why would they be following me?"

"I don't know, I was just gonna ask you that."

When they reached Tcheco's rented Centaurus, Bellacosa hesitated getting in, but, unable to resist an opportunity to make a few dollars, he did, regretting it immediately. Bellacosa hadn't been a car passenger in a while, and this fact, on top of the thing with the goons, made him uneasy. He looked around with fluttering suspicion as Tcheco sped away from Warwick Avenue, downtown, and said, "I'll bring you back to your car, don't worry. I'm just gonna drive around so we can talk for a minute. Your name is Esteban

Bellacosa, right? Don't freak out. Haven't you wondered how I know your name? You must be very trusting of people. How unlike the trend of the day, *amigo*. I'm a reporter. That's my job. How I make a living, and I try to do good by it. It's important to have good people in journalism, especially today. Hardly anybody is worth a shit anymore. The poets are as much at fault for what the fuck's going on in the world as the politicians.

"My name is Paco Herbert, see. Here's my international press card," he said, showing Bellacosa. "I have a syndicated column that runs in three different papers, in Buenos Aires, Prague, and *La Jornada* in Mexico City. I'm the one who exposed the big issue with the crystal-kind drug among people in the syndicates, and street kids who get it dirt cheap. A lot of them even cook it now. Last year I ran a series also about a Father Canchola. A priest originally from around here in South Texas, that now teaches English to kids in Costa Rica. He speaks French, too, and also teaches verse. Very interesting story about this priest, which is why I couldn't run only one column. When he was a boy he and two friends started crossing drugs across the river on a horse. Before the Border Protectors got souped up by the government and they built those fortress walls along the border, had tanks set up, the infrared watchtowers and all that. Anyway, one of his friends was named Freddy Santos, and together with another kid, they got connected with bad people. From Mexico they crossed what must've been hundreds of pounds' worth of drugs back then. And they were just kids, before things got really bloody and savage in the days of the drug wars. The people up top still had that old-world code of honor. But these boys weren't really a part of that, they weren't criminals in their minds. The way I understood the story from Father Canchola, anyway. These were just kids, like I said. There was less paranoia in those days, less surveillance and technology. The mythology of the old west and revolutionary bandits was still fresh. These boys made a lot of money, and when the times changed and the dead bodies started piling up, all three of them quit the business. All except for Freddy Santos, who ended up killed for trying to steal money from a deal he made with one of the big families down here, supposedly. Rogelio Canchola, when the weight of the evil he participated in seeped into his spirit, joined the seminary, to become a Catholic priest. He moved to South America and even got a college diploma. He supports himself well teaching English now and is able to travel the world. The third one. Their friend. He stayed down here. And. Well. You know what happened to him."

At first, Bellacosa got the feeling he was being shaken down and listened carefully for any tone of aggression. He hesitated saying anything and tried looking into Paco Herbert's eyes as he drove along and finished the story. Bellacosa thought of staying silent, then under his breath said, "Father Canchola, *ey? Pinche* Rogelio, *cabrón*."

Paco Herbert took his eyes off the road and looked at Bellacosa. In turn, Bellacosa stared at an abandoned, rusted tractor as they passed it by. He noticed his hands had been sweating profusely and lightly wiped them on his pants.

"I knew about Freddy's death. Everybody did. It was in the papers a lot at the time, and how they found his body in such a gruesome manner. Damn. I haven't thought of those guys in some time, to be honest."

It suddenly struck Bellacosa that he never caught the goons following him with his own eyes. It had been Paco Herbert who'd noticed and warned him and led him to this trap.

"You're the one chasing me around, then. And not those goons? Was this some kind of dirty trick?"

"No, no, please don't get the wrong impression," Paco said. "Just so you know, I never printed your name in any of those articles. But I know Father Canchola well, and consider him a friend. I've spent Christmas at his house. He may have done all those crazy things with you, but he's a changed man. Funny, that's one of the highest compliments you can give a man, that he's changed. But that man's a changed man for the better, like a worm turned into a butterfly. Except, what do we say when they turn for the worse, do we say he went from worm to maggot?" He paused.

"I'm driving us somewhere, Esteban Bellacosa. Somewhere I've been curious to check out. I came to South Texas from Buenos Aires on a totally different assignment, and I want you to know it was an act of chance when we met at the counter in Baby Grand Central. I heard one of the waitresses call your name once, and to make sure I just had to do a little asking with Miss Colleen Rae back there. I'm thirty-three and single now. Sometimes I think I need a woman again. But most of the time I don't know what it is I want. I like my job, meeting new people. Maybe I get a little obsessive about getting into a story, maybe I talk too much, but it never gets me in trouble because I'm good to others. Now, about the job I mentioned earlier. I wasn't kidding around with that. The connections I made in the case of Father Canchola, when your name came up, they had nothing but good things to say about you. You did well in the screen-printing business you started down here, they tell me. With your wife?"

"Yes."

"And most of all, you kept your mouth shut. All this time. Nobody has ever found you. I tried tracking you down for an interview back then. Everybody I talked to said you stayed in Mexico. In Reinahermosa. I never thought to look across the border in South Texas, especially after the United States Border Reform. Because, well, these boys were Mexican boys. I never would've thought that you were a Texan-born Mexican, a citizen of the States. Ho-lee shit. And that I found you without really looking for you, that's the real wonder of it."

They were somewhere along the border in the small town of Rio Hondo, on a two-lane narrow unpaved road at a high elevation, and about half a mile down was a Border Protectors watchtower with its green sensors flashing. Paco

Herbert parked just close enough to look down toward the border walls and they could see the sparkling Rio Grande flowing eastward. He sprung out of the car as if anxious for something, and Bellacosa followed.

Paco Herbert said, "The watchtowers, look at that. Didn't know they'd built one there. It wasn't labeled on the map. I checked. They got them every five miles from here to Southern California."

For a moment Bellacosa remained silent, walked toward a dry mesquite tree with musket branches, and took it all in. He could easily imagine how the area was in his boyhood, even in the presence of the border walls and the distant watchtower.

Visions from those days then came to him with the power of an ocean liner returning to shore. As if unable to believe certain details himself, Bellacosa said, "This is the first spot where I'd cross with Rogelio and Freddy in those days. We all must have been twelve or eleven years old. I'd pick up a heavy-loaded mare from the man who offered us the job, named Charly. It would always be a mare. With bags packed tight so the merchandise wouldn't soak. Charly had a mustache like the silent film character from the streets, so everybody called him this. One of us kids would ride the mare across, and the other two would swim along, to help the mare in the river's deeper pockets. On this side, where we're standing, waited the Americans. They'd unpack the bags and hand us the money. Can you believe grown men handing kids all that money? They did. This is quite funny to me now, seeing all this. I'm glad there's a watchtower over there. I think I'm glad. But I still don't understand what you want. You want an interview with me? For a running story you've been working on, about my old friend Canchola, the priest?"

"No," Paco said. "Not at all, actually. I told you these things more than anything to point out the series of coincidences that have happened to lead us here. My assignment here now has nothing to do with you. I came to South Texas for research. I finally have the lead I've wanted. The biggest lead, probably, in my entire career. Tickets for an underground dinner. You know what I'm referring to? It's being held the next county over, in Calantula. The only way to get tickets is by the pair, so that's how my people managed it. Believe me, I thought about asking that pretty punk rock waitress at the Grand, but don't really think it's the kind of thing to spring on a first date. I'm not a member of the Government Daily or anything like that. I'm not looking to get anybody in trouble. I'm a journalist, like R. Murrow, abiding by the Truth-perception standards of the day. I would go alone if I could. But these people that put these dinners together are suspicious of singles. They fear those who can stand to eat this dinner alone. It'll probably be glamorous and all that. Swanky. And we will have to eat and try everything they serve, no matter how disgusting it is in reality. A high-class affair, in other words. *De etiqueta*. And I have the feeling I can trust you. Right, Esteban?"

"What kind of journalism is this, what are the ethics with you blackmailing me?"

"Hey, I know how this looks. You can say no and we can forget about this. But you have to understand I'm in a bind. I don't know anybody else down here. My previous connections have moved on. I've lost touch. You don't have to help me, but I have to find somebody quickly. By this evening. I'm offering you two hundred dollars in American. What do you say?"

BELLACOSA AGREED to the job on the drive back downtown, under one condition: that he be the driver. Paco Herbert had no objection, since it was a long drive and he was unfamiliar with those remote parts of South Texas.

Bellacosa picked him up at exactly 7:00 p.m. on the corner of Sixth and Giuletta in south-central MacArthur. The first thing Bellacosa noticed was Paco Herbert's beige-and-brown shined shoes, in a style he associated with the Mexican actor Tin-Tan. He also wore a trench coat with blue jeans and a long-sleeved, pearl-snapped western shirt, also blue.

Paco said, "*Coño, amigo.* You have one of those stereos from way back in here. I wasn't expecting this, I made a CD for the occasion. It's one we've had going around at the office in Argentina of old propaganda songs from the old American wars. A lot of them are pretty poppy and good, you'd be surprised. The wars have sponsored some nice catchy hits."

"Wait a minute here," Bellacosa said. "I have a device, actually, my wife made me get a device installed down here. Here it is, see. You can control it from those buttons there."

Paco Herbert popped in the CD and brought the levels down to his liking.

"My condolences, by the way. About your wife."

There was silence for a few road signs, then Paco Herbert said, "Can you tell me something about what it's like? To be a widower?"

"What do you mean? About what? About how it feels? That's an inappropriate question to me."

Silence stared down on them like a gargoyle. Paco Herbert took a crooked cigarette out of his coat pocket and played with it in his fingers.

"I mean, what have been your overall feelings after her passing away? Besides sorrow, the things that come when our loved ones leave us. I don't mean to be pushing this on you, not trying to be intrusive. Answer only if you feel comfortable. This is probably just me going into robot mode and trying to read the present moment as an assignment."

"What kind of an accent is that you have?" Bellacosa snapped.

Paco Herbert laughed. "My accent? I was born in Yugoslavia, *cabrón*. I can speak four languages. Was raised in a community of women, so I grew up with many mothers and sisters. My biological father was an ethnomusicologist. Didn't see him a lot growing up until I got interested in the university. Things in Yugoslavia got pretty bad by then and I had to leave anyway. I wanted to be a writer when I was younger."

"What about your mothers?"

"My Mama Tila and Mama Yulia live down in Cuzco, in one of those eco-communities with my Mama Lux and my sister Xochitl. Mama Sol and Mama Silvina we buried. Last year. They died within a few days of each other. That happened to you, too, right? With your daughter, then your wife dying so close together?"

"I don't know," Bellacosa sighed. "I wouldn't put it quite like that. My wife, when she had our daughter, it was in the years of the food shortage. Before the filtering and all that. We'd been trying to be parents for a long time already. Our daughter, Yadira. She was born with a vitamin deficiency in her blood. That worsened as she got older. Of course we didn't find out until it was too late. When she passed away nothing could be the same. She was only four years old. My wife took it the hardest. And died of grief. I thought that phrase was an exaggeration before, but I've seen it happen in my life. Because my wife died of grief."

The old Jeep was the only idling automobile at a railroad intersection with no traffic light at the edge of the city, waiting for the last boxcar of a freight train to pass by. When it did Bellacosa made sure there wasn't a chaser, stepped on the gas, and drove over the tracks. Paco Herbert had already lit his crooked cigarette. Bellacosa pinched a

Herzegovina Flor from his pack and used the vehicle's built-in lighter to spark it.

"Tell me more about this. About the assignment you are working on," Bellacosa said, exhaling smoke.

Paco Herbert got taller in his seat and cranked the volume a notch on the stereo.

"Of course, yes. I'm glad you agreed to this, first of all. I would've got into a little trouble if I didn't find anybody, since I don't know if this opportunity will ever come again. It cost my bosses *buena plata*; they got a loan from a big investor for these tickets, a rich believer in the cause. I'll pay for all your gas, and here's the promised cash. In advance. I trust you. I want you to know that, Bellacosa. My people scored me these tickets, like I said, after two years of infiltrating circles of the black-market culinary world, and getting deep in it. But this should be, believe it or not, a pretty regular and safe affair, from the accounts that I've gathered. I myself am not worried, but it's okay if you are, and if you want we can talk about it."

"I don't think I'm worried, but tell me more about all of it. About these black-market dinners."

"Well, what do you know?"

"I suppose I only know what other people know. What they've been saying in the news and you can read in the papers."

"Okay, all right. That's totally fair. Where do I begin? The rules," Paco said, suddenly serious. "The important thing to know is that no matter who is there and who talks to you, and if you get into a conversation with anybody at all, you can't ask them about who they are, personally. Nor what it is they do for a living. That one especially. There's probably gonna be all kinds of big shots and motherfucking fat cats. But that's also the best part, because nobody is going to ask us anything about ourselves, either. It's great, that way we don't have to get our story straight or anything. This is a complicated network, where the money funnels through a certain channel where only the necessary information is disclosed. I just got the address a little over an hour ago from my people. They're always moving, always having these dinners in different spots. And guess how much each pair of tickets is. Guess. Seven hundred ninety-nine million cubic pesos. That's how much I would make in twenty-five years, Bellacosa. If I'm lucky. And if they don't retire me early. So these are some serious high rollers we will be surrounded with. In other words, respected people in society. High-class types. You can talk about the food, even the order of the day, as long as it's not too outlandish or offensive. But I don't have to tell you, you understand all this, right? I only bring it up in case somebody there is a fast talker, you never know when it comes to rich strangers."

"What is the actual address to this place?"

Paco Herbert read the address aloud from a torn piece of notebook paper.

"I think I know that place. Strange, yes. I'm familiar with that area."

"Is that right? You been there already? How?"

"I had some business near there not very long ago. Was there to get a rig, you know, one of those used to dig through thick surfaces, like asphalt."

"Or some kind of rock, maybe. The side of a cliff," Paco mused.

"I imagine it could, yes. I have a client who does construction down in Mexico who needed one."

"Yes, you're like a scout or something."

"I find equipment. Cars. Even motorcycles, for people looking for something specific and have the money. I take a small cut."

"Excuse me," Paco interrupted, "but I've got to tell you another thing. About the meal again. Whatever it is, we have to eat it. Did I already mention this? We can't have them giving us the wonky eye for leaving our plates half-full. I need to know your ethics with this."

"Ethics?" Bellacosa asked. "Okay. Then I need to ask you in plain terms. What we're doing now is, we're attending one of those underground feasts? Connected to the filtering syndicates? Where they prepare meals of filtered animals, like the chicken ancestor birds and pandas?"

Paco Herbert fished another cigarette from his coat pocket, this one crooked almost at a forty-five-degree angle, and with his fingers tried to straighten it before lighting it.

"In essence, yes. They rotate the chefs and people working the kitchens in this network. Everybody gets paid big bucks. Word tonight is they got some chefs from northwest Spain running the joint. You ever been to Spain, Bellacosa?"

"Wait, I don't understand. What is your purpose? Why do you even want to come out here and get involved with all this?"

Paco Herbert turned to Bellacosa, leaning his elbow on the passenger door, and made a face as if trying to remember a famous speech.

"Well. That's a good question. I don't know. Look at me. You think my job pays me shit? You think I'd rather not be out at some bar trying to tell a pretty young thing how I always carry *The Portable Coleridge* and know his vision of 'Kubla Khan' by memory? There's a bunch of other things I'd rather be doing. Also, if you knew quite well where we were going and what was expected to happen, then why did you agree to come along? Maybe for the same reason that I'm this far into doing this, too. Knowing the rumors and obscure facts, you and me are the kind that don't mind the unknown. We are the people who face the world, and not simply for the challenge, or to prove a point. But to witness it, to know the facts at least for ourselves. I just happen to be in a position where I'm able to maybe communicate those facts and get them out on a wide level, to expose the corruption hindering our collective spirit in its continual ascent. We can't let this evil slow it down. It's my job to report our setbacks and celebrate what makes us flourish. I'm not here just getting my kicks. At least not as far as the meal ticket goes. I need to be there, inside, to properly communicate it. I need to see for myself what it's like and how it works, and then expose it. Lay it bare. And the meal, well. It will probably be one of the greatest dishes I'll ever have. Certainly the most expensive, *coño*, like I said. Damn. But. As far as the moral and possibly karmic consequences of eating an animal that is not natural, that God intended to be dead forever and ever, I'm not even thinking about that. I'm already past it, in fact. And you? Do you stand all right with it? If not, please talk to me."

"I think . . . that I'm okay with it," Bellacosa said. "The worst that can happen is I die, and that's fine by me. But it just occurred to me now when you said these animals, that should be long dead from this planet, weren't made by God. If you think about it, *we* are God-made. You and me. Humans. Everyday people. Even these people in the filtering syndicates. So even if they are creating these animals artificially through filtering, then God has a hand in that, too. The animals have to be God-made as well. Wouldn't you think so?"

"Either way," Paco Herbert said, "it's sick. This is the part I'm least proud of, but I have no problem doing it. If it's closer to putting an end to this culinary prehistoric chickenshit, or what have you, I'd pluck the bird and cook it myself."

EIGHT

THE WEATHER TURNED COLD, AND IT STARTED TO DRIZZLE in South Texas. Deep in the plump darkness of Calantula County, Bellacosa wondered about the true fate of the Aranaña Indian farmer Tranquilino, as they passed the doghouse-sized mailbox in front of the land where his trailer no longer stood.

"Here we go," Paco Herbert said. "This is the password right here, but I don't know how they're going to ask for it."

On a white business card the words "*pollo asado*" were typed out.

Bellacosa remembered the nauseating feeling from the day the deal for the 7900 Rig went bad, when he'd approached the same address and smelled the phantom, synthetic smell in the air. It had given him a sense of otherworldly doom that was making his stomach turn once again. He recalled the cuts and bruises along Tranquilino's face, and in a flash saw the fate of his brother in the fate of that Aranaña Indian farmer. Bellacosa for the first time felt remorse over leaving Tranquilino to deal with his own problems, and wondered about his own complicity for doing business with Leone McMasters.

It stopped drizzling when they turned into the narrow, unpaved road. About twenty feet from where the sealed gate was located there was a parked military vehicle with a grenade launcher and machine gun bolted on the rear bed, with one soldier wearing a bulletproof vest and helmet manning both. Two men out of uniform stood under a wide, anchored umbrella about five feet from the gate. One of them held a clipboard along with a small flashlight; the other had an automatic weapon and some kind of communication headgear with tiny flashing green lights that at a distance resembled fireflies.

Out of nowhere, on Paco Herbert's side, another armed man with headgear knocked rapidly on the window and in perfect English ordered for it to be lowered and the lights of the Jeep shut off. The man with the clipboard leaned down and, in the most polite way, as he flashed an unintrusive light on their faces, said, "*Buenas noches*, good evening. Do you gentlemen have a password written down?"

There was silence as Paco Herbert held up the card with the password. The man took the card, read through his clipboard without the light, and checked the password from the list.

"Enjoy, gentlemen. Just drive right in there until you reach the second gate, they'll tell you where to park. And please keep your headlights off."

Bellacosa drove the old Jeep past the grim gate that was like an open mouth with jagged teeth, the driveway a gravel tongue carved on the South Texas soil leading them over a hill. A thick, jellylike shrubbery ran under the foliage of perching mesquite trees, where the light of the condor moon seeped through. If there were still coyotes certainly one would be howling, because their lover was once the South Texas moon, but they are doomed to be separated forever now; the fact that the coyotes were missing made their forbidden love all the more tragic.

The ground leveled out upon approaching the second gate, where the men in the same firefly headgear had their weapons holstered and opened up the gate no questions asked. A faceless man waving neon batons instructed Bellacosa on where to park, and Bellacosa obeyed, following a row of five other vehicles of recent models, different makes.

When Bellacosa and Paco Herbert stepped off and locked the old Jeep, a voice in the dark said, "Right over there, gentlemen."

They followed a strangely smooth granite walkway, and at a football field's distance there was an oddly shaped Civil War–era house lit only from the front, its size indeterminable; green, but even the color seemed to shift in the darkness. Hidden in the dark space between the parking lot and the house were a few armed soldiers, all of them wearing the firefly headgear. The house had a second-story porch with unused chairs and tables. Christmas lights wrapped around lime trees on the lawn, where a woman in a silver dress stood drinking white wine. She greeted Bellacosa and Paco Herbert in a very welcoming, pleasant manner.

They returned the formality. Bellacosa recognized a Mozart piano sonata piping from the house itself, when a young cocktail waitress carrying a tray with red and white wineglasses intercepted them. She said, "Welcome, gentlemen, *bienvenidos*. Do you prefer to be waited on in English or Spanish this evening?"

Paco Herbert half shrugged his shoulders and turned to Bellacosa, then said, "*Inglés* is fine."

"Excellent. Please grab a glass, we have a 1978 Pinot Noir from the Menoculpta casks in Argentina, and a white Australian Zinfandel from the Jemima Ünger centenary batch."

They both chose the red.

By the right rail of the wide yellow stairs leading up the front porch sat an old man wearing an epaulet jacket and a young woman wearing a pastel-colored dress poufed at the shoulders. Between them wiggled a hooved animal that perplexed Bellacosa and Paco Herbert. In the dim lighting it looked like a pig with tiny ears, but it acted very doglike, with its front legs erect. A slurping, salivating tongue hung out of its mouth, which was actually a beak, like a chicken's or rooster's. It had the dark green skin of a crocodile, with rivulets shining like a fine pair of boots, and somebody had tied a handkerchief with the border-disarmament symbol around its neck. The girl in the pastel dress was petting the animal slowly as the older man drank his Zinfandel.

"Is the server still bringing her a carrot?" the girl asked the man in the epaulet jacket. She had an English accent.

Just then the cocktail waitress swooped down and handed the girl a couple of carrots on a ceramic plate and a napkin. "Thank you so much," the girl said.

The creature got visibly excited, though it remained in its seated position. The girl dangled a carrot over its mouth and slowly lowered it as the piglike reptile delighted in the treat, breaking off chunks with its beak and eating gluttonously.

Bellacosa and Paco Herbert watched her feed it another carrot, and afterward the girl told them, "Her name is Porgy."

"What do you call this kind of animal?" Bellacosa asked.

"It's a Trufflepig," she said. "Is this your first time with one? Personally, it's my favorite part of these outings. They love carrots. The server will bring you one if you ask, then you can feed it to her."

"So it's a she?" Paco Herbert asked.

The girl in the pastel dress laughed and, petting the Trufflepig, said, "No, I don't believe they have a sex, actually. She just seems very girlish to me. Look at her. How happy she is. Such a sweetie."

"It's surprising how still she is, and yet how excited," Paco Herbert exclaimed.

"Aw, well, that's because she can't walk. See."

She nudged the Trufflepig, and spun it around with her hands. Its hooves shifted to remain balanced as its stumpy tail wiggled, but other than this it didn't seem to move, and was delighted in the way the girl played with it.

More than any other time in recent memory, Bellacosa was at a loss for words. He leaned down and petted the creature hesitantly. Its skin was colder than the night and felt like expensive plastic.

"Just don't touch her around the beak, that's how she breathes, see. I don't think she'll actually bite you, however."

Suddenly Porgy the Trufflepig made something like soft panting sounds and squeezed a stream of clear milk out of its eyes.

"She likes you," the girl said.

Paco Herbert also petted it and the old man in the epaulet lifted his glass. "Cheers," the old man said to those around him.

Everybody including the girl toasted, although she didn't have a drink.

Bellacosa felt it would be a good idea to mingle elsewhere. Paco Herbert began conversing with a silver-haired man, already sharing big laughs. As Bellacosa moved away he looked down at the Trufflepig once again, the English girl in the pastel dress smiling right at him.

Chuckling nervously, Bellacosa and Paco Herbert stood side by side again, a bit removed from the other people in attendance; there were about eight, the girl in the pastel dress being the youngest. Everybody was making a pleasant evening of it, promenading on the lawn, sipping drinks at their own leisure.

There was a red-faced man with graying hair and a mustache in a black suit and yellow tie by a short palm tree. Accompanying him was a blonde in her late twenties, wearing a tight evening gown that matched his hair. The man kept one arm around her waist, so there was no mistaking whom she was with to any admirer. He spoke to her in Spanish and she responded in English.

Another couple was standing around one of the glowing lime trees. They were middle-aged, drinking red wine, cracking jokes to one another, and dressed as if they were audience members at an opera in a different time and place: she with an exotic fur draped around her sleeveless gown, he with a three-piece suit, bow tie, and pince-nez, which he constantly removed and put back on. One suspected they'd never spent a dull moment in their long lives together.

A bald man who looked like a land baron with many serfs to his name sat at the far left end of the downstairs porch. He was the only person in attendance, besides the girl, who was not drinking. A young man, presumably his son, sat by a few exotic vermilion potted plants on the edge of the porch, laughing to himself and drinking a High Life tallboy.

The girl in the pastel dress with the Trufflepig stood on the porch steps and began reciting:

"Una giovane donna di Tolosa
bell' e gentil, d'onesta leggiadria,
è tant'e dritta e simigliante cosa
ne' suoi dolci occhi, della donna mia,"

while from the lake of darkness between the house and parking lot two men in their mid-thirties resembling grungy artists emerged. That's also when Bellacosa spotted the bane of the past week of his life: the 7900 Rig, silhouetted at a quiet distance like a scarecrow against the bottle-glass, smoky night. It was by a couple of other machines that sat prostrate, like giant primates weary of worshipping the hills. Bellacosa made a move toward the machine, and sensing his sudden jolt in curiosity Paco Herbert gently grabbed his arm to stop him. Bellacosa shot him a wry smile, and sipped on his wine.

"Good evening to everybody," one of the grungy men said. He wore black skinny jeans with a leather jacket and carried a small umbrella. The other man was bearded and, unlike his friend, not wearing sunglasses.

"Can I get everyone's attention, please?"

The commanding voice that said this belonged to a woman of indeterminable age. Her hair was auburn and she wore business attire, with black high-heeled shoes.

The ten dinner guests, along with Paco Herbert and Bellacosa, directed their attention to this woman, who was standing on the middle of the porch stairs.

"First of all," she said with a smile, "I would like to

welcome all of you on behalf of the partners and myself. My name for this meal is Josie, and I'm sure you've met Michaela, who will be your server tonight. Just a quick rundown for you about proper etiquette that is expected of our guests. Remember that it is courteous to talk and share, and it is encouraged. But personal information inquired about or disclosed will not be tolerated. This includes with our staff, who have been trained to refrain even from making eye contact with you. We ask that you be respectful and mind the manners of the old court at this house, which was built in Pennsylvania around 1857. Drinks are unlimited and we trust everyone here is mature enough to hold their alcohol. As you've noticed, we have a couple of Trufflepigs for your enjoyment, and we ask that you be gentle with them. Aside from these formalities, we are confident you will enjoy tonight's one-of-a-kind dinner, which I am pleased to announce: Appetizers to the meal tonight will be lightly fried gizzards of Mare aux Songes dodo birds, partnered with our homemade aioli sauce. Our chef, originally from Seville, has specially prepared for you tonight Steak Charlemagne. Our culinary doctors have perfected the filtering of the lost bull species that roamed the green countryside of Italy and France in the days of Charlemagne. A bull revered during its time by both the French and the Romans, until a plague that was later traced to the tree nut the bulls were attracted to killed them off. It is served in sixteen-ounce portions, cooked in butter made from the fat of the Pampa blue-billed goose. Six hundred years after the

Charlemagne bull died off, this goose from the same region followed suit. It will be served with Mayan scallops prepared in the traditional style, and green beans. Another staple of the night will be Galapagos stew, or Galapagos Gumbo, as it is widely known. It contains rainbow trout and Pieria gulf salmon. The chef promises a Cajun twist to this old favorite. Stay tuned for dessert. All the wines were handpicked by our chef and myself, and were imported for this specific meal. If anybody needs anything or has any comments I ask that you approach only me. Many thanks. And again, welcome."

A couple of stout, brown-skinned men wearing white suits went around carrying what appeared to be fried alligator, with a dipping sauce, on nicely arranged trays. Looking down at it, Bellacosa told himself that it must be the dodo bird. The word "dodo" suddenly reminded him of American children name-calling one another. When a tray floated by, Bellacosa and Paco Herbert each grabbed a strip and dipped it in the floral-patterned ramekin with aioli.

They both ate like it was nothing.

"Dodo gizzards, huh," Bellacosa muttered. He wanted to laugh. They tasted like any old fried fish or chicken nugget. It occurred to Bellacosa that this whole dinner could be some kind of elaborate scam. That nothing they'd consume would actually come from extinct, filtered animals. They were working the placebo effect, and all these people who paid *buena plata* were fools.

Murmurs of approval fluttered like polite bats among the dinner guests.

Suddenly the grungy man wearing sunglasses said, loud enough for all to hear, "Charlemagne steak, huh? For a second I thought they were filtering the man himself back to life, and they'd be serving us his balls."

The old man wearing the epaulet was all good times, and was the only person to laugh a natural, effortless laugh, along with the grungy bearded man. The other guests fidgeted. Michaela the server pretended not to hear.

Bellacosa spotted Josie greeting guests individually, and shaking everyone's hand. When she got to Paco Herbert and Bellacosa she did the same and also thanked them. As Josie walked away both of them noticed the firefly headgear hidden in her hair, wrapped around her left ear.

The twelve guests were asked kindly to shuffle inside the house, where they were assured that there was very comfortable seating available.

The girl in the pastel dress carried in the Trufflepig and placed it on a small marble table by a bust of Pallas Athena in the vestibule. The guests moved toward the lounging area of the house, and the girl stood by the threshold petting the Trufflepig. Although she didn't see him standing behind her, the girl felt Bellacosa's presence as he stared at the Trufflepig in quiet amazement. Under the electric candlelight he clearly saw its beaded, jungle-green flesh, and its stumpy tail, which looked like a cigar someone had put out on its back. The Trufflepig made light panting sounds from its beak, and its pink, drooling tongue looked fake as it reflected off the shiny table. Once again Bellacosa mustered the courage to pet it. For a second he convinced himself this creature wasn't real. But he kept his hand on it and felt its inner warmth, its breathing. The Trufflepig was definitely not an illusion nor a machine.

"Hard to believe how obedient it is," Bellacosa said quietly to the girl. "It doesn't run around and bother anyone, getting in the way like a misbehaving animal."

"She would if she could, I'm sure. But she can't. It's the way her body is structured that prohibits any movement. Which is why they probably died off. But here she is, right? Alive again. It's interesting, don't you think? How the Trufflepig has reappeared. Even in this filtered way. After the Aranaña tribe came back."

"How do you mean?"

The girl smiled at Bellacosa, like it was he who was the younger, inexperienced one. She looked around to make sure they were alone, and eyed her old-man companion in the lounging room with the others. "What do you mean, how do I mean? You older generation are a weird bunch. I try to tell my father, but he's of that old mentality and doesn't understand, either. You know the Aranaña tribe, right?"

"Yes. The Indians from down here, of course."

"Calling them that is insensitive. They're a tribe. They are the original natives from these parts, but they were gone for a long time. Like over four hundred years. Nobody was ever really sure that they even existed. And a generation or two ago a lot of them came back. From the desert, they say. And their children and grandchildren are as much a part of our society now as any other race."

"Okay. Yes, that part I think is true."

"Well, don't you think that's super weird?"

"I don't understand what this has to do with the Trufflepig."

The girl in the pastel dress seemed suddenly put off by their exchange. "I mean. You know the Trufflepig is the deity creature the Aranaña worshipped. What they called Huixtepeltinicopatl. It was written in old scrolls that were supposedly destroyed forever. I'm sure you've heard."

Bellacosa half shook his head and half nodded. He was about to say something, then the girl picked up the Trufflepig. "Excuse me," she said, "I have to go now," and joined the others.

Bellacosa warily followed suit. The lounging area was very tastefully decorated, a lot of desert tones along the fine rugs and antebellum wooden walls, which seemed to expand then shrink like the house was breathing. The ceiling was high, with strong wooden beams running across the length of the house, and dim lamps were scattered throughout, keeping every corner well lit. There was a large dry aquarium with a fake island setting in the middle of the room, and inside were what appeared to be strangely shaped, blue-gray-feathered baby chicks, only they weren't running around pecking each other, but instead were waddling, following an invisible trail of circles and loops, occasionally bumping into each other only to continue the opposite way like tiny bumper cars. They were baby dodo birds. Paco Herbert was leaning toward the aquarium, getting a good look at them.

Bellacosa realized he had tracked in mud and felt embarrassed. He walked back out the entrance, where on the porch was Josie very stoically listening to the tall, thin, serf-owning-looking man. He seemed agitated, like he was registering a complaint. His mustache crawled as he tacked his words together and gesticulated the way angry businessmen do in silent films.

Bellacosa made eye contact with Josie and shot her a smile that expressed sympathy and a plea for forgiveness, as if he was associated with this man.

He wiped the mud off in a thick patch of dewy grass and managed to chuckle as he saw the 7900 Rig once again. When he walked back Josie and the serf-owner were gone. He made sure the mud stains on the rug weren't much, then saw a middle-aged lady with volcano-brown hair and a spray bottle, who had cleaned his mess. She smiled at Bellacosa as if they were old playground friends, which threw him off and left him speechless. She seemed a gentle soul, out of place there. He thanked her quietly and didn't quite make out the words she mouthed as he made his way back to the lounging room.

NINE

THE TWO MEN RESEMBLING GRUNGY ARTISTS WHO WERE the last to arrive were having white wine and laughing boisterously in front of a rectangular glass case propped up at waist level by the crackling fireplace. Bellacosa picked up vibes from the serf-owner that he was disturbed by the presence of these men. The serf-owner gave airs of being above not only them, but the other guests as well. He hovered by the fireplace and red velvet couches, the kind you see naked Renaissance ladies lying on in paintings. His son was finishing off his tallboy and admiring a work of art on a panoramic canvas, an image seemingly of the American frontier: cowboys driving cattle across a shallow stream in a junglelike terrain with red snakes coiled around sharinga rubber trees. The setting was very unlike the landscape of Texas, or the old west.

"That's a rough life and a half," Bellacosa heard the young man say, staring deeply at the painting.

The serf-owner was making direct eye contact with Bellacosa. Instinctively, Bellacosa almost introduced himself, then remembered the rules, and merely shook the serf-owner's hand. The three of them exchanged mild formalities, then there was a moment when they gazed at the painting, as if it was a window and the cattle drive was happening in front of them.

Bellacosa moved toward the rectangular glass case where the grungy artists were standing, and saw what they were laughing at. There were five shrunken heads with dark brown skin tones, done in the traditional way attributed to the Aranaña tribe, with the actual skulls also shrunken. They were the size of softballs and looked like skinned squirrels with their mouths sewn shut, rather than humans. All the shrunken heads had their weblike, frizzed hair hanging about a foot down and each was accompanied by a bronze plaque with a golden border. They had their eyes shut in lamentation, their mouths stitched using *huarango* thorns in the cicatrix pattern, and seemed to be holding a séance filled with eternal supplication, their souls' own purgatory trapped inside each skull. The plaques all read that the men who these heads belonged to were pure-blooded warrior descendants of the Mapuche Indians in South America. Bellacosa had never heard of such a thing. They must've carried an immense street value.

The bearded, grungy man said to Bellacosa, "Can you

believe they trust people not to steal the heads of these savages right out of here? Who's got a hammer?"

Bellacosa felt a fine-grained horror. *Sagrado horror*, as his ancestors would say. It struck him as more sinister than ever that the reports in the papers and media about the shrunken heads concerned real people. The media was also just people reporting on people, and it was people getting their heads cut off, it was real people doing the cutting, then the shrinking, then the smuggling, and selling. It wasn't some monster or cheap science-fiction alien conquest, but people creating all the horror, enslaving one another at all cost in a world where more and more syndicates and absolute power reigned supreme.

The grungy men were making racist jokes about the Mapuche Indians and the heads. One of them said, "They sew their mouths shut while they're alive, to keep their souls inside before beheading them, but these wetbacks don't have a soul. The people collecting them don't know what they're doing, we oughta steal them just to teach them a lesson. I don't even mind skipping the stupid meal, let's just pick up a pizza."

The two stout men in white suits were going around again with another round of the notorious dodo gizzards. Bellacosa felt sick to his stomach and reluctantly grabbed another. He looked over at Paco Herbert and saw him waving one sauce-dipped gizzard at him, like a baby's arm saying hello. Bellacosa averted his eyes from the aquarium of dodos to the left of Paco Herbert as he bit into the fried gizzard, ignoring also the ongoing slurs between the grungy men.

The girl in the pastel dress and the old man in the epaulet were at a farther end of the house, sitting at a small obsidian table. They were playing the card game speed bathhouse, and were slapping the table in rapid succession as the girl dealt the cards. A dark blue-and-black eel about a foot thick and ten feet long was mounted on an attractive varnished oak frame above them. It had morbid yellow eyes, and Bellacosa moved toward the creature's head as he held on to the rest of his dodo-gizzard strip.

"She's already got twenty-five bucks on me," the old man said to Bellacosa in a playful yet worried manner, while dealing the cards. "I don't know how she got so good at the game." He was slightly sweating as the girl in the pastel dress petted the Trufflepig on the table by her side.

"I told you, Father. The street-hustle tutorials at the public library. I'm a third-level street hustler already, and getting better. Me and Veronica have been going two days a week."

"I'll never understand kids these days."

"What is it you don't understand? I can explain it to you. Anybody can do it if they dedicate as much time as Veronica and I have. Bathhouse!" she exclaimed, slapping one hand down on the table. "I win again."

"Oh, I'll wire you the money when we get to the house."

Everybody, with the exception of Paco Herbert and Bellacosa, had taken a seat somewhere in the lounge area by now. Paco Herbert moved on to the shrunken-head display in the glass case, reading the plaques.

Bellacosa, with his eyes on the dodos that resembled a mad hatter's windup toys, thought that if there was a hell and he was sent there, he hoped it wouldn't be for eating this fried filtered dodo. He chewed and swallowed once again. It was actually delicious. He checked in with his bowels. They'd been agreeable with everything thus far, to which he felt grateful.

Maybe God is the mad hatter, Bellacosa thought. *We are all his windup toys.*

Josie rang a dinner bell and in a few moments all the guests were directed to the back section of the house, where the dining area was located. Twelve chairs lined up on the outer rim of a strange table shaped like a boomerang. Michaela filled water and wineglasses as the twelve guests all took their seats. The silverware was from the Romanov Dynasty. Each guest had a silver chalice that depicted a different scene from the life of Alexander Nevsky, which they used to drink Bordeaux from the vineyard of Eleanor of Aquitaine. Every guest was given their own bottle for themselves.

Bellacosa sat at the last seat farthest from the door, and to his left sat a very detached and introspective Paco Herbert. At the opposite end of the table, the girl in the pastel dress sat on the first chair, her father next to her. The middle-aged couple sat to her father's right, then the two grungy types, then the gray-haired man and his wife, then the serf-owner with his son to Paco Herbert's immediate left. The place looked like a Hollywood movie set, and not a cheap one. A dim, medieval chandelier hung from a thick chain in the middle of the ceiling; the flames of the candles placed around the room floated as if held by invisible hands in a vigil. Panoramic pastoral paintings hung from two of the walls, and a couple of abstracts surrounded the door.

Michaela and the suited servers carried out the Spanish chef's recipe for Galapagos Gumbo, which was reportedly the most highly coveted black-market dish. What gave it the Cajun twist, Michaela noted, was the newly perfected Carpathian trench bass, killed off the coast of Louisiana during the Industrial Revolution. Its spices were also derived from the king conch tortoise. Each bowl was served in an authentic tortoise shell.

Bellacosa didn't know that the king conch tortoise was known for its peculiar concave shape, like a Spanish knight's helmet. He admired its texture and the way it rested on the table. The soup was served with diced radishes, green onions, and a wedge of parsley. The steam from the Galapagos Gumbo floated around the room in the shape of many hands, with fingers that elongated and multiplied, making everyone's mouths water. Bellacosa waited until the others started in. The girl in pastel was the first to taste its broth. Paco Herbert was the second. Shortly after, everybody was finished with the Galapagos Gumbo and ready for the next course. All their faces were glowing with splendor. Bellacosa and Paco Herbert simply smiled as the others engaged in their own conversations and statements of approval. Michaela went around refilling drinks when the main course came out, the sixteen-ounce Steak Charlemagne, cooked with the Pampa blue-billed-goose butter and served with the Mayan scallops and green beans in a large, eggshell-colored plate.

Josie hovered over the entire dinner and the hidden, grumbling kitchen in the back of the house. She paced in and out of rooms and whispered into her headset with stiff ventriloquist lips. She walked to the front door with a big smile at one point, looked around the lawn and the darkness, signaled to somebody from afar, then walked back to the guests like a woman who could make a fortune on the stage.

Michaela was either on drugs or born to be a server—her movements and reflexes were fluid, and she responded to needs on the spot. The serf-owner was really making her dance, repeatedly asking her for napkins, requesting more ice cubes, complaining of cork pieces floating in his bottle of Bordeaux, which nobody else could see. A replacement wine was brought anyway, just to appease him. He wiped his mouth gently and darted nasty looks at the grungy types when they chewed or spoke loudly. Even when they proposed a toast to everybody in the room the serf-owner appeared annoyed.

Every time Bellacosa would look up he'd catch the girl in the pastel dress staring his way. Perhaps he was mistaken and she was looking at a decoration hanging behind him, but there was nothing interesting on that part of the wall when he looked. He felt nothing at all sexual in their communication, and took the whole thing rather lightly. Then he couldn't help for a moment but think about his dead daughter and his wife. He remembered what an old friend had told him about grief when the time came to bury his daughter, Yadira: the dead, for the rest of our lives, will keep following us, finding ways to tell us they are still among us, lending the living a hand. Then after his wife passed away he'd notice gestures or expressions in strange women, a smile or gaze that took him back to the woman he loved for many years and then buried. It'd been almost ten years since Yadira had died, and the strangest thing about the girl in the pastel dress was that in her eyes he saw not only his wife, Lupita, but also the spirit of his daughter.

Bellacosa ate his meal thinking of pleasant things, too, and drank the finest red wine he'd ever had. It must've truly been the blood of Christ. *One day it will happen*, he thought. *It is only a matter of time before they bring Christ back through the filtering process, and we will kill him over many times just to keep bottling his blood. They'll use it to cook the meat instead of olive oil, and afterward to get plastered drunk.* Bellacosa looked around for the Trufflepig but didn't see it anywhere. The girl in the pastel dress smiled, in a half-mocking manner this time, as if she could read his thoughts. He cut and chewed the Steak Charlemagne. The goose butter was melted like a sun over the tender meat, pink in the middle to perfection, the kind of steak that grew on trees in the days of Adam and Eve. The scallops and green beans were also exceptional. Thinking of the Trufflepig again, Bellacosa wondered if that was the name assigned by Adam himself, and laughed. He turned to Paco Herbert, who also seemed to be enjoying the meal. For a second he almost told him the joke, then simply waved his fork and forgot all about it.

The first to order dessert were the middle-aged couple and the girl in the pastel dress. There were three options, Michaela informed them: the Chevalier Royale Cheesecake, the House Flan, made from the eggs of Moroccan quail and topped with Scandinavian caramel, and the Chef's Crema Catalana. Bellacosa requested the Chevalier Royale Cheesecake to go, since he felt quite full, and Paco Herbert the Crema Catalana.

After the dinner, in the lounging area, the middle-aged couple started to tango without any music. The grungy types clapped beats and hooted them on. The girl in the pastel dress requested a dance with her father, and together they danced something very formal and old-fashioned. The middle-aged couple were transported to a ghetto in Buenos Aires where the tango was born, and the girl in the pastel dress and her father to a nineteenth-century Rothschild gala. The grungy types continued to clap time as the dodo chicks ran around in the aquarium like frantic toy soldiers. The serf-owner and his son, the gray-haired man and his wife, and Paco Herbert and Bellacosa, along with the five shrunken Mapuche Indian heads, merely looked on in cold silence.

TEN

EVERYBODY TIPPED WELL, HAD THE LEFTOVER WINES RE-sealed, crossed the empty field in jovial spirits, and ignored the guards scattered around the property in the panther twilight. Bellacosa and Paco Herbert got in the old Jeep, put their dessert and bottles in the back. From a distance the oblong estate looked like a washed-up Noah's Ark, the thick of it concealed by the darkness in the Valley. The armed men who had greeted them earlier at the gates waved good-night as the dinner guests' vehicles drove out. The night had gone over for them without an incident.

Driving once more through the outskirts of Calantula County, Bellacosa turned the stereo up, and the voice of Eddie Cantor was saying, "Many of them risk their lives for victory in the air. Surely the least we can do on the home front is to lend our dollars to Uncle Sam for war bonds. No matter what we've done before, we must do more right now. Figure out the total of your family income. Calculate your necessary living expenses and the extra for more war bonds in a savings payroll bank. Yes, figure it out for yourself, and you'll find you can increase your purchase of war bonds every week or every payday. Your investment in victory and peace."

Then it went from sounding like an advertisement to something of a radio play, and Eddie Cantor lowered his voice to ominous music: "One of our planes went missing. Two hours overdue. One of our planes went missing with all its soldiers, too. The signals stopped coming. We couldn't hear a word. And suddenly through the humming: *Coming in on a wing and a prayer, coming in on a wing and a prayer. Though there's one moment gone, we can still carry on, coming in on a wing and a prayer . . .*"

"That animal," Bellacosa finally said, over the loud stereo. "Did you see the animal again after we started eating?"

Paco Herbert said, "Which animal?" He grabbed and uncorked his leftover wine, took a long chug without spilling a drop, and with his fingers started eating his dessert.

THEY DISCUSSED their impressions and went over details about the dinner and the guests until they ran out of steam and got back to MacArthur. Bellacosa dropped Paco Herbert off at the place he was staying, and both agreed to meet and discuss further in a few days, after they'd had time to digest everything properly.

Bellacosa started to feel very dehydrated, and the memory of the clear, milky residue that emitted from the Trufflepig's eyes rained down on him as if from the stars.

He parked along the street in his neighborhood and, walking to his front door, noticed the smell of broth cooking in the air, thick with vegetables and meat. He thought it was probably a bit late for anybody to be cooking, but after the night he'd just had, who the hell was he to tell anybody how to have their dinner?

Impulsively, before he walked into his shack, Bellacosa did a little stretch. He hadn't been stretching as regularly as he'd been accustomed to, and this day had really run a number on his back muscles. He leaned forward and touched his toes, bent backward, swiveled side to side, and his back gave a healthy crack that made him groan.

"That was a great dinner," he said to himself, "but too bad it had to be a dinner." It was the tongue-in-cheek slogan of the FBI branch in charge of black-market dinners in the state of Texas, usually juxtaposed over an image of a person behind bars. Bellacosa said it without any irony as he jiggled a key into the doorknob and entered his shack.

The smell of the broth was wafting like fog along a harbor inside his place.

Bellacosa thought, *Did I leave something on, or what?*

He paced rapidly toward the kitchen, leaving the front door wide open. There were vegetables and chicken bones boiling in a big pot, with all the lights of the shack turned off. Looking into the boiling soup, Bellacosa realized he hadn't cooked a meal in this place probably ever.

Something clicked behind him and he suddenly feared that as soon as he turned around there would be trouble. That an intruder was already plotting to kill him.

A cloaked figure shut the front door slowly while sitting on the easy chair in the shadows.

Spooked, Bellacosa exclaimed, "*Quien fregados está aquí*," in the most menacing way he could, holding the bottle of red wine like a weapon.

The figure stood up and Bellacosa saw its balding silhouette with patches of thin, disheveled hair in front of the blue windowpane. Bellacosa felt that he'd been transported to a place more like a graveyard than his shack, as the boiling pot gurgled in the kitchen, and the bloody smell of flesh torn apart by machines pulled at his nerves.

The balding figure said, "*Soy yo, hermano.* Oswaldo. Don't turn on the lights, please. Not that." The voice carried a noticeable speech impediment.

Bellacosa swiftly set the bottle of wine on the kitchen counter. Oswaldo appeared unstable and deranged, but grounded in his composure. He wore a brown trench coat, a style Bellacosa hadn't seen in years. In the darkness, Bellacosa felt his brother was looking at him yet not, and he couldn't directly make out his eyes.

He hugged his brother, whose death he'd already lamentably come to terms with in his own grieving manner.

"Oswaldo," Bellacosa said. "Oswaldo, what happened to you, my brother?"

"Look what they did to me," he wheezed. "I haven't looked in a mirror. A mirror is too bright for me. What does it matter? *Ya está hecho.* It is done. I'm finally becoming accustomed again to talking, see? You wouldn't believe. You wouldn't believe how a *huarango* thorn burns when it pierces your flesh. Imagine. Imagine them all over your mouth. Like this. They were going to shrink my head. They were going to shrink my head yet didn't. I saw them. I saw them do it to a lot of others. Women, too. Young. Kids. All ages with dark skin. It's hard to believe, brother. I can't repeat those things again to another human. It went through my mind that one day . . . I should go to mass to confess and tell a priest now, now that I'm not what I was, a shrunken head to be. Sorry, sorry. I can't feel myself talk and it comes out too fast not making sense at times. There's somebody trying to become the new kingpin out there. Men were moving a group of us to another, to a different location. But there was an accident. And I remember running. I remember the river. There was smoke going up like this, like this, in little pieces like confetti. Don't remember how until a man found me. A Border Protector, of all people. Who is secretly part of the Phantom Recruits. He took me to a woman who was something like an angel, and I thanked God that I was still alive. Strange, because I had begged Him to kill me, before. To end it all rather than keep seeing them do it, to cut the head off another person and to suffer. And to be fated the same fate."

Bellacosa brought the broth down to a low boil, and Oswaldo sat in the easy chair by the door, next to the shrine of candles for his wife, Lupita, his daughter, Yadira, and the dead. There was also the picture of Oswaldo as a young boy, which he'd recently added. When Bellacosa sat down on a stool and faced Oswaldo, he tried to really find his eyes in the dark living room. Bellacosa asked why he couldn't turn on the lights, and Oswaldo replied because he no longer had his old eyes.

"*Como*?" Bellacosa asked, slightly afraid, feeling a deep dread for his brother that was, like the broth, slowly boiling.

"Yes. The headhunters in Sindicato Unidos. They were going to shrink my head and sell it. Doing it the way they suppose the Aranañas did. The Arananã doctor working for them started the process, the process with me, and my soul, and I'm sensitive to all light now. The doctor inserted the spirit called *altalumbre*, and sewed all our mouths shut. To keep our real spirits inside our skulls, our holy ghost forever fighting, never here nor there. Get it? The Aranaña Indians. They knew this about people, about our souls. People think the Aranaña used actual souls as currency. That this was their sustainability as a race for a long time, this untouchable fabric which makes us human, our souls. See? Even though in their core people make them out to be idiots, and are discriminated against by us, by all the people.

Aranaña descendants have the most demanding, degrading jobs and are discouraged from education, through—through political influences. It's all a disguise. *Una máscara*, it's a mask the Aranaña have to wear, just like other people. Brother, I am not myself anymore. Bright lights make me blind, and only in the nighttime do I have energy. I don't know why I was made to survive, you see, you see? I survived, I am here. Right, brother? I am here with you."

"Yes, yes you are, Oswaldo."

"I am here but I am not here. This is my new mask, the one I am made to wear now. Like the Aranaña. I used your kitchen. I can't eat and hope you are not, not hungry. *Perdón*. The thing is that I have a worm growing. A worm that is always inside me, always growing. Every day. The only way to get it out is with a broth, or it gets bigger. And when it's out, a new one starts over, and time to cook another broth. The thing is, also, that I'm here and I am not here."

In a fit of desperation Bellacosa said, "I tried to find you. Remember Manolo, from when we were boys? He's the head detective they got in Reinahermosa now. He's been helping me out."

Devoid of emotion, Oswaldo interrupted: "That's who did it. Manolo, from the neighborhood. *Se lo va llevar el diablo*. It was that *perro*."

"No," Bellacosa said. "That can't be."

Oswaldo's body lightly trembled, then he grabbed ahold of the side of the chair and lifted himself up.

"Yes. Somebody figured out I owned a couple abandoned

buildings. They started using them for their dirty business. When I reported them to the police they came and got me. But with the kingpin Pacheco dead there's a new war on the rise. Listen. I listen to myself saying these things and my mouth stings. So much. When I speak. But it's not really me, brother, can you see this, too, that it's not me? My eyes can't adjust to the bright light of day, tell me what now if I can't do that? Is my mouth sealed shut again? My mouth was shut. With the *huarango* thorns, my mouth was shut, and my soul was trapped to fight the spirit *altalumbre* too long, too long. I'm shaken up inside. We're not really here, but we are. Past, present, and future. Father, Son, and the Holy Ghost. Every Aranaña is all three, brother. Brother, you. You and all the others are only sons. We can live only in one world. But the Aranaña live in all three. You understand me, right? Each of them is a trinity, and sons are only a part of that trinity. We are stuck in the present, and they are perpetual. Sons can gain enlightenment by learning the Father and the Holy Ghost through many, many lifetimes. The Aranaña don't need lifetimes. They are lifetimes. Understand, brother? The place I am in now is a difficult place, where are the birds, where are the stars? I am no longer a son. No longer anything, can you see that? I can't achieve enlightenment, happiness. Or love. I don't have a soul in me, or the one that was there is lost. Shaken up. So I've contacted my sons, Luis and Ricardito. And sent my ex-wife a note, too. I hope I can see my boys one last time. As a father I think I've done good to them, though I know they resent me. My sons are old enough to be their own men, as you know. In the divorce they took their mother's side."

Oswaldo had moved into the kitchen and Bellacosa stood up and followed him. Before the stove, Bellacosa watched his brother's features. A nerve on the right side of Oswaldo's face was twitching, and for the first time Bellacosa saw the wounds where the *huarango* thorns had been sewn around his mouth. They looked like tiny mouths themselves, as if God decided more were needed to attain true silence. They'd been bleeding and it was unclear to Bellacosa whether they were healing or infected. Oswaldo was mumbling something about the broth and Bellacosa placed his hand on his brother's shoulder as he stirred the pot with a wooden spoon.

Bellacosa said, "I'm very sorry about everything, Oswaldo. Tell me what I can do."

"I no longer know what sorry means, Esteban. Don't feel sorry. I can't feel anything, just the sound of the words. There are a lot of things impossible to me now. Look at me. Who am I? Am I a ghost? I think that I am. But something about me is still human, can still yearn. It burns out more and more every moment, but there's still a yearning in there, in here. I was made to live this whole time for something. The Border Protector that found me, he's in with the Phantom Recruits. I'm helping him. I'm helping him with the little I can remember. This big thing is happening, a great big voice in the deep night tells me. I listen to the shadows, they know the evil hiding in their crevices. The *viejita* he took me to, she's a descendant of Arañaña, and still in touch with the old, true culture. She can get me to the other side now. I just have to go to her and she can finish it. Finish the process. But the only way to finish it is by death. If I die. This, how you see me now. This is the only way I can keep living if I live. She warned me the longer I lived with this the more tormenting it all becomes. With the worm, the worm inside of me, always growing, always needing to get it out. But I need to say goodbye to my sons. To my family. I wasn't thinking of saving myself."

Oswaldo carried the pot to the living room and set it on the tiled floor.

"I wanted to see you, too, brother. You were always the gifted one of the two of us. I can see that now. I was never there for you or your family. I was never there for Mother. I held things about our childhood against all people, and against you. But I never considered that we were both only boys. And Mother and Father, they were only kids, too, when they had us. But we were all affected, affected deeply after Father died and we were left all alone. Mother couldn't even read. And I carried only the bad things that happened with me into old age. And those are my sins. I never gave you the money you needed. For you when your daughter died. Or when Lupita passed away, this is true. My sons, I know that both my sons are evil-spirited young men. That's what they are, and I know now the reason is because they took, they took from me. And what do I have now? I was made to survive for something, and what I can do I will do, from now until my true end. Manolo, they're getting Manolo, the Phantom Recruits know all about him. Rest assured of that. He's getting tied in with crooked Americans with money. But not for long. This big thing is happening, you'll see. In this soup, you know what's in here? It's real coyote bones. The only way to get rid of this worm inside me."

Bellacosa was on his feet when his brother grabbed the handles of the pot as if they were the ears of the coyote itself.

Oswaldo said, "Talking tires me. I can't talk anymore. You don't have to be here to watch me do this."

He was on his knees before the pot, like a drunk about to hurl into the toilet, and with his mouth wide open breathed in the steam of the coyote bones and vegetable broth. He did it in grinding heaves, like it was painful to his body.

Bellacosa watched his brother retch a couple of times, then his body began to shake wildly, his face turning red then purple. Suddenly, with an obscene, shocking grace, a pearly worm an inch and a half thick slid out of his throat and his mouth and into the hot broth. Oswaldo's throat gurgled and the length of the tapeworm seemed interminable. He heaved and heaved and finally the pale tail of the tapeworm showed and the ordeal was over. Oswaldo gasped for air and his complexion turned pallid again. He made quick arrangements to his composure and began excusing himself excessively, almost sobbing, and insisted he had to leave before it got too close to the light of dawn.

"Nonsense. Where do you have to go?" Bellacosa exclaimed, and urged him to stay.

Oswaldo took deep breaths and with the help of Bellacosa propped himself on the easy chair and passed out. Bellacosa ran his hand over his brother's head and in the darkness his eyes began to tear up.

Bellacosa locked the front door. He walked to the kitchen and poured himself a glass of water, downed it, and poured another. He went to the restroom, finished, and walked back to the living room to find Oswaldo gone and the front door wide open.

Bellacosa cursed, ran outside, looked all around and, strangely, up toward the sky in search of him. He got in the old Jeep, but quickly saw his efforts were in vain. Oswaldo had fled into the night, with the shadows of the trees as his wings. Back inside the shack, Bellacosa sat exhausted and defeated in his living room and stared into the coyote broth with the tapeworm swimming around for a really long time before flushing it down the toilet, bones and all, and threw the pot away. He drank another glass from the bottle of Bordeaux, listening to his favorite Bach string quartets, and when he passed out he did so on the easy chair Oswaldo had used in the tiny living room.

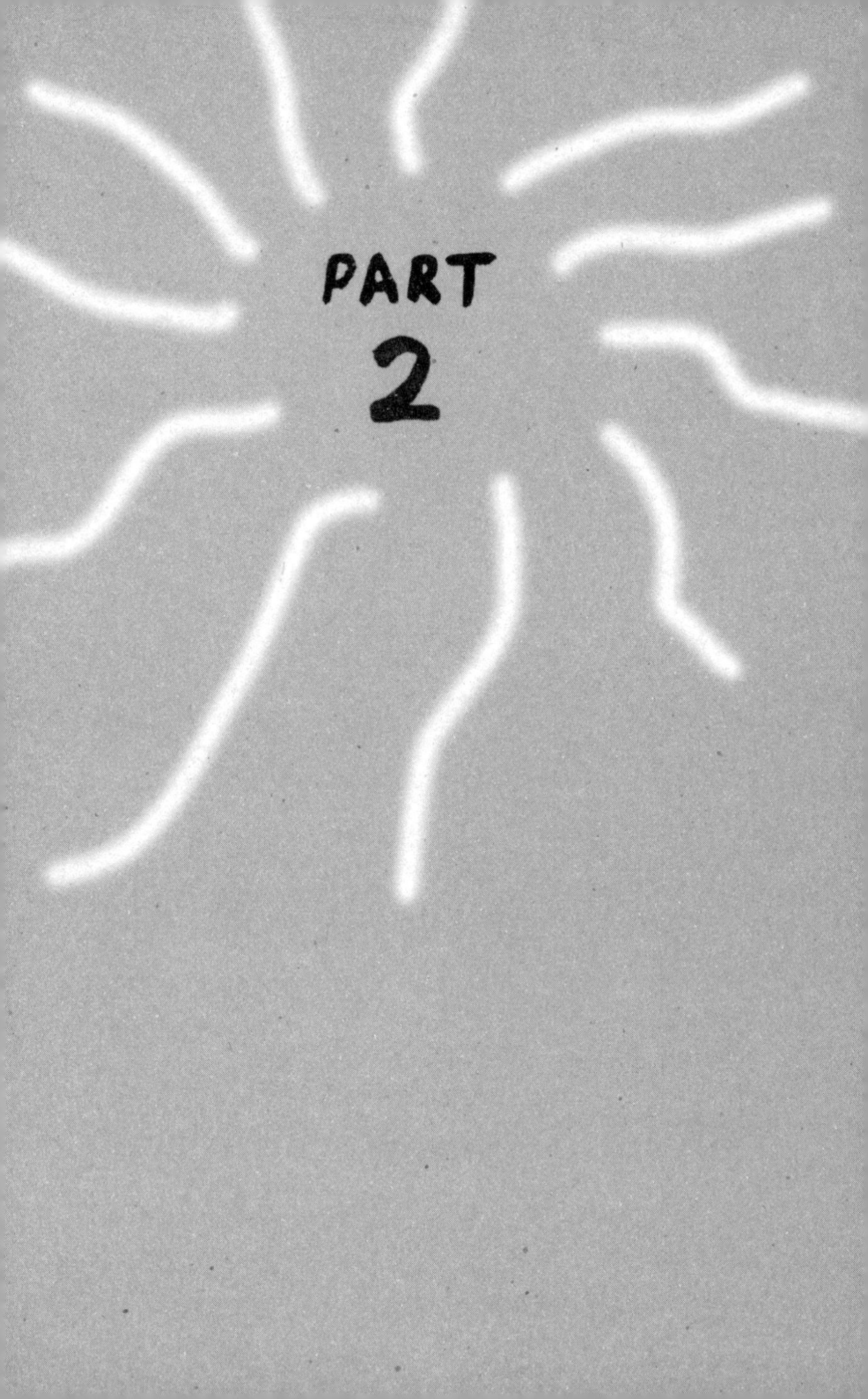

PART 2

ELEVEN

SOMETHING BIG WENT DOWN SOUTH OF THE BORDER. THE foreign press dubbed it the most elaborate art heist in history, and in Mexico it was felt as the worst blow to the nation and roots of its culture since the taking of Texas: Thirteen Olmec heads from across the country were stolen in armed robberies. Thieves had successfully made off with twelve Olmec heads from Veracruz, as well as the head on the Reinahermosa-MacArthur International Bridge. Each head weighed between 8 and 41.87 metric tons.

In San Lorenzo, Veracruz, two eighteen-wheelers with cooler units and ten pickup trucks filled with armed men reportedly took over Las Ruinas Nuestro Palacio and, using Gargantua forklifts, stole monuments 5, 15, 17, 53, 61, 66, 89, 23, 24, and 42, with mild gunfire and three deaths.

In La Venta, Tabasco, at the touristy Parque Museo, the

armed security guards were old-timers, and had been sipping on a communal bottle of Presidente whiskey on their night shift. They defended the five Olmec heads filled with liquid courage against fourteen sober traffickers, and somehow came out unscathed, their adrenaline pumping high while surrounded by bodies as the police and ambulances arrived. The guards were lauded as heroes, defenders of *La Patria*, and photographs of them posing by the saved Olmec heads, along with old mug shots of the assailants, were published rampantly in the media.

At the locations of Olmec head monuments A and Q in Tres Zapotes, Veracruz, it was only one eighteen-wheeler and a flatbed with a crew of no more than eleven men, and all the security guards were paid off. There was no conflict or even mild resistance.

The heist of Olmec head L, which stood alone on the Texas-Mexico border and weighed 16.3 metric tons, was pulled off in a similar fashion. Security cameras there didn't register any footage, and no witnesses came forward reporting foul play. Neither the American Border Protectors nor the Customs Military of Mexico knew which direction the thieves even ran, north or south. What took the Olmec civilization hundreds of years to build and transport, this syndicate, in what appeared to be a carefully planned military-style operation, made vanish overnight. Outrage befell the country, people took to the streets, blocked highways, set fire to vehicles; universities and museums went on strike to organize and attend public demonstrations. No syndicate came forward to admit responsibility, which was far from their modus operandi. The Mexican Marines had soldiers stationed at the remaining five heads at Parque Museo La Venta, in Tabasco. The Reinahermosa-MacArthur International Bridge was closed off for a full investigation and life along the border grew stranger yet again.

Out of precaution, the British Army was temporarily stationed at Stonehenge, and a trained team from the UN was deployed to monitor all activity on Easter Island. Tourists couldn't help but catch an air of fear blowing over their shoulders at the ruins of Rome and Pompeii, and even at the Louvre and Statue of Liberty security was beefed up.

Though immediately no motives were known, it was rumored among the people that the Olmec heads had been bought off in a private, underground auction held in the western hills, hosted by an elite Scandinavian impresario. Others said the heist was instigated as a competitive bet between rival syndicates. The most daring still whispered that the thieves were actually the government itself, that those elected into power had sold the Olmec heads in a clandestine business deal to fuel their own private accounts. Candles and handwritten notes were placed by natives and tourists at the site of El Angel de la Independencia; offerings and handmade sculptures of the heads were placed at Tres Zapotes, an act denounced as deeply offensive by the right-wing newspaper *El Sureño*, confusing many and enraging some. Besides the twenty-one missing young biology students from Universidad la Reforma who'd been found decapitated in a mass grave, no singular criminal act had ever provoked as vehement an outburst from the Mexican people.

WHILE THE WORLD MASTICATED over these revelations, Bellacosa, in the days after the dinner, was closed off from it all. He allowed himself to sleep in, and after stretching, he walked over to El Carretón Taco Million, picked up two tacos to go with potatoes, eggs, and refried beans on freshly made corn tortillas with tomatillo salsa, and ate them sitting barefoot at the counter dividing his kitchen and living room.

Remembering his unfinished business, Bellacosa told himself there was no avoiding it anymore. He dialed his client Don Villaseñor's number, which went straight to voice mail. He thought it over, pinched through the crevices in his wallet, and found the slip of paper with Don Villaseñor's second office phone number and dialed.

"*Bueno*," a male voice he didn't recognize on the other end answered, crawling out the speaker like a black, hairy spider.

Bellacosa was about to say something, then hesitated. It was quiet in the background, which was unusual for a weekday at Don Villaseñor's office. The man on the other end was chewing on something that didn't sound edible, like the end of a stapler or a pool cue.

He hung up the phone feeling suspicious of everybody,

and began thinking about his brother, then about that *hijo de la chingada* Manolo, whom he'd been paying off for information and who had been Oswaldo's captor and torturer all along. The tomatillo salsa from breakfast had been spicy and Bellacosa was filled with rage. He didn't remember the last time he felt this way, and he stood in front of the sink drinking glass after glass of water. He breathed in profoundly and forced into his mind the spiritual side of the equation: that the Fates had a say in everything and that Manolo would get what was his in the end; and so would Oswaldo; and so would he, Bellacosa.

Still, he entertained the fantasy of revenge, getting back at a corrupt police detective like Manolo, by extension taking his revenge on the syndicates and all the evil men in this world. *Los hombres malos*, like the farmer Tranquilino had said. Then Bellacosa reflected on that man, Tranquilino, and remembered the way he'd described being attacked in front of his family while his wife was violated.

When pigs fly, Bellacosa thought. *That's what the saying used to be, but nowadays we see pigs fly every day. Fat, super-rich, homicidal, stinking of impunity, greedy for even more power and making the weak suffer. The saying should be, "When pigs fry their own bacon,"* a voice peeling down from the kitchen's blue wallpaper seemed to respond.

Bellacosa showered and got in his old Jeep, turned the stereo up after adjusting the needle for a clean signal. The speakers rattled: "*And in the yellow cigs we watch the limelight fall, and we tip our way to the Holy Land, y'all, tip our way to the Holy Land, y'all—*" The song was catchy enough that he could ignore it.

He thought about driving to see his friend Ximena and have her read his coffee grounds again, then, stuck to his old ways, told himself he didn't want to be a bother. When he discovered his pack of cigarettes was empty he made a U-turn on Tenth Street and went looking for a store instead.

Bellacosa drove into Edinburgh City and parked at the far end of a Hatfield's Supercenter, where everything was always cheaper. As he walked in a young man with a blue Hatfield's vest said, "Welcome to Hatfield's Supercenter. If you can find it cheaper we'll match it," in a muddy, monotonous voice. As Bellacosa made it deeper into the store, he heard the young man repeat the phrase many times over.

Bellacosa wandered through a few aisles of snack food and beverages in a daze. He ended up in front of stacks of brand-new color replicas all broadcasting different networks, when he remembered what he came for. He bought a pack of Herzegovina Flor cigarettes, cracked it open, and sparked one as soon as he was outside again. It was cool and breezy, police sirens could be heard from the expressway, and for a few puffs of smoke the world in South Texas made sense to Bellacosa. Shoppers wheeled carts in and out of Hatfield's at an aardvark's pace, and Bellacosa watched as two men his age pushed a train of them back into the store.

"The next police officer I see I am going to pull out and give a good *sacudida*, and beat the shit out of him. I'm going to pull that copper out and sock it to him real good, make him feel it. I've never called the police for anything in my life, but if I do it'll be only for this. If it's a lady officer I'll let her be, but I hope it's a strong, arrogant, disgusting male cop," Bellacosa said, thinking of Manolo and clenching his teeth with anger as he drove out of the Hatfield's Supercenter parking lot.

Bellacosa recalled the girl in the pastel dress at dinner, and for the hundred-and-twelfth time wondered who the hell the other people could have been. He had a distinct memory of each of the other ten guests, like characters in a board game. The images of the shrunken Mapuche heads, and the baby chick dodos in the aquarium, running around like fools on a holographic desert island, couldn't escape him.

Then his thoughts turned to Oswaldo. It broke Bellacosa's heart to think of his brother in this new terrible way. The figure that had appeared to him was no longer his brother, but a man with a death sentence. He'd been hexed. Bellacosa could see that Oswaldo had come to terms with the fact that there was no way back to his old life, and had his own personal business now to straighten out—of which visiting him at his shack was a part.

He drove to the restaurant El Caballo Ballo. It was pricier than anything at Baby Grand Central, but he wasn't very hungry and only looking for a cup of black coffee. Also, the joint was owned by his client Don Villaseñor. Now that he had spent some of the fifteen grand he owed him,

Bellacosa planned to ask Don Villaseñor for a loan of three grand and refund him only twelve thousand.

Bellacosa didn't recognize the stylish hostess wearing a gold-sequined outfit at El Caballo Ballo. She directed him to sit where he liked and he thanked her.

He made his way toward the back and noticed there was another occupied table, with a blonde lady in a ponytail and business attire, sitting across from a man Bellacosa recognized as the mayor of MacArthur, Luis Mercedesanto Paz. Bellacosa scowled inwardly and clenched his right fist in his coat pocket.

"*Ingeniero*," Bellacosa heard from behind him. It was the waiter Quintero, a barrel of a man who always dressed sharply, with a rock of copal quartz as a left earring. Quintero also had a couple of gold chains and rings on both pinkie fingers, and his hair was slicked back and to the side.

"*Qué onda*, Quintero," Bellacosa said, and the men shook hands. Bellacosa liked Quintero, though he rarely got along with male waiters, and always seemed to attract the poorer of the bunch. But Quintero was different, always sniffing around and ready to report the order of the day with a good sense of justice. He had no gauge for humor but had charisma, and always called him Ingeniero, though Bellacosa lacked every sense of an academic degree, much less one in engineering.

"Sit wherever you like, Ingeniero. I'll be with you shortly."

Bellacosa sat far from the mayor and the lady, and put

them away from his mind. When Quintero came back Bellacosa asked for a cup of black coffee, and they brewed a fresh pot just for him.

Quintero brought a mug over with sugar packets and cream as Bellacosa asked him, "*Oye,* Quintero, has Don Villaseñor returned? From his trip in Mexico? I was doing a job for him and can't quite reach him, even at his offices."

The waiter, wearing a silly grin that didn't express humor, said, "No, Ingeniero. El Patrón was taken by *los hombres.* They kidnapped him, *no mames.*"

"Kidnapped him? How do you mean?"

"It happened about five days ago. He was leaving his office in Piedras Negras, they took him along with two friends going to a business lunch. And men with machine guns and masks put them in a truck, *no mames.* They found the two friends outside the city, naked with their hands tied and bodies burned, and nobody knows what happened to Don Villaseñor."

"*No me diga.* Don Villaseñor? But he is already a little old, no, to have dealings with those people? The man is older than me."

"Who knows, Ingeniero," Quintero said. "They never tell us anything, we're just employees at his restaurant here. I only know because of the things I pick up here and there. I tell you, because of your business relationship to Don Villaseñor. You are sometimes on his payroll, correct? I'm sorry to tell you, but if he owes you money you're probably not getting it today. They say they're asking a lot for his ransom. Don Villaseñor has money and connections in Mexico, maybe these people caught wind of it. They're the same people who have dealings with the fake animals, *no mames. Les vale madre a esos cabrónes.*"

Quintero excused himself and took a pitcher of unsweetened iced tea to his other table. He asked the blonde lady and the mayor a few questions, had a few laughs, then walked to the back of the restaurant. Bellacosa sipped carefully at the steaming coffee, and it was good.

On a napkin, using the black ballpoint pen he always carried, he started doodling.

When Quintero walked by he smiled that humorless smile again and said, looking down at the napkin, "What's that? The Huixtepeltinicopatl?"

"The what?" Bellacosa exclaimed.

"*El cerdo de los sueños. No mames,* Ingeniero, why are you drawing that? Somebody's going to catch you, and then what?"

Quintero quickly moved away from Bellacosa. Drinking his coffee, Bellacosa took a good look at his little sketch: a very amateur rendition of the Trufflepig he'd met at the illegal dinner. "The pig of dreams?" he asked himself, repeating what Quintero had said.

MEANWHILE, on the other side of town, Paco Herbert sat on an aluminum table painted like a chessboard at a taqueria named Yum-Yum. He was reviewing notes he'd scribbled hastily in his blue notebook that read: "old house /

fancy / loony dodos / fried dodos / spicy sauce, yellow, damn / guests except one middle-aged / teenage girl / the pig / skin like alligator / beak / disgusting / stub for tail / salivating / can't move / harmless / with teenage girl likes / mounted heads / mounted eels / skeleton visions / heads of Mapuche / commemorating plaques / steak, Charlemagne bull / old king / remember no guests made eye contact / remember girl, she spoke to Bellacosa / French wine / goose fat sauce / find the bird / the Galapagos soup, standard staple, and gizzards / the pig gone / concerto music speakers / short waiters / hip waitress / Josie, fake name / meal satisfactory / Aranaña, pig connection according to Bellacosa / lizard pig / beady eyes / fed carrots / casual environ / nothing threatening / top-dollar clientele."

Paco Herbert was eating *sopes* with refried beans and *queso fresco* dowsed in Yum-Yum's red house salsa. He nodded, flipped through the notebook, reading through every single word.

He popped an orange upper, swallowed it with tropical punch soda, and walked three blocks to the city library, sat at one of their booths, and hooked up to an information thread. First he searched for the native Aranaña tribe. He came across current articles about the Olmec heads heist and minor immigration and labor disputes in Cameron County. Then he got distracted and walked outside, called his employer's only office in the States, which patched him through to his boss in South America. It was a madhouse at their end and Cecilia sounded to him like the scribbles in his notebook. Paco Herbert was able to make out the phrases: "Insanity / scandal / where the hell are you / this information quick / thirteen of the Olmec heads / disappeared / filtering syndicates / still a mystery / tied in to the filtering / hijacking indigenous articles and culture and crafts / conspiracy / new struggle for power / corruption up high all the way down the ladder / elected officials / what are you still doing in South Texas / the action's farther south / can't hear a thing / call back with real results / no more cash flow your way / growing bad reputation / ruin us / eyes wide open / better hear back soon."

Paco Herbert hung up, walked back to the information thread in the library, and, after considering how to specify his search, typed "Aranaña" and "pig," then hit enter. It yielded zero results. He typed in only "Aranaña," at first with the "ñ," then using the "n," and two monographs came up, which he immediately queued up. He searched again for "pig" and hundreds of articles resulted. He felt stupid and narrowed it to "reptile skin pig beak hooves," and yielded articles related to veterinary studies and a couple of books for children on natural habitats and parts of animals.

Paco Herbert walked to the front desk and a middle-aged woman made him sign for the monographs he queued. One was *Understanding Native Texans* by Joel Campos Phillips, the other was a book on metaphysics called *Reflections of Our Collective Psyche*, by Johanna Crowfoot-Skye. He started with the former, and in the table of contents immediately noticed a few lines had been blacked out very carefully—pages seventy-seven through eighty-one, which were missing entirely from the book.

Paco Herbert got a strange feeling he was on to something, and looked over his shoulders. There were only everyday-looking people and young students scuttling around the library while the sleepy security guard read a medieval fantasy paperback. Paco Herbert glanced over to the only other person who knew what he had queued, the librarian, but she was busy, looking bored. He opened *Reflections of Our Collective Psyche*, and it didn't have a table of contents. He skimmed through it page by page until he got to pages thirty-six through thirty-nine, which weren't removed but blacked out, in a much sloppier fashion than the methodical job performed with *Understanding Native Texans*.

He looked at the publication dates of both books. The history book was published twenty years prior, and the metaphysical one was only five years old. He jotted down their publishing houses. Back in the information thread he searched "Olmec heads," queued *The Idiot's Guide to Mexican Monuments*, and signed for it at the desk. He made a couple of calls to check the state of his finances in both work and personal accounts, summoned a taxicab, and paid to be driven to Mission Public Library thirty minutes away with the company card. He performed the same searches there as in MacArthur. There they only carried *Understanding Native Texans*, and in the table of contents the same lines were blacked out and the same pages were missing. Handling the book, Paco Herbert's hands were drenched in sweat, his heart was pumping hard, and from a tin in his coat pocket he pulled an orange pill and swallowed it dry. He walked to the men's room and washed his face, dried it with paper towels, rinsed his mouth. When he spit the water into the sink it came out bright pink.

Paco Herbert needed a smoke and outside sparked one of his Caballero Lights on a bench, chatting up one of the young librarians on lunch break. She had tattoos of scripture he recognized as Armenian.

"Is this Armenian?" he asked her.

"It is," she said, genuinely surprised. "You know the language?"

"My fiancée is Armenian. Well, my ex-fiancée."

"Really? I don't know. I felt I needed to get them. To commemorate my ancestors and all. Pay tribute."

The librarian checked the time, then hastily packed up her lunch and excused herself.

"Thank you for telling me that," Paco Herbert said, stubbing out his cigarette.

"No problem. Thank you for asking. Most of the time men just grab my arm to try and make out what it is."

Running on mercurial instinct, Paco Herbert hurried back inside and searched for "El Gordo Pacheco," and queued the most recently published monograph on his life and the rise of filtering syndicates, how their power structures worked. He also searched for scientific studies on the Rosokhovatsky Filtering Method, which had been the most effective way to extract and filter fruits, vegetables, and animal species. He found two studies along with a nature publication entitled *Mother Balance.* The studies were put out by Jamestown University Press in Connecticut. One was called *Complete Rosokhovatsky,* which was a thick university-level textbook, and the other was *Filtering Sciences Today.* Paco Herbert signed for all the books, called another taxicab, and later locked himself at his place near downtown MacArthur, with some coffee and serious drugs for all the reading he had ahead of him.

TWELVE

THE PUBLIC CLASSICS NETWORK WAS AIRING A BLACK-AND-white Cagney picture, *Frankie's Ride*. Cagney played Frankie McClint, a poor boy from the Bronx who made it big in the bootlegging racket during Prohibition. Never knowing his own father, the only real paternal figure Frankie rebelled against in his life was Father Andrews, the Irish Catholic priest. The famous scene of the picture was playing—Father Andrews is pleading with a sharply dressed, wisecracking Cagney to quit the bootlegging business and become a positive role model for the neighborhood youths.

"Don't you see, Frankie, that these boys have grown up idolizing you? You've got them picking pockets and running numbers. And for what, I wonder? I wonder, Frankie, do you ever see anything of yourself in these boys anymore?"

"Firstly, Father," Cagney responds, slyly fixing the cuff

links on his suit, "if you're accusing me of asking these boys to commit crimes then you are mistaken. I'm a businessman, not a barbarian. These boys have a right to be boys, and if they're able to contribute a little to their families then nobody can argue that what they're doing is entirely bad. Now, if I'm supposed to lose sleep because my success has an influence on these boys' futures, then you are sorely out of line, Father. We all know the hero you'd like them to have is up there on the cross, and the Church ain't putting food on the table for any of these youngsters."

"That's where you're wrong, Frankie. What the Church puts on the table goes a lot farther than food."

Bellacosa was watching and enjoying the picture. It was his second time catching it as it aired, but he had never seen it from the beginning. The depiction of poverty in those old pictures, for Bellacosa, always reminded him of his boyhood in Reinahermosa. It didn't matter if the film was Italian, German, Swedish, Japanese. The poverty depicted, especially in the two decades of cinema around World War II, was always a visceral, universal poverty. Once he'd seen a Japanese film about a murder in the Tokyo ghetto, and he felt he knew the smell of those shantytown, underworld locations, the rubble of the buildings, the children playing in trash heaps looking for diamond rings. If the actors had been Mexican he would've sworn it was a picture about his own childhood.

Bellacosa didn't care to watch Cagney die in the unfortunate climax again and turned off the black-and-white replica, put it back in the closet. He walked over to his altar, grabbed the stick of white sage by the picture of his wife holding their daughter, moments after her birth. He lit the stick and watched the white sage burn a green smoke that carried the smell of something infinite, like it was cut from the tree of life itself, and he placed it on the onyx rock. He grabbed the Bengali quartz crystal, the agave stone, midnight-rose-quartz rock, the jawbone of the Texas coyote. The stones he placed in a glass jar with Himalayan pink salt mixed in water to clear their energies, and the bone he placed on the windowsill to absorb cold sunshine. He grabbed the old silver Mexican coin with an etching of the priest Miguel Hidalgo and finally got the accumulated gunk out of it using baby oil and a cloth. He wiped his wife's sunglasses clean, wiped the tiny simian and lion marble sculptures, and rang one of the gray bells his wife gave out to people as gifts the week after their daughter died.

When Bellacosa felt he was getting too emotional about his family again he took a long, hot shower, shaved, and after he dressed and combed his hair put his pair of ostrich-knee Wingham shoes away. He shined his backup pair of the same-style shoes, slipped them on, and admired them in the long, vertical hallway mirror.

The Cagney picture, finding his brother, Oswaldo, in the condition he was in, and all the recent events were doing a number on Bellacosa's sense of emotional equilibrium. Thinking of his boyhood, he had a hard time accepting that what he'd done then was wrong: crossing drugs with the other boys, selling them to men who drove them farther north—though these were still considered serious crimes, in those days the brutality just hadn't caught up. To him, they were still boys playing at marbles—there were rules and everybody played fairly. This had allowed Bellacosa to make a lot more money than he did shining shoes in the very beginning, and he'd moved his mother into a respectable place, paid Oswaldo's way through the Dental Academy of Merida. It wasn't until later that the synthetic drug crystal-kind entered the market. The violence and addictions that followed forced a change in perspective, paving the way for the legalization of certain drugs and controlled substances, but by that time Bellacosa had already met his future wife, Lupita.

Together they mapped out their future, and when Bellacosa was ready to tell his partners, Rogelio Canchola and Freddy Santos, and their employer that he was quitting, he didn't have to anymore. The trafficking and production of crystal-kind was slowly gaining way, as was the bloodshed and betrayal up and down the chain of command. Somebody on the American side turned out to be an informant during a standard deal, there was a raid, and a couple of the higher-ups got caught and sentenced. Rogelio disappeared, and Bellacosa, until learning otherwise from Paco Herbert, assumed he'd been killed, like Freddy was. Bellacosa laid low in Mexico shortly after marrying Lupita, and they moved to Mission, in South Texas, on their second anniversary. Lupita applied for U.S. citizenship and they invested in equipment to start their own screen-printing business. They did well for themselves for many years, screen-printing uniforms and class shirts for elementary and high schools across the Rio Grande Valley.

Still, putting everything into context with history and modern trafficking and now filtering, Bellacosa couldn't believe what he'd gotten away with in those days. For never having killed anybody, he got pretty ahead of the game as a boy and a young man. *How far could I have gotten if I would have stayed*, he wondered, but knew the answer had to be: not much further at all. He dropped it, as fate would have it, at the perfect time, and always he had Lupita to thank. When she was alive he never dared harbor the "what if," but now he couldn't help but imagine what could have happened, how much more money he could've made on the side in those days with the occasional deal. Instead of suffering through the years of the food shortage, struggling hard to have the life with a wife and child his own mother once wished for him, then burying all of them and slowly aging into a lonely, broke old man.

Bellacosa pictured his good, patient wife, standing next to him in a lucid way no photograph could show. Though they'd had many trying moments, though he could have been a better husband, and not a day went by since her death he didn't beg for her forgiveness, Bellacosa suddenly wished for a chance to do it all again. He remembered Job and how he'd lost it all in a cruel, sadistic test of his love of God, and how as an old man he was rewarded with a real chance at a family and a prosperous, normal life. As his pain was steeping, Bellacosa reminded himself that the cosmos has a plan for everybody, even widowers who've lost everything. He didn't allow himself to think of things being unfair, and unlike Job, Bellacosa was unsure of his faith toward any God. He didn't wish for anything to be easier, only for another crack at it, a chance to be able to love his wife again, to show his dying daughter something meaningful, more than what he was able to offer when confronted with the reality of her imminent death.

It was a shame Bellacosa wasn't really a drinking man. Alcohol never sat well with him, and he always asked himself what there was for a non-drinking man to quench his sorrows. In spite of himself, he uncorked the rest of the Bordeaux and said, "Just to get rid of it, then I'm done."

In recent months he'd also grown fond of old music from all over the world. If it was Mexican, great; if not it didn't really matter, so long as the musicians played non-amplified, acoustic instruments—what they call Depression Era music, especially. He walked to the old Jeep, grabbed the disc of World War II songs that Paco Herbert had left behind, walked back to his place, and popped it into the audiobox. He listened to the songs into the evening, some humble and folksy, others clearly arranged for propaganda purposes, with high production value and orchestras. At a certain point he did a little dance in his shack holding the glass of wine, with his other arm around an invisible partner. He enjoyed simply holding the glass, not really drinking, listening to songs about Hitler, evil, hope, Yokohama, and patriotism in those old days he never lived through.

When the disc ended it was nighttime. Bellacosa set the untouched glass of wine down, put on his Wingham shoes, and took a drive in the old Jeep. He drove through the historical district in Mission, then closer to the border, to hidden spots he thought maybe Oswaldo could be, like the abandoned monastery, the run-down BigTex warehouse, and the shady side of Will Shuppe Park. He decided to cross into Reinahermosa and visit the old neighborhood where they lived their formative years, hoping to find some kind of answer, and his hands began to sweat as he imagined an encounter with Manolo Segura. When the old Jeep neared the international bridge Bellacosa saw yellow police tape and two Border Protector tanks set up in front of barricaded toll booths like the steel boots of colossal titans. Uniformed officers standing guard shone lights on Bellacosa's face and a voice from a bullhorn blared, "Move along, the bridge is closed off for investigation by state and federal law. Move along. You can cross at the Pharr-Progreso Bridge."

As he drove away Bellacosa noticed news vans for several networks that'd been corralled, and a reporter was doing a live report in Arabic on the sidewalk, while the local station crew tore down their own equipment.

None of this seemed out of the ordinary to Bellacosa, but he took it as a sign not to cross into Mexico at all, to calm down, and drive back home.

He thought again of his client Don Villaseñor, and hoped what the waiter Quintero had said about the kidnapping was misinformation. With him missing, Bellacosa was at a loss for what to do, whom to answer to, and the money he owed from the failed 7900 Rig purchase was just sitting in his bank account, tempting him. Though it wasn't a huge amount, he could live on that for a good stretch of time, considering his discipline and minimalist lifestyle. But it didn't feel right. He hadn't worked for it and the money wasn't his.

Bellacosa stopped to pump gas, picked up the day's edition of *The Bugle of Plenty*, folded it, and didn't read the headline until he was walking into his shack. It read: "Thirteen Olmec Heads Stolen Overnight." He read the entire article, sipping at the red wine, and finally understood all the fuss at the Reinahermosa-MacArthur International Bridge. They'd taken the Olmec head that'd been a gift from the ex-president of Mexico Miguel Redondo to Sigifredo Mueller, the acting mayor of Reinahermosa twenty years back. He read the article a second time and it seemed more like a piece of absurd fiction than news. Bellacosa couldn't believe the audacity of these thieves, these men. *In this world, it is only men who are guilty of anything, men of flesh and bones and gravity and sin*, he reminded himself.

He turned on the ceiling fan and cracked open the door to his shack. Sitting on the easy chair his brother had used during their encounter, Bellacosa smoked a Herzegovina

Flor, and fell asleep to an a capella number playing on the audiobox called "Stalin Wasn't Stallin'."

A few hours later Bellacosa was startled awake by a cold, sticky hand lightly tapping on his left wrist, and he hopped to his feet, his heart dry-heaving. It was a small, old woman with curlers in her hair and a baby-blue bathrobe covering her entire small frame. She was holding a burning candle that emitted a good amount of gray light, and after a few seconds Bellacosa recognized her as his landlady.

"*Ay, señora*, what a surprise," Bellacosa stammered, realizing he'd been busted smoking indoors.

"I'm sorry for waking you, *joven* Esteban. I didn't mean to give you a fright. You had your door open so I helped myself in. Please forgive me for this trespass, I had no right."

"No, no problem at all, *señora*, how can I help you? I'm at your service."

"Come with me, *por favor, joven* Esteban."

The landlady was very formal and old-fashioned, from a distinguished family in Mexico City whose lineage could be traced back to the Toscana neighborhood in Rome. She was about thirty years his senior and Bellacosa got a huge kick from her referring to him as *joven*—young man. They entered her large, tastefully decorated house, and she led him up a balustrade staircase to a master bedroom with a golden threshold. She held the candle close to the side of a large bed with blue and yellow covers, and there was Don Castañeda, her husband, beholding the kind of peace reserved only for the sleeping.

Doña Castañeda said, "I had a dream where my husband kissed me. And he told me, 'I'll see you soon, *mi amor*,' and jumped into a fountain carrying an umbrella, turning very small as he did. This took place at a train station, surrounded by people hurrying in every direction. When I awoke he was already this way."

Even before he reached to take his pulse, Bellacosa understood the patriarch was dead. He no longer looked peaceful, but like a general in mourning, the war long over. Doña Castañeda placed the candle on the bureau by the bed and held the old man's hand as Bellacosa dialed the paramedics. He stayed in the room until they arrived shortly thereafter, and a young black medic who spoke Spanish took information from Doña Castañeda with patience. Emotion hadn't yet settled in the old woman, so what she recounted was merely factual. The events hadn't been articulated into actual feelings for her, and Bellacosa tried to remember how much time passed after the deaths of his wife and daughter until he admitted they were gone. Probably no time at all was his answer.

Bellacosa offered to give her a ride to MacArthur Memorial Hospital, where they were taking him, but Doña Castañeda insisted it wasn't necessary. The old woman removed her curlers, changed into something more formidable, and drove herself to the hospital filled with quiet pride.

He admired her freight train determination and tried to imagine what she could've looked like at his age. Bellacosa checked the time. It was 2:45 a.m. He walked over to his shack, which smelled like an ashtray to him, and opened the doors and windows to get the air circulating. After turning the lights off he sat in total darkness on the easy chair until he found himself dozing, then went to bed.

THIRTEEN

BELLACOSA WOKE UP WITH A CLEAR IMAGE OF OSWALDO, the *huarango* thorn holes around his mouth, and regrettably accepted what they'd done to his brother. Which to him meant they had done the same thing to the neighbors' brothers as well; which meant they would also take the neighbors and one day they would come and take him, too. Bellacosa felt there was a constant, unspoken war and the battlefield was always somewhere in the map of the collective brain. He thought about Don Castañeda now gone, *que en paz descanse,* and wondered what the world looked like to that old man in his final days. He remembered the girl in the pastel dress, along with the Trufflepig at the dinner—the girl being so comfortable around that terrible creature.

As he had his breakfast back at El Caballo Ballo, Bellacosa pulled out the crude sketch he'd previously made.

What was the word the girl in the pastel dress used for the Trufflepig, he asked himself. He'd also heard the waiter Quintero say it. It was like the name of a volcano.

Susanita, an older career waitress with a tiny diamond engraved in one of her teeth that flashed with her smile, refilled his coffee without asking, and brought him an extra ramekin of tomatillo-cilantro salsa. Bellacosa looked around to see if Quintero was creeping around before his shift, and thanked Susanita kindly.

Holding up the napkin, Bellacosa asked, "Susanita, do you know what this animal is?"

Susanita appeared shocked and embarrassed, like Bellacosa had flashed her his dick. She denied knowing what it was, blushed, looked down and to the side. Bellacosa could see she was lying, somehow felt sorry for her, and did not press the matter further.

He ate his *chilaquiles oaxaqueños* humming a World War II folk song, and sipped his coffee thoughtfully. The vibe was dense and uneasy with the staff of El Caballo Ballo, and he didn't bother asking about Don Villaseñor.

After breakfast he decided it was finally time to find Paco Herbert. Bellacosa had a lot of questions, and was confident Paco was the only person he could trust to ask. Funny, Bellacosa hadn't felt anybody to be a friend in a long time, and Paco Herbert felt more and more like a friend, though the reporter was at least twenty years younger than him. He questioned his own judgment in this, but managed to shrug it off, and he parked the old Jeep along Baldemar

Avenue in downtown MacArthur and walked to Baby Grand Central.

On the sidewalk he was stopped by the *chilango* anarchist man who sold toys from the old world like tops, yo-yos, and *baleros*, all of which he'd whittled himself from Valley mesquite. "One for the independence, *señor.*"

Bellacosa didn't know what he meant and asked him to repeat it. The man replied, "When you support the independence of one, you support the independence of all. Revolution first starts with the wrongful imprisonment of an exceptional individual. We old-timers have to remind the proletariats of this, otherwise they'll catch them like El Tigre de Santa Inez. You remember him? He was the thief of the small area of Durango they once called Santa Inez. He was a master thief before such a thing was common. He'd break into business establishments, banks, and people's homes, all at odd hours of the day, and nobody ever seemed to notice him, since he was always well groomed and carried himself like a cultured prince among men. Well, remember now how they caught him? This guy, who the press and people dubbed El Tigre for his cunning ability, never did much with the money and artifacts he stole. He hoarded everything in various holes he dug by the wilderness in the mountainside. He was living out there, too. When the authorities discovered this they sent a few teams out there and guess how they caught him? With his pants down in the middle of taking a huge shit. They let him wipe himself with those soft banana leaves before arresting him. That's why we have that saying now, 'You caught me like El Tigre de Santa Inez.' Meaning, you caught me at my most vulnerable, when I was taking a shit, *jajaja*."

Bellacosa sighed and asked him how much for a *balero*, and the man replied, "*Seis*."

This seemed too much and Bellacosa offered the man five dollars, wondering what kind of anarchist this crazy man was, charging so much for two pieces of wood tied together with a string.

"*Sobres*," the man said, and gave Bellacosa the one he secretly felt proudest of.

Bellacosa walked with the *balero* into Baby Grand Central, past the older southern woman who ran La Frutería Andes as she laughed like a yodeling bird at a Spanish game show on her little black-and-white replica. He approached Marselita's and saw Colleen Rae working the counter, but no Paco Herbert. It was emptying out as a group of suited men walked away laughing and shoving one another in caveman-like praise. Colleen Rae had a scowling, offended look on her face.

When she saw Bellacosa approaching she winced her eyes and told him, "You know what that pig just said to me?"

"Which one?"

"The one with the goatee and neck tattoo. I don't even want to repeat it, just know it was misogynistic and repulsive. And look at all his idiot work friends laughing. They didn't tip me a cent and left their stations filthy. Look."

Very calmly, Bellacosa walked toward them, and got in front of the man described by Colleen Rae.

Bellacosa said, "Excuse me."

The men all stopped laughing between the Middle Eastern couple's stand selling local honey and bark from all over the world and the stand belonging to the Chilean man who fixed watches and sold Mexican junk food. Colleen Rae didn't mean for Bellacosa to react as such and, fearing trouble, left the Marselita's stand. The cook in the back washed his hands and looked over their way.

The man's shoddily executed neck tattoo was of a harpooned mermaid. Very aggressively, he said, "What's this? You have something to say to me, old man?"

"I don't have anything to say. But you do. To apologize to this young woman for disrespecting her, and for disrespecting yourself."

"Excuse me, old man?" Neck-Tattoo replied, and from thin air the man produced a blade, while three men beside him grabbed Bellacosa by the arms and legs, one of them administering a hold that prevented much struggle. Bellacosa dropped the *balero* as they carried him outside Baby Grand Central. The three men pinned him down hard on the sidewalk, as Neck-Tattoo pressed the blade to Bellacosa's left cheek. There was loud cursing on Colleen Rae's part, and commotion among people and passersby, when suddenly a voice said, "Ricky, we can't do this. We got a meeting in a few minutes."

Just like that, the gang of them fled calmly toward an office building on the next block—central offices for Hatfield's Supercenters, and the tallest building in MacArthur, Texas. A couple of young strangers helped Bellacosa to his feet. A heavyset woman in a blue tank top was outraged, protesting in a rapid Spanish nobody understood, and spit on the sidewalk. It had all happened so fast Bellacosa felt a little embarrassed—a man his age, being shown up by a pack of twentysomethings.

Colleen Rae suddenly emerged from the arches of Baby Grand Central in her smock, a revolver in her hand. Before anybody else could see, Bellacosa grabbed her by the shoulders and redirected her back inside, to Marselita's, and said, "C'mon, this isn't necessary."

Her teeth were clenched and in her eyes Bellacosa saw an anger that ran deeper and was more real than what he'd seen in any of those men. He let go of her and her body went limp. She slipped the revolver into her apron pocket and went into the women's room in Baby Grand Central. Bellacosa looked around as people went about their normal business again. He had forgotten that crazy things like this happen every day here. Then he felt something dripping down his chin and realized Neck-Tattoo had cut him.

Thirty minutes later Bellacosa was having *caldo de pollo*, with the *balero* he bought sitting by his water. Colleen Rae only had one other customer and she sat across from Bellacosa at the counter as he ate. "And you know what's sad," she said, "is that to guys like that, I'm just the waitress. That just because this is my job and my wages depend a lot on customers, some of them who are dicks like him, they feel entitled to treat me like shit. To talk to me like I am temporarily their property. The things people think they can get away with, when they start seeing you not as a person but as their property, like they own you. You know Raquelle? A girl who works here sometimes? She's the one I'm in a band with, we actually came down here and got jobs at this place because we wanted to see what it was like, you know. After reading all those articles about the border and the syndicates and how women are treated and everything. We couldn't imagine, and us being women tied to Mexican-American culture, we moved here to write our second album. To feed off all the energy, even the bad energy, and to change it to something positive, to music, to rock and roll that is hard-core and hopefully means something. We have a big show on Thursday, are you gonna come?" She smiled. "I haven't seen your friend in a while, is he still in town?"

"We haven't been in touch lately, but I'm looking for him. What do you know about him?"

"About Paco? He's nice. Very supportive. I gave him an advance copy of our record and he said he'd try to get it reviewed for the publication he works with."

"What's it called?"

"The record's called *Godiva Skydance/Bluebeard Soup*."

"*Ah si?* And what's the publication he works for?"

"I forgot. He said he would bring me some issues, but I

haven't seen him. Nor Raquelle. He's friends with her, too. You're right, your cut just sealed right up pretty fast there."

"Yeah, I still heal fast, for an old man like me," Bellacosa said. "Which is surprising."

"You're not that old. Anyway, what does any of that mean, age?"

"What does it mean? You're actually asking me? Okay. I think that's what age is. Healing faster. You still get all the pains everybody else does, but everything heals faster. At least for me. I don't know how it is for anybody else, so I'm not really sure."

"What else?"

"What else?" Bellacosa asked, rubbing his forehead. "I don't know. It's harder to make friends, I could say. Or maybe that's always hard."

Bellacosa grabbed the stick end of the *balero* so that the cup dangled from the nylon string like a pendulum and held it very still over the table, moving it slowly, and keeping his eye on the cup.

"Yeah, I think that one's always hard," Colleen Rae said. "That's why you hold on to the friends you got for a long time, and be good to them. Excuse me, let me get this guy his ticket. Your meal's on me today, by the way."

Bellacosa thought he misheard her so he didn't protest, simply grinned as if she said something funny, and kept his eye on the *balero*'s cup as he dangled it over the glass of water. Slowly, the cup began spinning counterclockwise on the string, acting like a dowsing rod. Despite the scuffle,

Bellacosa's mind was still on his brother. He set the *balero* down, looking around at all the faces of Baby Grand Central, half expecting to see him, and wondered what would happen if he actually did.

LATER IN THE DAY, driving aimlessly, Bellacosa recalled something Colleen Rae had said. She said the problem in this world is that wolves are still murdering grandmothers and disguising themselves as them in order to convince you nothing has changed and lure you into bed, where after raping you they eat your flesh and pick your bones clean. He'd never heard a young woman talk like that, and was both shocked and impressed by her harshness and depth. He was glad to be acquainted with a strong young person like her. He'd also been thinking over the Olmec heads heist, and the madness in how many different types of heads the syndicate wars were affecting. There had been protests not only in Mexico City but also in Reinahermosa, Monterrey, Guanajuato, Miguel Alemán, and Tijuana, with people demanding social justice, reform, and for the president's resignation. After years of gruesome violence and widespread fear, it seemed people were finally fed up and unafraid to confront the impunity in the country's municipal and federal governments, which had gradually been hijacked by the syndicates.

After the death of El Gordo Pacheco, the mass graves of the biology students, and now the disappearance of the thirteen Olmec heads, people wanted real change. Bellacosa swelled with emotion thinking about the young people having to fight every day just to have a chance at a bleak economic future. He thought of the first man emerging from the red earth, the Border Protectors sticking automatic weapons in his face, demanding to see the first man's papers. He felt it was he himself who was this first man from the red earth, and back to the red earth Bellacosa longed to return. He realized that over the past few weeks, for the first time since the death of his wife, he was regularly feeling down. He saw how the history of violence along the border had karmically doomed the dream of prospering and the pursuit of happiness not only for him, but for all his people, the people living along the borders of Mexico and the United States. He asked out loud what could become of his lot, now that he was old and had nothing left, now that everything was more fleeting than ever and all the old charms and haunts had turned to stone angels in the cemetery.

Bellacosa ended up driving along the edge of Goya Canal on the American side, gunning the gas as if he was to jump across a gorge. He slowed down, pulled over as the sun was setting, and got out of the old Jeep. The ground was muddy and the shrill rattle of cicadas along the embankment stabbed through the evening air like tiny ice picks. On a grassy patch he got down on one knee like the time he proposed to his wife. "Lupita," Bellacosa pleaded to the setting sun, the orange and red clouds like a bride's dress afire. "Lupita, *mi amor*, please never leave me. Please never leave me like I never left you."

THE FOLLOWING MORNING Bellacosa put on a dark blue suit and the last shoes Lupita had bought him, a pair of very worn but polished Franco Brunis, for the occasion of Don Castañeda's funeral. He was ready before dawn, well before the scheduled service, and decided to go to Café Charon to see if any of the old gang was there. It was a place where the clientele was made up entirely of retired, working-class Mexican-American men. The meals were cheap, the coffee was acceptable, and the conversations consisted exclusively of physical ailments and home remedies the men had discovered. The place wasn't much, but to these men it was a sanctuary. They'd drive their families mad if they had nowhere else to go in those morning hours.

MacArthur was foggy, like it was inside of a glass bottle where somebody had discarded a cigarette. Bellacosa had the radio off and was grateful for the silence, for the empty streets. The green lights were all in his favor. He remembered rumors of an incoming South Texas snowfall, but scoffed it off and didn't believe it. Bellacosa asked himself if it was a Sunday, then told himself it must be.

The sun was rising when he parked his car on Datepalm and Seventeenth Street, next to more beat-up-looking cars over a decade and a half old. When he walked inside Café Charon the bell hanging on the door clanked like an old guard dog with laryngitis. About fifteen men sat around at low tables throughout the small space, and a few lined up along the counter by the cash register and tip jar the employees shared. The family of young and middle-aged ladies who worked at the restaurant were always nice, and as Bellacosa found a spot for himself along the counter many smiles and nods greeted him. The men's faces in Café Charon were old and clean-shaven, some with finely trimmed mustaches; they all wore trousers with perfect creases, western-style shirts tucked in, with only the finest hats by their side.

Bellacosa recognized Don Rodrigo by his cane, and that weasel De La Roca, who still owed him fifty in American from an old World Series bet. He saw the Aranaña waiter Cuauhtémoc refilling coffee cups all around, wearing a blue bandanna harnessing his thick, inky hair. Bellacosa was glad to see him still at Charon, though there were definitely better places to work in town for a young, able-bodied man.

A heavyset man with sheer white hair was having a conversation with an even older man in a maroon shirt. The heavyset man was saying, "That's how you have it wrong, Teodoro. I remember my father used to tell us that when you're older and you pee, to save just a tiny bit, and get a dropper from the store. In your ears, squeeze a little drop of pee, to clear all the wax out."

"But who in God sakes would do that," the other man responded. "Who would want to smell like pee all day?"

"Teodoro, don't be silly. It's just a drop or two, and you will rinse your ears afterward. Who's going to smell like pee when it's just a drop and then you rinse? Don't exaggerate."

"My method is better. Grab a little coin, it could be a nickel, could be a dime. Those two work just fine. And stick them in your ears. With the reverberation from the material of the coin, you can hear everything much better."

At the counter, behind him and to the right, were two men Bellacosa didn't know. Their names were Macario and Leopoldo, and they were giving each other tips on indigestion.

"I'm going now three years doing it," Macario said. "With my *bicarbonato de sodio*. First thing in the morning, well before you put anything else in your stomach, mix a tablespoon of baking soda in a plain glass of water. Stir it up. Drink it all in one go, and that's it. It will clean your organism right up. You'll see. And just so you know, sexually speaking, I haven't been better with that since around the time I got married."

Leopoldo responded, "That will never work with the kind of stomach I have. Yes, Macario, we are both immigrants, but the way we digest is rooted in different places. I take what I call *La Combinación Perfecta*. Which is a tablet of multivitamins for gentlemen over fifty-five. Some vitamin C. And a combination of vitamin B_{25} and B_{12}. I haven't had the mildest cold going on ten years now."

Then a thin man, the only one wearing his hat indoors, interrupted and said, "Why don't you men try a piece of garlic. That way you don't have to go to the pharmacy and put all those chemicals in your body. Just cut up a piece of garlic and take it with a spoonful of honey, so it goes down better. The garlic dissolves in your blood and kills all your bad intestinal bacteria."

All three of them nodded as their coffees were topped off by Cuauhtémoc.

Bellacosa accepted a refill himself and finally read the chalkboard breakfast specials. It felt good to be there.

DON CASTAÑEDA'S SERVICE was held at Gonzalez Funeral Home. It was a modest turnout of mostly older folks; the casket was pearly white and matched the suit he'd be buried in. To Bellacosa, it was a shock to see an old man dressed in white, and he asked himself if he'd ever seen a depiction of an elderly angel. He clasped hands with the widow and kissed her cheek. She was dressed quite elegantly and took people's condolences with teary eyes full of affection. Bellacosa had taken a seat toward the back when a middle-aged lady walked into the chapel. She wore a black hat with a veil, a black dress, and loud high heels. Bellacosa sensed right away it was Castañeda's estranged daughter he'd heard about. When the widow saw her, the daughter wailed, and held the old woman's hands as the rest of the guests looked down or were also overtaken with emotion. Bellacosa felt he couldn't be around any longer and walked out, dipped his fingers in the basin of holy water and crossed himself, feeling the coattails of death walk beside him. He made it to the old Jeep and drove away.

Bellacosa lit a Herzegovina Flor and decided to listen to the news network to get death out of his mind. There was an interview with Senator Tim Haugher about immigration, and he was saying, "The argument isn't about the Border Protectors and their reach broadening with this merger, but how American tax dollars are getting spent. Now, with this measure, the United States will have the power to send troops into Mexico and make sure our borders are secure by starting the lookout within the region, by making sure the immigrant infiltration doesn't spread here—"

"But, Senator," the host interrupted, "what about reports, and the eyewitness accounts? After the first border wall and the second border wall, built from coast to coast, and after the proof that nothing is keeping people from crossing into this country, how can you insist that any of these extreme tactics are necessary? And what about the controversial third border wall proposition? Why does the government continue to throw money into the Border Protectors, and its operations, in the five years of its existence that have produced zero positive results?"

"Danielle, that's an inappropriate and uncalled-for attack on your part—"

"Senator, unfortunately we are running out of time, but one more question. What is your opinion on the reports that the immigrants, who came into this country not knowing English or Spanish, the ones anthropologists have dubbed descendants of the lost Aranaña natives, have actually arrived from within the country, appearing in the Ballí Desert from a yet-to-be-discovered underground tunnel?"

"Danielle, as you know, especially with the way things are now, we always have those crackpots claiming the supernatural as a legitimate source. I don't take any of these claims as valid, and I'm sure my colleagues and most of the American public can agree with me on that."

"Senator Tim Haugher, thank you for your time. This is Danielle Esperanza, going to commercial break. We'll be right back, South Texas."

FOURTEEN

WASHED IN THE BLOOD OF THE NOON HOUR, BELLACOSA reached Calantula County listening to Peruvian folk songs on the radio. A chord of regret had struck him at the funeral home, once again, about the Aranaña man that worked for Mr. McMasters, Tranquilino. He vividly recalled how childlike his fear was, the cuts along his face, his black eye, and the bruises around his neck.

I must be out of my mind now or something, Bellacosa thought. *Why didn't I help that man and his family on the spot? I was wrapped in my own business, with the 7900 Rig, and didn't even notice a situation when it was happening in front of me. I must be selfish like everybody else now,* chingado. *I am old but not that old that I've stopped thinking of others.*

He tried to remember every detail about their two

encounters: the chickens, the ants, the boy with the basketball jersey, his young wife behind the screen door, the black van–turned–chicken coop, the tank with poison strapped to his back, Tranquilino's dream of making the land functional again and selling naturally grown onions. He asked himself if Leone McMasters could really have been more directly involved in the whole thing.

Bellacosa then thought about Ximena's cups where she'd read his grounds, what she said about attracting energy and harnessing it, about what his life had become in so short a time span. He couldn't believe he was driving all the way back out here for an Indian, an Aranaña, no less. *Fuck it*, he thought. *I'm an Indian, too.*

He noticed a new sign posted on the road reading "Farm Road 151." Bellacosa pulled his map out from under the seat and didn't see the road labeled anywhere.

When he got to the plot of land where Tranquilino and his family lived, Bellacosa didn't see the doghouse-sized mailbox parallel to the road. He pulled over, stepped off the old Jeep, and heard the whirring of machines and the hollowed yelling of men at work. There were a score of workers in hard hats and vests laying a huge foundation on the property, big enough for a mall or warehouse. Cement trucks were scattered and feeding the ground mixed cement like giant insects pumping sugar out of their bellies. A couple of men in white shirts and hard hats stood outside a small beige trailer reading an architectural plan and holding the wide scroll open together. Fifty feet away from them, another man was surveying the workers by a sign that read "McM Construction." There was no indication that anybody had lived here, nor that it had once been farmland. The men discussing the scroll spotted Bellacosa and both waved with curiosity at him.

Bellacosa felt deep remorse for whatever fate Tranquilino and his family were now suffering. He was convinced it couldn't be good.

Bellacosa waved back to the men. He stood there for a moment and asked himself if he'd made a mistake and driven to the wrong spot, but it wasn't possible. This was definitely the land the ants had escaped to, where the chickens once ran loose after a storm, and the 7900 Rig disappeared.

He only got more curious, and he walked back to the old Jeep and drove toward the direction of the gate where the military truck had been stationed, outside the house where he and Paco Herbert had the clandestine dinner. It seemed like years had passed since that happened, but it'd been less than a week.

There was no gate at the entrance to the driveway that led over the hill, and Bellacosa stared at the ground before him with the vehicle parked. He clenched the steering wheel until his knuckles turned white, clicked his tongue like an ancient call of the wild. Then Bellacosa put the old Jeep in gear and drove in. He remembered there had been gravel paving the way, but it was missing; the ground was packed in cold and hard under the mesquite trees shaped like giant vultures.

He parked at the clearing as he'd been instructed during his visit, got out of the old Jeep, and gazed into the distance, looking for the old, shapeless house that seemed to come out from the darkness like a whale with its mouth wide open.

Bellacosa didn't see it. In its stead was a sign similar to the construction site one: "McM Properties." He walked in plain day over the granite walkway between the parking clearing and where the house used to be. Over to his far left, he spotted a couple of small shacks resembling slave quarters in the antebellum South. They had faded blue trim around the windows and appeared quite sturdy. He looked again toward the spot where the house had been located and saw only a patch of trampled grass and scores of compact haystacks scattered in no particular fashion throughout. The 7900 Rig was also nowhere to be found.

Impossible they could've hauled that house so fast, he thought. *They'd have to take it in pieces, have it hauled by a couple of flatbeds, or hundreds of burros.*

He walked through yellow ankle-length grass toward the slave quarters, saw the door was slightly open behind the ragged, dusty screen door. He knocked quietly and listened for any movement. When he sensed the approval of silence, he shoved the door open. It felt warm in there, like there was a radiator going, or something was baking in an oven.

Bellacosa, evoking the perverted old men from when he was a boy who catcalled the women going by, said in a loud voice, "*Arroz.*"

Nobody responded, nothing moved, and he walked inside the long, wide room. The place was empty except for a desk at the far end supporting a monitor with many tentacle-like cables that dug into the wooden wall. A calendar by the door from three years ago advertised a mechanic shop named Taller Armendáriz. The ground appeared recently swept, and Bellacosa could smell cheap pine cone deodorizer. He walked to the monitor and could feel that the heat was emitting from this machine. It clicked in strange sequences and slightly shook. The screen displayed a succession of six looping images in color and black-and-white, of apparently the same scene from various angles.

The images were of a warehouse with many aboveground muddy troughs about fifty feet long, like furrows of vegetables were being filtered and grown. People in white bodysuits walked around with clipboards as if inspecting the troughs, and there were men dressed in the Tejano style holding automatic weapons, as if they were goons overlooking prisoners. The color images revealed not vegetables, but slivers of flesh emerging from the mud in some of the troughs. The black-and-white cameras registered the flesh in a strange gray hue, like giant blades. The slivers looked like people to Bellacosa, as if they'd collectively been drowned naked in those furrows of a fake swamp.

It dawned on him that the images were not various angles of one place, but different locations. The people with clipboards and the goons were all standing and moving differently in every successive image. Bellacosa stared at the flicker of the monitor for an interminable moment, then thought about himself being in the room in the first place and got the creeps, and he pulled himself away from the images and the monitor.

Órale, viejo, he told himself, and hurried toward the door.

Two Border Protector trucks had rolled in and there was an officer scanning the plates and registration on the old Jeep, while another captured a three-dimensional portrait of it with a special camera. Two officers stood about twenty feet in front of Bellacosa with weapons drawn, and the light-skinned one with bad acne said, "*Manos arriba*. With your hands up."

A dozen automatic weapons then pointed at Bellacosa. He raised his arms and said, "I'm an American citizen. I have rights."

A muscular female officer said, "Right. Frontsquad, show this American here his rights."

Two officers approached Bellacosa in shuffles of alligator movements. One of them pressed what looked like an electronic vampire bat to Bellacosa's neck; it bit into his flesh and released a shock that brought Bellacosa to the ground, unconscious and shivering. The officers shackled his hands and his feet and carried him into one of the Border Protector vehicles as he convulsed.

An officer wearing a purple visor said into his radio, "We're gonna need the flatbed to come out here and haul a vehicle away. Here at the new McM Properties place. There was an intruder, but the situation is under control. Better get the paperwork going. Find its address of origin and have them leave it there. We don't want another incident with people asking questions. Barbecue tonight, to celebrate the big game. Don't forget to inform the rest of the crew, everybody. It's gonna be a nice one."

ON THE OTHER SIDE of the Valley, Paco Herbert was driving around in the Centaurus he'd managed to rent again with the last of his work stipend. He chewed on a piece of terebinth jerky, unable to stop adding up the things he'd read. He obsessed over the story of the great and final leader of the Aranaña tribe, Sopo, who was the first to vanish before their civilization mysteriously disappeared for hundreds and hundreds of years. It was the only account or legend he found published in any library's information thread.

Sometime in the fifteenth century, Sopo was the only son of the Aranaña emperor Tritbú and empress Bexexes. He was born on the day of the Eagle's Tooth under both sun and moon daggers. Immediately after Bexexes gave birth, strange things occurred: birdlike fruit sprouted on cacti and flew away; a crowd of people learned to whistle in unison to lift fish from a lake; a child spotted a red-feathered hare and chased it into the ground, never to return. Legend had it the Aranaña people crossed effortlessly between reality and the world of dreams. They believed both worlds to be one and the same, so the lions and reptiles Sopo slayed in dreams were real events witnessed by all. When the Vulture Age changed into the Amalpa Age and the ritualistic succession of power occurred, Tritbú and Bexexes were cast into the Crystal World, the world of dreams, at Laguna de Sil. Afterward, to fulfill his ascendance to power, Sopo had to climb their volcano god Huixtepeltinico and rescue what academics from a certain era referred to as "*el cerdo reptil*"—a term first coined by the Mexican historian Dr. Lazaro Carranza, somewhat crudely translated by himself as "the Trufflepig." This Trufflepig was not considered real by history's standards, and if it existed no skeletal remains have been discovered. The Aranaña believed that since Sopo climbed the volcano Huixtepeltinico and rescued his Trufflepig, every member of the Aranaña tribe had their own Trufflepig to rescue, too, and in dreams had to climb the volcano to retrieve it. It was also Dr. Lazaro Carranza who proposed the Trufflepigs were a sort of mascot of the Aranaña subconscious, accessible to them only in a dream state.

Scarcely anything of the Aranaña was known—their numbers or quotidian lives—except what was translated from scrolls written by Miguel Espinaplata de Marsé, the Spaniard who documented the Aranaña during the brief time he was acquainted with the tribe. This field writer alone is the only link modern history has to the Arananña natives. The idea that Espinaplata de Marsé, a failed playwright whose father studied with the father of Lope de Vega, fabricated the tribe and their infamous legend has not been unpopular.

Yet in the final section of the scrolls he states that Sopo, the Aranaña leader, after predicting unrest in the arriving age, chose to go off into the Crystal World not through the Laguna de Sil, as the ritual went, but through the Ballí Desert. Dr. Lazaro Carranza theorized that a different idea of a dream world began somewhere past the Ballí Desert, thus the leader Sopo, carrying his Trufflepig, walked into its silver horizon, and every day henceforth a new member of the Aranaña tribe followed suit with their own Trufflepig, until all of the Aranañas successfully disappeared. In his scrolls, Espinaplata de Marsé has almost no description of the Trufflepig, but there was supposedly a rough sketch that was very piglike, with hooves like a goat's and a beak like an eagle's. Unfortunately, the original scrolls went missing only a few years after their discovery in the ruins of a monastery, and Dr. Carranza was the only scholar to have studied them. He died in a car accident in Berlin around the time the Aranaña were rumored to have returned, and before he was able to publish a monograph on his findings, though fragments of his work were saved and cited by colleagues many years after his death. His research became a touchy matter for both Mexican and American governments, when they had to face the insurgence of Aranaña immigrants, and most of Carranza's work, Paco Herbert concluded, was suppressed.

The explanation that was chosen and bought by the history books and the press was that the Aranaña were refugees from Tlicolco Island in the southern Atlantic Ocean, which had been closed off from the rest of civilization for centuries. Two generations of Aranaña had turned over since then; many of them learned to speak Spanish or English and were successfully assimilated into Western culture. Hidden forces made sure their unstudied language and culture died off with the elder refugees.

Paco Herbert felt he was on to a big story now, not quite waving his hat in the air as he rode on the wild beast of it, but almost. Somebody, some entity, had been suppressing the knowledge and culture of the Aranaña. They'd gone through elaborate, if half-assed, means to even black out the few books that referred to them. But why? And the Trufflepig—after learning more about it, Paco Herbert couldn't believe he'd come so close to one. What the fuck was the Trufflepig? If this world and our dreams were really one and the same, then what were the dreams we experienced in sleep? What was this world we called reality?

He tried to work out an angle for Cecilia, his editor, chewing on the jerky and listening to Liberian gangster rap. Though Paco Herbert had seen the Trufflepig at the illegal dinner, he had a hard time connecting the two—what did this creature tied to the Aranaña have to do with the filtering syndicates and these dinners? And who was setting them up, now that the kingpin Pacheco was dead? The Mexican syndicates were too busy killing each other—the initial burst of violence needed time before things settled for it to be possible to see who had gained the most ground.

Paco Herbert's bulky cassette recorder sat on the passenger seat like a trained pug, determined to record the conversation he was planning to have with Bellacosa. The last of the daylight was burning. He wadded up the remaining jerky in its wrapper and threw it aside. It was time now to visit Bellacosa, to discuss what they remembered of the dinner, and to maybe share details with him of the things he'd learned.

When he got to North MacArthur it had been dark over an hour. He'd stopped at three different stores before he found the Pinot Noir he craved, Acuña Roble from the Nieves Estate. Paco Herbert didn't want to show up empty-handed.

When he pulled up to the big house, it seemed strange to him a widower with no children would live there. Then he noticed the big house actually shared a yard with a shed converted to a living quarters: Bellacosa's place.

Sitting in the Centaurus, Paco Herbert wondered if the rumors of snow could possibly be true. He thought he saw a hooded figure move between the rustling shadows under the birch trees, in the garden that the house and shack shared. Paco Herbert watched for any movement in the darkness and where the streetlights shone, feeling very aware of his caged sobriety. For a few seconds he got paranoid. Paco Herbert lowered his window slightly, and from his breast pocket pulled out a thin silver whistle about four inches long and blew on it, pointing outside. It hit a strange note and spread like a pungent cadmium-yellow smell carried by the wind. He heard a few barking dogs. But nothing moved or crept from the birch trees again. He grabbed the Pinot Noir and almost took the tape recorder, too, but changed his mind. Paco Herbert told himself he'd come back to grab it in due time, and got out of the car. The old Jeep was parked along the curb, which is why Paco Herbert knew Bellacosa was home.

MUMBLING TO HIMSELF and slowly walking in circles around a graveyard, Oswaldo clutched at a pain in his stomach and took notice of the headstones surrounding him. He panicked and asked himself where he was while trying to take deep breaths. The headstones turned to branches swaying with the wind, and then Oswaldo took notice of the birch trees, the rustling of the bougainvilleas and anaquas, as the pain in his stomach receded. Oswaldo was outside his brother's home. In the moonless night he kept forgetting how he got there and what his purpose was. Then the birch trees and the plants grew still and turned to headstones surrounding Oswaldo once again.

He mumbled to himself, slipped one hand in his coat

pocket, and kept playing with the large coins he kept in there, flipping them around, then clenching them like talismans. When Oswaldo pulled the coins out and saw they were actually coyote bones he admired their shine under the smoggy MacArthur sky. He shuffled the coyote bones around in his hand and they seemed to smile. That's when the reality of his life flashed before Oswaldo and the pain in his stomach returned. With the help of Angelo, the Border Protector who'd found him, Oswaldo had arranged a meeting with his sons by the old airport near the border. When they met he saw his sons cry for the first time as grown men. It was harder to arrange anything with his ex-wife, but one night he got to see her from afar, which proved sufficient for Oswaldo. The only thing remaining was to see his brother, Esteban, one last time.

Oswaldo felt his larger reality lowering slowly like a metallic curtain. Then he saw the bones, really saw the coyote bones resting in the palm of his hand. They seemed alive and eager to dance like a marionette. He mumbled something incoherently to himself, dropped to his knees, and with one hand dug a small hole in the cold ground. Oswaldo heard a strange whistle in the air and looked around in alarm. He threw the coyote bones into the dirt, mumbled louder to himself, and covered up the hole as all around his brother's neighborhood dogs began to bark. Oswaldo clutched at his stomach and tried to stand up, but slipped and fell by the bones he'd buried.

He swung like a pendulum between consciousness and

the beyond; the unmistakable sound of a shutting car door boomed over and over from a pipe-tunnel darkness, followed by footsteps, then a soft knocking on a door. Oswaldo found a pocket of gray adrenaline within himself that reminded him he was expecting his brother, and he sprung up, jumped over the short perimeter fence. In front of Bellacosa's door, holding a bottle of wine and about to light a cigarette, was Paco Herbert. Standing absolutely still, and obviously spooked, he whispered, "*Buena hora*," but the pain in Oswaldo's stomach had returned too painfully for him to respond, so he let out a groan instead.

—

BELLACOSA KNEW something bad had happened as he regained consciousness under bright orange lights. That he'd been in a car wreck or he'd been shot. He was on a stretcher, still wearing the dark blue suit and the Franco Brunis. He could barely move his fingers, but tried to feel his body for bandages or pain. There were no people around. He could hear electronic hummingbirds beeping from the lights beside him that shrunk, getting tighter and tighter, then popped open like Dalí's melting clocks toward the ceiling. Through a large window on the wall was a sad newsroom with nobody in it. Everything inside the newsroom was turned off and a darkness that opened like an infinite mouth emerged. Bellacosa looked into the mouth as it told him everything that had happened. In a half-conscious state, feeling not quite human, he panicked and tried to get up. He flopped around and in his weakness tried pushing himself upward. Though he wasn't strapped down, his efforts proved useless. He moved his rubbery lips to try talking and felt like a horse chewing tar, or an inebriated fish with long whiskers, and his limbs became one fin. He swam away like a fish, but he couldn't swim. Bellacosa was trapped. He saw a couple of empty stretchers in the same room; one appeared recently soiled, the other heavily bleached. He heard a distant sound grow into a loud echo and a door opened.

Two young scientists wearing eggshell-white bodysuits walked in along with a chubby, short man wearing a Smithson hat in the style of old westerns and dressed like he played *conjunto* music. In his arms he held what looked at first like a golden goose to Bellacosa, but turned into a gold-plated AK-47. The chubby man chewed gum loudly. He kept the weapon pointed at the young scientists in bodysuits, reminding them he could end it really fast for everybody whenever he wanted.

The chubby man waved the golden goose at the two scientists to hurry it up. One of them grabbed Bellacosa's ankles, the other pressed down on his shoulders to make sure Bellacosa lay flat, and together both scientists wheeled him out through a long, bright hallway that led through an open room like the vestibule of an empty hospital. Bellacosa was handled like he was a washed-up dolphin needing rehabilitation, but he felt more and more conscious and aware by the second.

The young scientist in front of the stretcher kicked a door open. In the new room, various young scientists in similar bodysuits buzzed around with loud footsteps, some wearing surgical face masks. Bellacosa tilted his head to the left and saw a group of nervous scientists monitoring equipment in a huddle, and looking through a window into a hospital-like room. Inside the shut room, propped on a cushioned, tall chair, Bellacosa saw a Trufflepig, like the kind they had at the clandestine dinner, only this one had sensors attached like a sinister wig on its body. The sensors led to machines displaying frantically changing readings with green digital numbers.

A few feet from the Trufflepig, harnessed to a gurney, was a very big, strong Mexican man with tattoos along his arms and face. His exposed torso and temples were also attached to sensors. The tattooed man was screaming in pain, his face red and sweaty, with bloodshot eyes like prairie dogs caught fire bulging out of their burrows. His gurney was violently shaking, while, in contrast, the Trufflepig lay absolutely calm and still. The screaming then stopped and the big, strong Mexican man wasn't moving anymore. He had given up the ghost. All the young scientists grew disappointed and resigned, like rabid fans tired of their soccer team losing. The door to the room was quickly opened and a couple more scientists walked in.

A young female scientist removed the sensors, first from the dead man, then from the Trufflepig's reptilian skin. They wheeled out the man's body as a bearded scientist read numbers off the machine that had been attached to him. "This guy just had four heart attacks. A new record," he said.

"What's the reading?" yelled a scientist surrounded by short tables with stacked and scattered files. He was outside the room with the Trufflepig, standing close to Bellacosa.

"A hundred and twenty-seven per minute until it shocked him out."

"God damn."

Two men dressed like *conjunto* players with AKs perched over the scientists like gargoyles on a desecrated church, looking mean. Unlike the chubby man's golden goose, their AKs were the color of old, rusted bumpers. The scientists were scraggly and disheveled, like they hadn't bathed in days. Some looked sleep-deprived, and others wired with energy to the point of spontaneous combustion. They didn't make eye contact with the armed men or one another.

Bellacosa was wheeled into the room with the Trufflepig, and he heard a voice say, "Do we have this one's information?" as if it came from a poltergeist floating in the air.

"We do. Chivo has it."

In the room, Bellacosa noticed something he couldn't see from the outside. It was an image, as if torn from a magazine, of a pyramid, taped to the wall they had him face. The pyramid was illustrated and it was unclear whether it was Mayan or Egyptian.

A young man with dark green rings around his eyes

stepped toward the poltergeist carrying a small wooden box with a leather wallet, keys with rings of the Eiffel Tower and El Angel de la Independencia, a lighter, and a pack of Herzegovina Flor cigarettes. His hands were shaking and suddenly he blurted, "I can't do this anymore," and dropped Bellacosa's belongings on the floor.

This jolted the composure of the men with guns, and they swooped down on the young scientists as if ready for a standoff.

"Chivo," yelled the young man at the lower elevation in the main room, "*chingado*, don't do this."

The man with the golden goose pointed the weapon at the two scientists who had wheeled Bellacosa in. The Trufflepig sat at the cushioned stool and had that clear, milky residue dripping from its eyes. The bearded scientist wiped the residue away with a red cloth. Lying there, the Trufflepig was looking into Bellacosa's eyes. Things were starting to become very real for Bellacosa now.

Two armed men grabbed the scientist named Chivo. The poltergeist assumed the body of another young scientist with a thin mustache, coming to Chivo's defense: "He's tired. You haven't let him sleep for three days. He doesn't know what he's saying—"

"I'm tired, yes," Chivo said. "I'm tired of everything. Let them kill me, Marcos. I'd rather they kill me than do this again. Why do they still have us doing this? Putting the Trufflepig against these criminals, doing their dirty work for them, why? He's just gonna die. That's it. Big surprise.

What's fucking scientific about this? Why don't they do it themselves? Why do we have to do it?"

The chubby man pointed the golden AK at Marcos and asked, "*Qué dice? Qué dice?*" The chubby man lost his patience, slapped Chivo with his open hand a few times, and asked again, "*Qué dices, pinche mierda?*"

"Leave him alone," Marcos yelled in Spanish. "He needs rest, we've been working very hard for you."

Without warning, Chivo lunged at the chubby man with the golden AK like a wild animal deprived of red meat, but it was of no use. The men with rusted AKs grabbed Chivo and forced him down on his knees, and the chubby man hit Chivo many times on the head with the handle of the golden AK. Chivo lay motionless on the ground with his head bleeding. The short, chubby man wiped the blood from the golden AK on the leg of Chivo's bodysuit and told the armed men, "Put him in the freezer."

The two armed men dragged Chivo away. Just then, a couple of Border Protector officers walked into the main room with their weapons modestly holstered, like sentries assessing a situation. They crossed their arms and surveyed the frantic mock hospital room. The chubby man with the golden AK turned away from them and yelled, "*Órale, a trabajar,*" to nobody in particular, and the scientists' attention was back on the Trufflepig and Bellacosa.

A scientist placed his arms under Bellacosa's shoulders to lift him slightly. Another scientist carrying pills in a plastic cup squeezed Bellacosa's face to make him take them.

In his drowsiness, he resisted as much as he could, then Marcos returned with an oblong plastic tool that opened Bellacosa's mouth wide, and they all watched him swallow three orange capsules one by one. The men with the rusted AKs smiled and nodded, showing their crooked, dirty teeth. One of them winked at Bellacosa and the other made exaggerated kissing sounds.

The chubby man with the golden AK stood mesmerized by the Trufflepig as a young scientist reattached the sensors on its green skin. It was no bigger than a football helmet or a pumpkin, and its stumpy tail wiggled as its eyes teared with the gelatinous liquid.

Marcos wiped the Trufflepig of the residue and snapped his fingers at Bellacosa to make sure he had his attention. As another scientist attached sensors to Bellacosa's head and torso, Marcos said, "We gave you a very potent dose of ground peyote. What you saw happen to the man that was here before you—pay no attention to that. And what you heard our friend say, don't listen to any of that, either. That gangster died because he committed evil and his subconscious got him back. You're not going to be able to move anymore, but don't worry about that. I have to say, nobody has survived this test yet, but we've had nothing but the worst kind. Cold-blooded killers, people like that have different chemicals in their brains, their bodies. Committing unrepented sin knocks our chemicals off-balance each time, unless we do something about it. We are monitoring your heart rate. Remember now it's all in your mind. We are leaving you alone in the room with El Grillo Cri-Cri here. Don't be afraid of him. Where you're going, you'll learn more about him. Please tell us about it when you come back."

Marcos, remembering the pyramid illustration, stepped aside and tapped it with one finger in rapid succession. "Pay attention," he said. "Try to remember what you see. Watch for any old monuments. Like this. Any structure at all that looks ancient to you. We'll be here to hear about it. And find it together. Don't worry. We'll be watching from right out there, through that window."

From the window in the room, one of the young scientists wearing a headset and looking at a monitor signaled everybody with a thumbs-up. All the armed men and scientists except for Marcos exited the mock hospital room.

"All right," Marcos continued. He stood over Bellacosa as he lay there in a reclining position, and looked into his eyes. Marcos tried to think of something he hadn't told any of them before, words of consolation or warning or behest. But he could think of nothing except Chivo, his close friend the armed men had beaten and dragged away, and his face quivered.

"What's his name?" one of the scientists outside asked.

Marcos had grabbed Bellacosa's wallet and pulled it out of his bodysuit pocket, opened it.

"Esteban Moises Bellacosa Dolíd," Marcos said.

"No way," the same voice outside replied, as if being put on. "Is he Aranaña?"

"I don't know. Doesn't look it. Who can even tell any of these things anymore? What does he look like to you?"

"He looks Basque," a different voice said. "Not from around here, for sure."

"What kind of surname is that? Usually these guys are named Garza, or Rodriguez, with first names like Lalo, or Chema."

"He looks more *mojado* than any of us put together," said a scientist who'd been crying. "This guy ain't Basque or anything, he's clearly Mexican as fuck, with a Mexican-as-fuck name."

It was difficult to laugh, but a few of the young scientists laughed, and so did the men with guns, though they didn't know why.

"Mr. Dolíd," a female scientist outside the room said, as everybody quieted and tempered themselves to the present situation. "First off, God be with you, sir. Please forgive us for this. These men are making us work this way for bad Border Protectors. And the man who owns this lot. We are treated as their slaves. All we want is to have a fair chance at life. The opportunity to be with our families and to fall in love and have a future. But please, if anything happens to you, sir, don't haunt us. Atone for your sins now if you have them, whatever that means to you, spiritually, or scientifically. But if you don't, that's fine, too. Remember the Trufflepig, sir, because you'll be dreaming its dream. Don't be scared. And if you have to haunt somebody, please haunt any of these evil men—"

"*Qué dice esta vieja?*" one of the men with the rusted AKs said.

Marcos signaled for her to wrap it up. He tried to think of something to add, then just patted Bellacosa's leg, patted the Trufflepig on its body, and left the room, closing the door behind him.

Bellacosa was face-to-face with the Trufflepig. The sensors made it appear electric, and there was something in the creature's eyes that absorbed him. Bellacosa swayed and immediately pulled back and turned a dark corner, where he fell into a sandy, catatonic state. The lights in the phosphorescent room blinked, and in the lightning flashes of darkness he felt a globular presence floating, and bright blue radiation. To his left there was a raft with huddled sailors. About a hundred yards to his right were the remains of a ship sinking into a coffee-colored ocean as a storm cackled and thunder clapped. There was a skull within a cloud looking down at him and the sailors. The survivors on the shore knew they were due for a longer, more painful death, stranded on a barren island. Bellacosa felt the pasture of his breathing, took some deep breaths of dandelions, sunflowers, of cattails by the lagoon, breaths of grapefruit orchards, then exhaled everything in a liquid breeze. Bellacosa, feeling the horror of complete freedom, saw his memories and life lessons run away from him, hand in hand down a hill. His memory was now the memory of all living things, and in a musky, chrome fog he saw the hourglass figure of a woman approaching. She carried a basket on her head and wore a thin dress like the skin of a tiger. Looking closer, Bellacosa concluded she was a beauty. As her body shook itself of the static fog, Bellacosa saw her face and head clearly. Instead of a human head this woman had a Trufflepig over her shoulders, like she'd emerged from a hieroglyphic on a pyramid wall. The Trufflepig sat on her neck, its four stumpy hooves dangling, reptilian skin like tiny switchblades sprouting from its pores. Bellacosa knew, suddenly, that this woman's body was the Trufflepig's body; that the woman was the Trufflepig. She had an eagle's beak, and a sharp, thin tongue.

Bellacosa said to himself, "This is Lady Eve."

Then he said, "I emerged from the red mud. I am Sir Adam."

Hand in hand they walked into the capsicum fog.

FIFTEEN

BELLACOSA AWOKE TO FOOTSTEPS AND A BLENDER. A LOUD replica in the living room was playing Spanish network news about the food shortage riots in Jasper, Illinois, and Sacramento, California.

Lupita knocked on their bedroom door and said, "*Órale.* Get up already." She was licking yogurt from a large wooden spoon and wearing a purple bathrobe.

Bellacosa showered and dressed for work, slipped on a pair of white Velcro tennis shoes that were easy on his feet, put the replica on mute, and joined his wife and teenage daughter for breakfast.

Bellacosa had *huevos revueltos* with corn tortillas, Lupita had yogurt with granola, and Yadira barely touched her cereal and stared into the screen on her tablet.

"Yadi, c'mon, what can be so important on your tablet this early in the morning?" Bellacosa said in a low voice.

"What?" Yadira responded.

"See, you can't even listen to me, you're entirely unaware of your surroundings. All of you kids of your generation, I don't know."

"I'm not doing anything wrong. Mom, tell him I'm not doing anything. I'm just doing the same thing you guys are doing, which is catching up on the news. I hate watching the replica, I prefer to read it the old-fashioned way, on my tablet."

"I'm driving you to school this morning," Bellacosa declared.

"What, why? That's totally unfair, what did I do? You guys promised I could take the car every day from now until graduation. You're not being fair. Mom, would you tell him he's not being fair, please?"

"He has a point, Yadira. We've told you many times, no phones at the table."

"But I wasn't even on my phone. I was reading the news on the tablet. You guys are staring at the replica while we sit here. What am I supposed to do? Just eat my sad cereal and look at your faces?"

After breakfast, Bellacosa drove his daughter, Yadira, to MacArthur North High School in the MacroStar Ultra, his loyal work van of many years. Yadira clenched her teeth the whole way, and when they pulled up to the school she hopped out and slammed the door shut without uttering a word.

As Bellacosa drove away he lowered his window and lit up a cheap Windjumper cigarette. There was no stereo in the work van and Bellacosa whistled an indistinct, melodic tune.

He passed a bearded man selling walnuts in sandwich bags at an intersection, and Bellacosa waved a no-thank-you gesture. The bearded man threw him the peace sign as he drove away.

RGV Uniforms was located in dirty downtown by the overpass, near the airport. Despite the occasional landing or takeoff, it was a quiet, calm morning, and Bellacosa thought he heard birds chirping in the palm trees. He saw his assistant Diego's beat-up Murciélago parked out front. Bellacosa was glad the young man was already there: Diego was strong and hardworking, had come from a good family in Puebla famous for breeding the best fighting roosters. Diego had moved to the States when his family fell on tough times after Mexico's economic collapse, with the plan to train roosters the traditional way, like he'd learned back home. But nobody bothered to tell Diego the cockfighting business had been outlawed in the States a long time back. Diego found out the hard way, when the FBI raided a cockfighting ring out in La Feria and took his rooster and his money. Luckily, Diego got away and wasn't sent to work at one of the many deportation camps. One day he walked into RGV Uniforms asking for any kind of work, and Bellacosa sympathized with Diego, trained him in the craft of screen-printing. That was three years ago, and Bellacosa had been fair to Diego in his wages, wasn't a crook like most business owners in South Texas. Diego got ahead in his life, had a wife and a baby boy on the way. It was all thanks to the contracts Bellacosa had acquired with the independent school districts, who needed his uniforms. If it wasn't for them, Bellacosa and Diego would really be in trouble.

They had a contract for Cantú Elementary due at the end of the day, and Bellacosa felt confident they were ahead of schedule, with Diego already working on it.

Bellacosa walked into the shop and saw the strong young man on the ground, as if he'd fainted, paperwork scattered around him like plucked, broken wings. The cash register was open and all the money inside gone, except the coins. Bellacosa crouched toward Diego. He didn't know exactly how to check his vitals, but as soon as he touched Diego's neck he came back to and exclaimed, "*Qué onda, güeyes!*"

"Are you okay, Diego?"

"What happened?"

"What happened, Diego?"

"What is this?" Diego said, picking himself up.

Diego swung his fists as if getting in a brawl with invisible drunks and unaware of Bellacosa's presence. Bellacosa got out of his way and watched him swing until, panting, Diego stopped himself and recognized his boss. Bellacosa heard a distant ringing, as if from a bell tower in a phantom cathedral.

Moments later, Bellacosa got the coffeepot going as Diego sorted out the paperwork on the ground, feeling confused and embarrassed. They locked the doors to the shop and Bellacosa listened to Diego's story.

A group of men had forced their way in when Diego opened. They didn't take anything because the money was still in the safe and Diego told them he didn't know the combination.

"They kept asking about you," Diego said. "They knew your name and about your family. They mentioned the name of my wife and knew her age and that she was pregnant. That's when I got upset. Two of them grabbed me and the one doing the talking laughed. I don't remember anything after that, just you waking me up, *patrón*."

"They didn't say why they came here?" Bellacosa asked.

"Not that I remember. They did also mention your brother."

"My brother? Oswaldo?"

"Oswaldo, that's the name."

"What did they say?"

"I don't know. I can't remember, *patrón*."

Diego was shaken up. Bellacosa insisted he go home for the day and get some rest, told him he could finish off the Cantú Elementary contract and deliver it himself. Although Diego protested, he eventually gave in, thinking of his wife's safety.

Diego said, "These are the kind of men who go around now all the time in my village causing trouble. They are nothing but talk holding a machete or gun, but wouldn't last a round with one of my roosters."

CANTÚ ELEMENTARY had changed its mascot in the middle of the semester, after the school board and community vote went through, and in the back of the shop Bellacosa skipped lunch to finish screen-printing one hundred and eighty dark blue T-shirts. The T-shirts had an illustration featuring the new school mascot—the Trufflepig—along with the school's name in silver print. In the illustration the Trufflepig was charging like a bull and screaming, its eyes angry, almost possessed, and Bellacosa finished the shirts without giving the creature much thought.

At one point he heard a strange, gurgling sound from outside, and staring at the design on a medium-sized shirt he imagined for a second that it had come from that Trufflepig illustration.

Bellacosa delivered the shirts to the administration building of Cantú Elementary after boxing them up and loading them in the MacroStar Ultra. The people there were nice, for school administrators. They seemed unaffected by the odds stacked against them in trying to teach the youth of today—these kids would steal your wallet if you dropped your guard.

Bellacosa thought of his daughter on the drive back to

RGV Uniforms and admitted he'd been harsh with her in the morning. He was disturbed by Diego's earlier encounter. He feared the sins of his youth had caught up to him, and asked himself, if they knew so much about Diego, what could they know about him?

Bellacosa reflected upon his small business. Lupita hardly came into the shop anymore. Only once or twice a week, to help him with Diego's payroll, or to catch up with the paperwork for the coming tax season. He felt she'd distanced herself from the business to distance herself also from him. Bellacosa knew they hadn't had much romance the last few years and their marriage was suffering. Though they were able to make a good living now, after working on the business so hard for many years, it had consumed them, and he had no choice but to keep it going. This was their American Dream, to be a family in MacArthur, Texas, as opposed to Reinahermosa, Mexico, the city where they'd met and which they still considered a kind of home.

The only hope they really had now was to keep growing and expand the business. To open another shop, maybe in the next county, Calantula or Starr or Yver. To make a little bit of extra dough. Perhaps Diego could run one of them and make a better living for his family, too.

Bellacosa thought about the things he missed from his childhood. He admittedly missed the thrill of crossing over drugs and money into the U.S. *We were so stupid then*, Bellacosa thought. *We didn't know the weight of what we were doing. Warnings back then were just lies adults told, but glowing in that innocence and the amount of money we made, that was something like power.*

Bellacosa sparked up another Windjumper cigarette, thinking of these daring, naive days. He also missed the period before he and Lupita agreed to quit smoking, for their health. He missed sharing cigarettes with her on car rides, even on the back porch, discussing finances or having an argument. But as the attitude on smoking changed, they agreed to be a positive influence on Yadira, and he reminded himself that, despite the little spat with his daughter, he was a responsible, providing father. That he and Lupita were good parents. They worked hard together, owned their own house, and had invested in their daughter's education—all things that in some way also gradually dissolved their affection for each other.

Driving down Twenty-Third Street, Bellacosa asked himself, *But what could I have done differently all along,* chingado, *to not end up this way?*

The only answer he had was that he could have stuck to the drug game in his early years. He could have grown into a man while trying to keep rising in power and remaining a bachelor. He could have renounced his American citizenship and stayed in Mexico for good.

If I did those things, odds are I wouldn't be alive on this earth. Just like Freddy and Canchola. They stuck with it and now they're dead or disappeared.

Bellacosa had run into Freddy Santos's sister many times

in the past, and always avoided eye contact with her. He was afraid she'd ask him questions of the old days.

Just as mysteriously as all those memories came to him, they went away, and Bellacosa was grateful for everything he had in the world. He was honest, sent the bills on time, had built his credit history and maintained it.

About half a block away from the screen-printing shop, a black Blazer driving in front of him came to a complete stop. He tried going around it when another black Blazer with tinted windows blocked him to the left and Bellacosa slammed on the brakes. Four teenagers dressed in the Tejano fashion came out of the first Blazer and the window of the Blazer to his left rolled down. A boy in a suit behind the wheel greeted Bellacosa, playing at being tough and bigger than he actually was.

As the other four teenagers stood around Bellacosa's work van, the boy said, "Your name is Esteban Bellacosa, is that right? Is that your business over there? RGV Uniforms?"

Looking him in the eyes, Bellacosa said, "*Así es.*"

"It's a very nice business," the boy continued. "You have some sophisticated machinery in there. It looks like it cost a lot of money. Machinery that took sacrifice and hard work to acquire. If something happened to that equipment it would hurt your business. Is that right?"

Without talking, Bellacosa responded in the affirmative.

The boy said, "We are the Zuetzales around here. It

didn't come to our attention until recently your business is in our territory. But don't look so worried. That only means we are going to collect payment from you. Starting tomorrow."

"But I pay rent to my landlord of many years, Don Villaseñor."

"Let us worry about Don Villaseñor. We are your friends now, Esteban Bellacosa. We will watch that your business stays safe. We'll come by tomorrow morning, shortly after you open. Don't be late this time. I want you to remember that we approached you here like friends. Look around. None of us are armed. And that *pi-po-pe* that works for you? We didn't even touch him. He fell to the ground on his own and started squirming like a worm."

The teenagers surrounding Bellacosa's work van chuckled in unison.

"Welcome to the Zuetzal neighborhood, Esteban Bellacosa."

ON THE DRIVE back home, after closing up shop early for the day, Bellacosa took his time getting there. He drove through the Sharyland neighborhood of MacArthur, and walking on the shoulder of the road he saw the bearded man who'd been selling walnuts earlier. Bellacosa pulled over and offered to give the man a lift.

"Where are you heading?"

"To the border," the bearded man said.

Bellacosa signaled him to hop on. For a few minutes they rode in silence. The bearded man smelled like many layers of back roads and sweat. He sat with his back straight, staring at Bellacosa with an attentive grin. Thinking him to be deranged or a pervert, Bellacosa stopped the van and was about to kick the bearded man out, when he saw it was his brother, Oswaldo. They hadn't seen each other in many years, and Bellacosa was at a loss for what to say.

As they rode along in the van, Oswaldo said, "I ran into some trouble in life, brother, and have been laying low. There are men looking for me, who say I have taken their money. That I owe it to them. I lost my job and social status. My family want nothing to do with me. And these men, when they find me, they will kill me. I know where that money is, brother, only I can't show my face there. If you can drive me there I'll take you. I'll tell you everything you need to know. We can split it down the middle. You are the only family I have left, brother. What do you say?"

They drove to the edge of the Rio Grande by the ghost town of Madero. There was no bridge, not even one border wall dividing the United States and Mexico. Bellacosa saw a piebald mare tied to a mesquite with a bucket of water at its side and Oswaldo signaled him to stop. He jumped out of the van, ran toward the piebald mare, and mounted it. Bellacosa stayed behind the wheel and watched Oswaldo ride the mare, splashing across the shallow, waxy river into Mexico at a gallop.

THAT EVENING, Bellacosa had a pleasant dinner with his family. They all sat together at the table with the electronics turned off. Lupita had been looking up recipes from the Southwest that had gone out of fashion for a project, and prepared *flautas San Quilmas*. Yadira had a good day in school and received two different acceptance letters from top universities. Quick to put the disturbing events of the day behind him, Bellacosa told a non-dirty joke he heard from a customer a while back, involving gold, an immigrant, and a bullfrog with a sore tongue that discloses words of wisdom.

After dinner Bellacosa washed the dishes and Lupita announced she'd finished a new piñata for the bazaar during the weekend. She'd been wanting to branch off into another business about a year back and had learned the art of making piñatas. Lupita rented a booth at the MacArthur Bazaar and was happy selling them there, until she felt confident enough to find a location and open her own shop.

Yadira, Lupita, and Bellacosa walked into the shed they'd built that was Lupita's studio, and Yadira said, "Oh my God, Mom, wow. This is amazing."

Lupita had made a piñata in the form of a Trufflepig. It had yellow hooves and dark green skin with a yellow beak, made out of papier-mâché.

Bellacosa said, "What kind of thing is this?"

"What do you mean?" Lupita said. "You don't like it?"

"No, I like it. I like it, of course. I just thought. I don't know."

"Don't listen to Dad, Mom. This is incredibly bad-A. Somebody is totally gonna buy this."

Lupita got mixed signals from Bellacosa when she asked him to elaborate, and, being confused himself, he couldn't come up with anything. He slept on the couch that night and awoke before anybody the next morning, brewed some medium-roast coffee from Chiapas. He made eggs with beans and salsa, the way his mother did for him and Oswaldo. When Lupita woke up he felt an iciness from her, which put him in a funky mood again.

Yadira drove herself to school in the car they had financed for her, and Bellacosa whistled quietly in the van on the drive to work again.

Suddenly he said out loud to himself, "I will grow old with my Lupita. This is just a rough patch. We will come out stronger after all this. I will be a less stubborn man with our marriage and we will learn to live in peace and be happy."

The two black Blazers were outside his shop ten minutes before opening time, along with Diego's Murciélago. There was something about these tough guys that he didn't believe, that didn't quite scare him. Nevertheless, Bellacosa decided he was going to the authorities in the afternoon.

When he walked in the same four unarmed teenagers were waiting for him, and Bellacosa saw Diego on the ground once again, shaking like he had been electrocuted.

"Diego," Bellacosa said, and moved toward him as the four teenagers grabbed and subdued Bellacosa against the wall. Diego was convulsing ravenously. From the back room the boy wearing the sharp suit emerged like he'd just had a meeting with the undertaker, grinning like a crocodile and exposing his matchstick teeth.

"What's wrong with your friend here?" the boy said. "You oughta make him see a doctor. I think he might be an epileptic. It can be serious, you know. And the man has dependents."

The boy's fist turned into a vampire bat and it bit Bellacosa on his neck.

Bellacosa heard strange sounds circling, as if the stars had climbed down and started barking, as if the earth below him had turned into clay humans speaking all at once about the future. Bellacosa heard the song of the Sirens, the lyre of the passed-out man, felt himself cold and with jelly-like hands.

When Bellacosa came to he was in the dark trunk of a moving vehicle—probably in Diego's Murciélago. He felt sticky with blood. Although he couldn't see, Bellacosa knew he wasn't bleeding. Then he felt the body next to him, and a very deep sadness came over him. It was Diego, and he didn't give signs of life. The car skidded to a stop, the trunk was opened, and the blue light of day blasted in like an unwelcome mariachi.

They'd zip-tied Bellacosa's wrists together on his back. Four silhouettes pulled Diego and him out of the trunk. They were suddenly surrounded by thick snow. There was snow on the ground, toward the hills, on the still treetops that looked down like old schoolteachers, and there were long tire tracks the vehicle had made on the Styrofoam terrain. Feeling the slippery ground beneath him, Bellacosa figured they were over a frozen lake.

When he saw Diego's body unconscious over the ice, he saw his own brother, his own blood, lying there like a suitcase full of flesh and bones, waiting to be inspected by customs. Bellacosa's eyes finally adjusted to the inferior daylight. The four teenagers who pulled him out of the trunk were armed and wore dark sunglasses and silver boots. In a quick gesture, the boy leader signaled the other four to commence, as if rehearsing a scene.

One of the teenagers grabbed Bellacosa by his work shirt and pushed him to start walking. Bellacosa heard a sound again from afar, something between beeping and the yelping of a bloodhound. It was persistent yet subtle. The teenagers were confident in their wolfpack movements, and none of them responded to hearing the sound. Getting a mental hold on himself, Bellacosa thought about what was happening: that these boys were there to kill him. He looked up at the gray sky as if it was a safe waiting to be cracked, and the light snow over the frozen lake was like a Sunday pastry.

What beautiful battlefields we tread on, Bellacosa said to himself.

He looked down at his white Velcro tennis shoes walking over the crystal-blue ice and didn't recognize them. He lost his traction, slipped, fell forward on the side of his face. As if it was a sick joke, the four teenagers and the boy leader lost their balance and followed suit. Lying there, looking into the frozen lake, Bellacosa saw a structure submerged in the ice. As the armed teenagers cursed and picked themselves up, a gun went off that hurt nobody, and Bellacosa lay there as if he'd found the source of the song of the Sirens, and was beginning to be seduced by it. He saw that the structure in the ice was not a ship or a vessel and it was made of bricks. A house? A building? It was a pyramid the size of a shopping mall. It rested in the dark depths with a wise and infinite patience, knowing one day the ice would thaw and it would emerge, setting foot on the shore like a great amphibian. Bellacosa was struck dumb at the sight of this submerged pyramid. As he stood up he asked the teenagers, "Which lake is this?"

"Laguna Ballí," responded the last of the teenagers to get to his feet.

Bellacosa heard that strange, distant sound again. It wheezed like a balloon with a slow leak and rang like an alarm from the valley of snow.

From the lake's horizon appeared a small green dot making its way toward them. Bellacosa strained his eyes to see it and said, "There is no Laguna Ballí. Ballí is the South Texas desert."

The figure on the ice effortlessly glided toward them. It was a Trufflepig, its hooves skating on the ice. It stopped about ten feet in front of them. The Trufflepig cast its odd, beady eyeballs over the teenagers and Bellacosa like tiny rain clouds, and its stumpy tail wiggled obscenely. As they gazed at it, the Trufflepig brayed loudly out of its beak, like a deranged donkey at the garbage dump; like the bird of the apocalypse; like all of creation crawling out of a deep, dark nothingness. The Trufflepig brayed and brayed, as the armed teenagers covered their ears. Bellacosa tried with his shoulders, as his hands were zip-tied.

Everything slowed down, to where the braying reached cavernous lows, then in a flash it all sped up. The boy leader held up his pistol, pointed it at the Trufflepig. Bellacosa let out a primitive battle cry, jumped and kicked in the air like he never had in his life, and with his foot made contact with the boy's pistol—

Bellacosa's body rolled off the gurney in the mock hospital room, as his right foot kicked in the air. With the sensors attached to his body, he hit the floor, wearing the blue suit and Franco Brunis. Bellacosa panicked for a moment and felt around for the ice as the Trufflepig in the room continued to bray for all it was worth. Bellacosa's face was dripping with sweat like a wet mop. For a second he wasn't sure it was actually sweat and wiped some of it with his sleeves. He got up and looked at the Trufflepig's jaundiced eyes, as it lay on the crib-like cushioned high chair, the sensors on its small body. It stopped braying.

The silence came down like a guillotine.

Bellacosa removed the leechlike sensors from his body, buttoned his shirt. He moved toward the window and saw a massacre had occurred. He opened the door of the mock hospital room and heard light whimpering. The scientists, in their white bodysuits, were covered in blood. None of them moved. The armed men were also shot up, one of them twitching and holding a pistol, and the chubby man who had the golden AK was dying alongside him. The golden AK was missing.

Bellacosa considered the possibility that it was him who was dead. He remembered his wife and his daughter the way he'd just seen them, like the reality he'd experienced was a stove he forgot to turn off. He felt desperate to get back to them. His heart beat fast and he panicked, looking down at the shot-up young scientists and thinking about his wife and the business they'd started; about his teenage daughter graduating high school and going off to college; about his homeless, wandering brother, Oswaldo.

When Bellacosa looked back at the stoic Trufflepig he began to realize that none of those things had actually happened, and he quietly sobbed as he remembered his wife and his daughter and their painful deaths. He saw his four-year-old daughter with the color of her skin drained out in the months before her death. His chest heaved as he looked down at the ridiculous Trufflepig. He wanted to shake it; to destroy the terrible creature. Then he wanted to embrace it like a filthy teddy bear after a bombing. Bellacosa didn't know what it was, but the Trufflepig had brought him closer to his dead wife and his dead daughter, to his life if it had taken a different direction. He slapped his own head to force himself to stop crying. He pictured his wife's face as he saw it in the ultra-vivid dream, and his daughter's, got emotional again, and gently this time tried to push those feelings aside.

On the floor, Bellacosa saw his wallet and his keys and grabbed them. He was half-afraid to open the door of the main room, pictured the Border Protectors stomping in at any moment. If anybody took a look at this they'd conclude it was he who killed everybody. He opened the door, which led to a long, gloomy corridor with a blinking green light at the far end. He was about to make a break for it when he looked back at the Trufflepig. Bellacosa walked carefully around the blood and bodies and wondered what the hell had happened. It didn't appear there had been a struggle or much of a fight among them. Bellacosa thought maybe the Border Protectors did it themselves to pin it on him, that he was the patsy of this unspeakable crime.

Bellacosa removed the sensors from the Trufflepig. He grabbed it, carefully at first, until he was sure the animal didn't mind, then he walked out of the room carrying it confidently down the long corridor. The Trufflepig wasn't slippery like he'd imagined, but scaly and dry, and Bellacosa had a firm grip on it. The Trufflepig salivated from its eyes and wiggled its tiny feet and stumpy tail. Bellacosa walked briskly down the dark corridor, thinking at any moment the floor would give or turn to quicksand, and down they would go. When he reached the blinking green light, he saw it was a switch on the wall, and the corridor made a sharp turn into a room that gurgled, as if housing many large aquariums.

He almost didn't, but Bellacosa flipped the switch with the green light, and, like some divination, a warehouse as big as a gymnasium lit up. He jumped back and turned the switch back off. A few seconds later he changed his mind and flipped it again, and as the lights came on the gurgling immediately seemed to get louder.

The effects of the peyote, having dissipated for a while, flared up. Bellacosa held the Trufflepig under his arm tightly like a stolen car stereo. Illuminated beneath the lights of the warehouse were aboveground troughs, lined up parallel to each other like furrows of onions growing in a field—about a score of them, at least fifty yards in length. Bellacosa felt not horror, but a deep revelation, even when he saw the muddy soil in the troughs sprouting bare limbs of gender-ambiguous adults. The sight was creepily familiar: he had seen this image before. Various pipes and tubes ran through the length of the troughs, and small machines pumped either gas or fluids in and out of them like artificial arteries.

Rows of mirrors hung from the ceiling, just slightly lower than the lights. Bellacosa thought, *The body parts need a reflection of themselves to grow, like the earth reflects itself from the sky, and vice versa.*

He felt very attuned to the artificial life growing around him, felt a certain pride to be walking among it. Bellacosa moved down one of the rows in the middle of the huge room, then stopped. He hallucinated the shack in Calantula County, where he was now sure he'd been born. Bellacosa saw his mother, his father, and when he focused on the trough closest to him clearly saw an adult's shoulder, next to a foot and the hairless scalp of another person submerged in the dark mud.

Patterns of scalps and limbs were growing out of every trough, some of them emerging more confidently, like flesh-colored daisies from the black, cake-like soil. He looked up and saw the neck and lens of a camera pointing at him from the ceiling, and he was transported to the slave quarters on the property where he had the illegal dinner, standing in that stuffy room, watching the wired-up monitor, as it flicked through images from different security cameras. He made sure there was only one camera set up in the warehouse.

Ten feet in front of him, Bellacosa saw a dark-complexioned young scientist in a bodysuit, shot up dead on the cement floor. Standing there, holding the Trufflepig and hallucinating again on the peyote he'd been forced to take, Bellacosa heard nails being pried off an old gazebo. He wasn't sure if the prying was coming from the dead young scientist or from the bodies being grown in the troughs. He heard the dragging of chains by dead, unforgiven armies, and the nails became doomed moans, growing in clusters like garlic cloves, and the carved-out shapes and shadows under the lights became cavalrymen, then a lynch mob, and they were coming for Bellacosa.

The warehouse went dark, and an alarm sounded with a circling-banshee red light. Bellacosa started to run, looking for an exit. He ran through the gurgling troughs, which became more like purgatorial supplications under the frantic alarm. He was desperate, and the Trufflepig was his only friend.

Bellacosa pushed open something heavy that felt like a door and he was outside. It was nighttime. There were a few lampposts giving off a turmeric light in a lot with many large warehouses and hidden crickets. Bellacosa heard humans hollering at a vague distance as the alarm sounded and the red pulsating light flapped its wings around like a buzzard circling on its prey. He had no idea who the enemy was, what had happened, or why they cared about him. He looked the Trufflepig in the eyes, like a pup he couldn't keep. Bellacosa had an ominous feeling the Trufflepig must be left behind. That his survival depended on leaving it.

Immediately, he thought the opposite, that his survival actually depended on this creature. Again, he remembered his wife and daughter. Though he was positive the new memories of them weren't real, he knew the Trufflepig had something to do with materializing them. The peyote had probably helped, and Bellacosa felt he was coming down off it again. He found a dark edge by the side of the warehouse, and there were loud hangar sounds coming from all around, creating a dust storm of noise.

Shots rang out, and Bellacosa heard the zooming of vehicles. Suddenly loud gunfire burst in rapid succession, from a machine gun at a distance. Creeping with his back against the dark warehouse wall, clutching the Trufflepig, Bellacosa got to a well-lighted area in the hangar and hid in the shadows again, trying to find where the shots came from.

Bellacosa saw Marcos, the young scientist, running backward, holding something bright like his forearms were on fire—the golden AK-47. He was being surrounded by an exaggerated number of Border Protectors. Marcos went for another mad dash of firing rounds that shot nobody, then a bullet picked him off and he hit the ground. Officers approached his body cautiously, as if he was still a threat. The Trufflepig had a mean streak of clear residue running down its eyes, like pulpy tears, and Bellacosa recalled the same thing had happened when the armed men beat up the other young scientist, Chivo.

Bellacosa saw the attention of his captors had been concentrated on Marcos's spree, and things would be back to normal for them very soon. He ran in the opposite direction on his toes. He didn't know why, but when he got to the end of the shadows he ran straight through the middle of the hangar. There was a wide, exposed area that he cut through, bathed in light and thinking he must be out of his damned mind.

But nothing happened.

The alarm in the hangar stopped circling the air. Bellacosa reached the last warehouse lined up in the lot, and toward the back of it found a patch in the fence with yellow "Caution" and "Warning" tape. A couple of trash bags were tied to the posts of the fence, too, as if covering up a break. Bellacosa thought it would be ridiculous if that's what it was. He drew back the edge of a black plastic bag flapping in the wind, and that's exactly what it was—a break in the fence. The night had temporarily busied itself with silence, and Bellacosa was suddenly so grateful that he could kiss the Trufflepig. But he didn't. He squeezed between the bags and the metallic fence to the other side, where neither the ground nor the sky was visible, and ran away carrying the Trufflepig into the unknown. When he looked behind he saw every building in the hangar lit up, and painted on their angled aluminum roofs were the letters "McM."

SIXTEEN

BELLACOSA REMEMBERED THE ADAGE *SI HAY PIQUETE HAY zancudo* as he approached a dimly lit closed gas station—if there's a bite there's a mosquito. A taxicab sat with its motor running by the gas pumps, its headlights turned off. The driver was smoking a wooden pipe, wearing a thick scarf and a derby hat. He laughed loudly to himself when he noticed Bellacosa approaching from the portico darkness.

"*Buenas noches,*" Bellacosa said, and the taxi driver lowered the window all the way and replied, "*Sobres,* where did you come from, friend? Where's your coat, they say it's gonna be snowfall by sunrise."

Bellacosa got into the taxicab and the driver turned on his lights and started rolling.

"I'm not even working right now," the driver said, "just

having a smoke before I get home. I live just down the road over there, but I'll take you wherever you'd like, no worries."

"That's very kind of you. North MacArthur, please. Many thanks."

"No problem, brother, no problem. I'm not even that sleepy yet. I'd just end up waking my wife. Slow night for me. I don't allow animals in my cab, by the way. I don't think any cab driver would allow that. Just for future reference. There's gonna be snow in the morning, and I feel a little carefree right now, so it doesn't matter. Are you a farmer? That's a funny-looking pig. What's his name?"

"His name? His name is Abuelito Kukú."

The cab driver laughed and ashed his wooden pipe in the ashtray, under the stick shift.

"Kukú? Like a grandfather clock? Haven't seen one of those in years. I don't think either of my grandfathers even had a clock like that, that struck around the midnight hour, and a bird came out and would go kukú, kukú."

His captors had left Bellacosa's wallet surprisingly intact, and when they reached his street in MacArthur he had just enough cash for the fare and a decent tip. Bellacosa saw his old Jeep was parked in an unusual spot, across from the house of the Padilla family.

"Keep the pig warm," the driver said.

Bellacosa got out of the cab and felt how cold the night had become. He held the Trufflepig close as an electric chill shuddered through his body. He had his keys, too, another tiny miracle. Bellacosa picked a chile from the *chile piquín* tree growing at the side of the shack, ate it, then walked inside.

He finally set the Trufflepig down, on his couch, walked to the bathroom, took a crap, and when he finished realized he hadn't seen the Trufflepig ever piss or shit.

Bellacosa took it out back, by the birch trees, and set it on the ground. The Trufflepig didn't even move. Bellacosa got down on all fours to look at the Trufflepig's face, as it stood there like a tree stump and stared back with sleepy eyes. Bellacosa felt tired and didn't care if it shat or pissed in the shack, took it back indoors, and set it on the couch again. He didn't trust falling asleep in the same room as the Trufflepig, locked the front door, shut off the lights. He closed the living room doors behind him, and also the one to his room, kicked off his dusty Franco Bruni shoes, and passed out without removing his dark blue suit.

After showering the next morning, Bellacosa sat on the easy chair by his altar and stared at the Trufflepig a good while. Only now was Bellacosa thinking of it as a living being. It stared back at him differently than any cat or dog, with lifeless eyes, like an armadillo, that were deceiving. He wasn't sure if its leathery green exterior was its skin or some kind of shell. Its hooves were rough and piglike, and in the morning light pouring through the blinds, Bellacosa took a good look at the beak. It was brighter than a rooster's beak, and larger. The Trufflepig was beginning to disturb Bellacosa. Then, strangely, the creature gave him some kind of assurance. He felt that if a Trufflepig could happen, that anything could happen, and Bellacosa began thinking of it as a kind of Tex-Mex platypus.

It occurred to Bellacosa that the people who'd taken him knew where he lived, and maybe they'd come looking for him when they saw their Trufflepig was missing. Bellacosa didn't know what to do with the Trufflepig or why he'd acted on taking it. He definitely couldn't be carrying it around town. Bellacosa spread a blanket in the bathtub and set the Trufflepig on it, along with a plastic cup filled with water. He found a bag of passable baby carrots in his refrigerator, and he sat on the toilet lid. The Trufflepig's stumpy tail wiggled slowly. Bellacosa chuckled as he fed the Trufflepig a baby carrot. The Trufflepig took in the carrot through its beak and chewed with hidden inner teeth. Bellacosa fed it another one, then left a few down by the bowl of water on the towel, like it was having a little picnic in the tub, and he shut the restroom door.

Inside the old Jeep nothing looked like it'd been ransacked or even inspected. Bellacosa stabbed the key in the ignition, hit it, and the Jeep came to life. He grabbed the tin of mints he kept in the glove compartment: his emergency stash of money was still there.

"*Puros milagritos*," Bellacosa said, slipping the bills into his wallet.

Bellacosa remembered the warnings of snow—*but where's the snow*, he asked himself in jest, knowing very well the meteorologists in the Valley were excitable and prone to exaggeration.

Bellacosa drove by Teatro Los Alamos, and the marquee read "*The Final Days of Kid Cabrito*," a biopic of the famous alcoholic boxer getting rave reviews, starring a young actor from South Texas, Salomon Gonzalez. He parked, bought a ticket, and walked into an already dark theater with the previews rolling. Bellacosa felt uneasy, like how Lee Harvey must have felt as they were coming to get him. He walked back out and got into the old Jeep, thinking, *I can't afford to be wasting time and money this way.*

Bellacosa wondered how to start looking for his brother, Oswaldo, and scratched his chest on the spot over his heart. He thought about the unresolved business he had with his client who had disappeared in Mexico, Don Villaseñor, and drove to his restaurant El Caballo Ballo to find it shut down, with a delinquency notice signed by the mayor posted on the door.

This was a strange surprise for Bellacosa, and as he drove away he began to recount the hallucination he'd had in the mock hospital room with the Trufflepig. Out of curiosity he drove to the place where his business, RGV Uniforms, once stood.

He got to the overpass by the airport, and there was a building painted the color of old gold, with a very decadent mural portraying gangsters and brown women with big breasts and short shorts, hanging around a couple of souped-up lowriders. The name of the business hovered above in a jaunty font, "Trujillo Cruizerz." A couple of mechanics were standing by a jacked-up Wild Child truck, drinking forties and smoking rolled cigarettes. They stared down Bellacosa until he passed and turned onto another street.

A whitewater sadness flowed through Bellacosa as he drove through the shady business district of downtown MacArthur. He felt like he'd temporarily experienced another life through the looking glass, and, stuck in this reality again, he felt cheated. *If we remember dreams more vividly than actual experiences, which would be the true reality? What if what you once thought to be a memory never existed?*

Bellacosa felt nauseated by the deaths he'd been so close to in the last few days, and how they'd felt like nothing. He knew somehow that those young scientists were the actual ones the syndicates made disappear, and the bodies that'd been reported by the media were other casualties. The syndicates were kidnapping new people, murdering them, using their bodies to take the place of the previous disappeared, in an endless cycle. Having seen the troughs with the torsos and limbs and scalps, and going over all the pieces, trying to put everything together, Bellacosa had an idea of what was happening in his world. He retched with the dry horror that Oswaldo was also another casualty. If the Border Protectors or the government or the syndicates, whoever it was running those warehouses, came to his shack and killed him, he wouldn't mind one bit anymore.

I'm a Mexican, Bellacosa thought. *Which means I am only human, and I've had enough.*

Desperate for any kind of answer, it was then Bellacosa finally decided to find the journalist Paco Herbert.

LESS THAN AN HOUR LATER Bellacosa was walking toward Baby Grand Central under a swollen purple sky that covered the city of MacArthur in fermented darkness.

"It's snowing, it's snowing," said a little fat boy wearing a parka, jumping up and down, and holding the hand of an old lady in a houndstooth babushka by the fruit stand. The vendors who had opened their shops despite the weather warnings lined up along the arches at the entrance with a few stray customers.

A waitress over at Marselita's with sandalwood-brown eyes was smiling, admiring the beginnings of snow with the others, when she spotted Bellacosa and signaled to the short, stocky cook that they had a customer.

"How you doing today?" the waitress said. She wore indigo lipstick with no other makeup.

"Good, good. And you? No Colleen Rae today?"

"What's wrong with good ol' me?"

"Nothing, apologies. I just can't seem to recognize anybody today. I come here all the time and was hoping to recognize at least one face."

"Do you know what you're having?"

Bellacosa looked over their small, laminated menu and peeked at who was working the kitchen. As if it was the most difficult decision he'd ever made, he placed his order.

The waitress gave the ticket to the cook and when she came back she and Bellacosa introduced themselves by their first names.

"You're not from around here, are you?" Bellacosa said.

"Why do you ask me that? Are you asking me that because I'm black? And there's a relatively low population of black people in South Texas and northern Mexico? Where do you think I'm from? I'm not gonna tell you, take a guess." She waited, with her arms crossed. "Nope. Nope. Nope. One more, one more. Nope. I'm gonna see what that other guy wants. In the meantime, think about it."

She brought Bellacosa coffee and water without him asking, and a menu for the suit who'd just arrived. Bellacosa recalled the men he'd had an altercation with in his last visit to Marselita's, and made sure this guy wasn't one of them. When the suit noticed Bellacosa eyeballing him, he scowled, then the waitress came back and said, "If you must know, I just moved here from Monterrey. In the state of Nuevo León."

"Ooooooooh," Bellacosa said, and acted like he'd just got shot through the heart. The waitress laughed at his theatrics, then hung around the cook for a few minutes. She came back with Bellacosa's food. The other customer didn't order much and disappeared, leaving money on the table. She collected it and wiped down that spot, then stood on her toes to see the snowfall a little better.

Bellacosa said, "You oughta go see it. I'll be fine, don't worry about me."

"That's okay," she said. "I've seen the snow. I mean, not down here, but it's snow. Little, sugary things falling from the sky. I've seen it. I'm over it. Give me glaciers, the hard shit. Give me Pluto. Pluto's not a planet anymore, is that weird to you? It was weird to my mom when it happened. There was a period there when we were growing up and really learning about math and science. You know, in school. And she'd just go on about how she'll never believe those science books again, because they had taught her when she was a girl that Pluto was the ninth planet. And then a long time went by and people decided it actually wasn't a planet, just a big rock of ice. It was always funny to me. I was always like, Mom, there's moons revolving around Saturn that are bigger than Pluto. Now, if Pluto is going to be a planet, shouldn't those moons also get to be planets? My mom's probably around your age, so you must have grown up with that, too. This guy only wanted a lemonade. Can you believe that? In this snowing weather?"

Bellacosa saw that the cook working the kitchen was making eye contact with him and laughing.

"What's this Indian laughing at?" Bellacosa said.

"Excuse me?" the waitress said. "The moment you got here you were being racist, sir. You people of the old generation, you're all like that. I have to remember the world is changing, that slowly we are changing the meaning of words meant to enslave us. My mother is also kinda like that. But only against people who are not black. She lives back home in Detroit—"

Bellacosa's eyes went big, and she slammed one hand down on the counter.

"Ooooh, look at that. You busted me now, yeah, that's

where I'm from. Learn it, son. But, as a young girl, I don't know. I always identified very much with Mexico. I read all their writers, like Dominguére, Carrasco, and Delia Silve-Caigacielos. She has one of my favorite lines of all time, which is, 'Pink like the gums of a great beast, was the wash-tub in my eye in the cathedral of you.' I like that she uses the word 'in' twice. I think that's what makes it for me. Anybody else would've changed it. Anyway, I'm bothering you, here you are. You're just trying to eat. And I'm yakking away."

She walked away and left him alone to his meal. The people who had gathered to watch the snow moved on and for a moment, as Bellacosa chewed his food, everything was quiet in Baby Grand Central.

"By the way," the waitress said. "This other guy came around earlier. Also asking who I was. He was looking for a man he described to me. He left something here for that man. Is this also your name?" The waitress pointed to his surname written on an envelope. Bellacosa took out his wal-let and showed her his license.

The waitress smiled. "Really?" she said. "You don't even look that old."

Bellacosa took the envelope and opened it with haste, as if it was an urgent telegram. It was a sepia-toned photo-graph of an indigenous woman wearing a birthday garland and nothing else, on location in some wooded area. He turned it over and saw it was actually a postcard, with a scribbled address.

The waitress passed by with a tray of silverware to wrap

and said, "Damn, sugar," peeking at the postcard, as Bellacosa held it up.

He looked at the photograph again, then put it in his coat pocket. The waitress started rolling silverware and Bellacosa said, "All you young women who work here are really something. How do they find all of you?"

"Well, Marselita's is part of the Tigirl Work and Travel Arts Project. Pretty much any independent, self-sustained business that signs up as a host can take any girl on to work part-time if they're passing through the area. Usually things that don't require a lot of training. Marselita's, though, they're the only host business along the border. This one has a huge turnover rate, as you probably know. Girls are always passing through. This one's one of the hardest jobs, actually. There's bookstores, sport shops, coffee shops, all kinds of host businesses that are much easier. People living along borders are weird. Not just this one, but every border of every country I've been to is just crazy. Except for Canada, but I don't count that. And I'm not saying that in any kind of way."

Bellacosa felt he could've stayed at Marselita's awhile longer. He was enjoying talking to the young waitress from Detroit. He set a large bill on the table and said, "I don't need the change."

"That's too much."

"It's just a piece of green paper with a pig's head on it," Bellacosa said, as he walked toward the arches and the snow. The waitress waved goodbye.

BRITO PARK wasn't very far. It was the city park where high school kids surreptitiously got stoned. There was a basketball court, tall oak trees everywhere, a drained, fenced-in swimming pool with a padlock at the entrance, and a statue of the South Texas bluesman Texas Joe Valles, where the kids gathered to play acoustic guitars and read subversive literature aloud.

Toward the northwestern side of the park stood the biggest oak tree in South Texas, with a commemorative plaque. From a distance Bellacosa could see an old office desk set up below its hulking branches. Sitting on a chair behind it was Paco Herbert, smoking a cigarette. The snow came down in a soft drizzle. An ashtray on the desk that resembled a big green leaf was filled with butts of Caballero Lights. Paco Herbert had a couple of blue one-subject notebooks with scribblings in black ink.

"*Qué onda, cuate,*" Paco Herbert said.

He stood to shake Bellacosa's hand, pulled out a small chair for him from under the desk.

"I like this weird park," Paco Herbert said. "I get a lot of work done here. It draws a strange crowd of people. *Coño,* how are you, friend? You look well rested. That looks like a good coat you're wearing, you got a nice scarf, too, and all the works. I, on the other hand, must look like a fucking bus stop in hell or something. So, sorry if I'm smelling bad a little bit here. Please, sit."

"Paco," Bellacosa interrupted. "I have to ask you something."

Paco Herbert perked up and said, "Sure. Anything."

"When we were at Marselita's before the dinner. Did you lie to me? About those men following me around? You never gave me a clear answer."

"Okay. I want you to know I'm not the kind of person that lies. So, no. I exaggerated a little, probably. I think now it was just a coincidence those guys were in there the same time as you for several days. You know Baby Grand Central, always the same clientele. But I apologize either way. Please forgive me. I was in a tight spot, as you can recall. I needed a companion. I'm sorry. I didn't mean to put my word on the line. Are we good?"

Bellacosa gave Paco Herbert a half-hearted nod. Paco Herbert motioned for him to sit down and Bellacosa took another look around Brito Park before doing so.

Paco Herbert followed suit. He grew excitable and said, "It's snowing. I can't believe that. It rarely happens here, doesn't it? And look at this desk. I don't know who brought it here, but I'm enjoying everything around so much. I drink coffee and try to get real work done at this park. The waitress gave you the note, I take it? Gorgeous girl. If it's the same one we're talking about. What've you been up to, Bellacosa? I'm glad you're around. I had a feeling we wouldn't cross paths again, I don't know why. Is that morbid? Sorry. I shouldn't say stuff like that out loud. I think it's safe to talk here, either way. Bellacosa, I think I'm losing my mind. Or that I've lost it. I've been reading. I don't even want to tell you what I've been reading. But I'm working on the story already. Which is great, because at this point I've exceeded the budget they gave me. And the sponsor who was supposed to pay for the dinner tickets bailed. Now the company lost all that cash and they're naturally blaming me. Shit. I need to have the story in four days. That's fine, because I feel I'm on the brink of something. What we saw the other night. At the dinner. That was just the beginning. Do you want to hear about it? What have you been doing, my man?"

Thinking over everything that had happened to him in the past few days, sitting on those chairs under the oak tree as it snowed, Bellacosa said, "I'll tell you. But you tell me first. What you've discovered since the dinner."

Paco Herbert shut one of his notebooks and shuffled through the other. Then, using restraint to stay seated, he told Bellacosa all he'd learned about the Aranaña, their view of reality and dreams, and how he believed the key to everything was a merging of modern science and the beliefs of old cultures.

"Remember, at the dinner, Bellacosa, the Trufflepig? I had no idea of anything about that animal when we were there. I didn't know even about the Aranaña people from down here, their mythology that's deliberately missing from your history. I am just some fucking journalist getting hired to write a story on fucking illegal dinners. That's it. But this

Trufflepig is a mythological creature. It never existed. The Aranañas' only surviving myth, which is almost impossible to track down, tells how they rescued their own Trufflepig, in their own dreams. You follow? The Aranaña, unlike other tribes that worship deities that resemble men, they worshipped this Trufflepig, which doesn't exist. Think of it as something like a phoenix bird. Or like a dragon. Animals there are no remnants of except in our minds, because they never really happened. They were a product of our world fiction." Paco Herbert jumped from the chair at the word "fiction," then crouched and looked around, as if for a moment he thought they were being watched.

"You'll have to forgive my enthusiasm," Paco Herbert said in a lower voice. "I've been up for days with little sleep, friend, drinking *chingos* of coffee. But I think I figured out what the Trufflepig is. What it represented to the Aranaña. The Trufflepig was some kind of mirror. A mirror reflecting who we are as people beyond time and space. A creature that reflects the ugliness of reality and embodies it in its being, by being just the way it is. Does that make sense to you at all? Like the Chinese calendar, where they have the Year of the Dog, Year of the Rooster. The Aranaña believed they were living through an age. And the Trufflepig was the deity of that age. They believed that reality and dreams were one and the same, because they were both things that were being perceived and imagined by the same deity. You get me? The same animal god. This age belonging to the Trufflepig."

Bellacosa had stood up and walked with Paco Herbert over a cold, wet caliche trail. The dark clouds enclosed the park like the ceiling of a Gothic cathedral, and it was impossible to tell what time of day it was in MacArthur.

"In their mythology," Paco Herbert continued, "the leader that saved the first Trufflepig disappeared forever when he walked into the Ballí Desert, carrying the Trufflepig. A couple generations ago, the Aranaña came back. From where? Who knows. Everybody said they came from some island that ran out of resources, that was cut off from civilization. But I'm willing to bet they all appeared in the place they disappeared. The Ballí Desert. I don't know if they came back all at once or one by one. But suddenly they were here. Since then, as you know, the Aranaña were assimilated the hard way into society. Maybe the hard way is the only way we get assimilated. The original Aranaña now are all dead, and so is their culture, pretty much. Almost nobody speaks the language. Not even here in South Texas, and this is where most of them still live. But look around. It's fucking snowing. Is this really South Texas? You think a fucking Trufflepig is dreaming all this? I'll tell you what I really think, Bellacosa. I think the reason the Aranaña came back was because that was the end of the Age of the Trufflepig. A few generations ago we entered a different age. What could that age be now? Who knows. Maybe the Age of the Dodo. What heathen beast could be imagining all of this right now?"

Paco Herbert held one hand out, as if reaching for a beverage, then stared at his fingers when he saw they were holding nothing.

"I don't know how we got mixed up in this together, Bellacosa. I've been feeling bad about it, and I must apologize. Thanks for all your help, for being a good sport. Your actions will be remembered in some way. This is just a small corner of the whole truth. But anyways, where did these Trufflepigs come from, really? You think that if the Arananãs reappeared in the desert that they each came back with their own Trufflepig, too? I don't think so. This entire thing is a delicate balance of complicated things and quite simple ones, of primitive and modern sciences. That's why I think the Trufflepig we saw was filtered. That there's a filtering lab somewhere along the border here, or up in the hills. Now, I have no clue what the life span of something like a Trufflepig is. Usually they can't keep anything filtered alive for more than a couple months. Which is why these underground dinners are ideal, unless you can sell the animals for the furs or something. Killing and selling filtered animals as food is a quick profit. But if this is true, and they're running a filtering lab for the Trufflepigs, then how many can there actually be out there? And what are the repercussions of all this? The filtering syndicates have been operating for a decade now, and there are tests and recorded patterns in the environment that tell us how the world is being affected by their actions.

"But," he said, gesticulating, using one notebook as a prop. "The horror is. That if they really *are* filtering these Trufflepigs. A creature that supposedly never existed. Then what else could they be filtering? And at what numbers? And why? Just for the novelty? Just to make money from rich people who want to flaunt their wealth by displaying these animals? Because I'm willing to bet it's not for the sake of science. If they could filter up a leprechaun, then what? I'm gonna be real with you now and tell you what really scares the shit out of me, Bellacosa. In whose hands does this technology now rest? In the filtering syndicates'? Because you better believe they're out there fighting for the control of it. One day whoever wins won't have it in their hands anymore. The world will adapt, and so will the government clampdown. But the technology will still be out there. And who will be in control of it then? Somebody's ruthlessly fighting for this power as we speak. That's what's really driving me to drink."

They were in the old Jeep now, and Bellacosa pulled into Cameroon's Express a few miles away. Bellacosa said, "It's my treat," and they each ordered short Americanos.

Though Paco Herbert lived only a block down, Bellacosa insisted on driving the Jeep, since the snow was falling steadily and the roads were emptying out.

Paco Herbert said, "There's something else I have to tell you, too. I found your brother, Oswaldo. When I tried looking for you at your place. A Border Protector's been helping him and driving him around, can you believe it? Did you know this? He won't let me turn on any lights around him. In my apartment. Anyway, he's passed out there right now, is what I'm trying to say. Unless he left. But I doubt that. He'll be glad to see you. I promised him I'd find and bring you. His story's gotta be heard, too, Bellacosa. He's a survivor. I'm also working his experience into my assignment. Somehow, somehow."

Paco Herbert's place was in the first level of an apartment house, the court in the middle already bearded with snow. They walked into his place; the smoky daylight crept in for a brief moment and Paco Herbert struck a match. He lit two candles in a ceramic teacup.

"He discovered these Bavarian candles don't hurt his eyes," Paco Herbert said.

Oswaldo was lying in the corner of Paco Herbert's sad, empty apartment. There were a few books, newspapers, and magazines scattered around, along with empty cups and an ashtray. The place reeked of cigarette smoke; you could feel it wafting in the air. Oswaldo was scrunched up in a fetal position, facing the wall. His balding head had patchy, disheveled tufts of hair, like he'd been electrocuted on the chair.

Paco Herbert and Bellacosa sat on the floor and in the Bavarian candlelight sipped their Americanos, waiting for Oswaldo to wake up, listening to the snow outside, and the wind scratching its face as it moaned. Bellacosa skimmed his eyes over the newspaper clippings tacked to the wall, which resembled a large map of the border told through tragedies. Oswaldo looked already dead. He didn't seem to be breathing. After an hour, as if summoned by a force, he awoke, and it was when Bellacosa finally saw his brother's face, with the pale, scabbing punctures around his mouth from the *huarango* thorns, that he decided to tell Paco Herbert everything that'd happened to him.

SEVENTEEN

LATER THAT NIGHT, FROM THE GULF OF MEXICO, A cloaked barge rolled into Port Camarena, and at a dispatch center paperwork was exchanged for a sensitive shipment that was to be unloaded and carried to the nuclear power plant in Corpus Christi. There were thirteen large, special-made wooden crates, which had to be unloaded using a Gargantua forklift due to their excessive weight. The heaviest of the crates was over forty metric tons. Though most of the dockworkers had never seen snow, they worked as if it was just another day in the busy port. A balding man in a heavy wool jacket operated the Gargantua forklift, chewing on a piece of tobacco, as cigarette-smoking men directed him, since he couldn't see where he was going because of the immensity of each crate. The shipment was scheduled to be on the road by dawn, and at 4:13 a.m. the last crate was unloaded. Nine wide-load eighteen-wheelers with "McM Imports" logos drove out of Port Camarena, through Brownsville, Texas, and instead of heading north, toward Corpus Christi, they headed out west against the last of the snow.

An hour and twenty minutes later they arrived at a warehouse hangar located in Starr County. One by one the wide-load eighteen-wheelers reversed along the dock of Warehouse #8QA, in the back of the hangar-lot. There were many other warehouses in the hangar-lot, with workers noisily unloading pallets and crates with jacks and forklifts.

Inside Warehouse #8QA, two Gargantua forklifts were ready, so by the time the first truck docked up, the workers started. Toward the back of the warehouse, in a heated office, a small group of men was gathered, overlooking the work through a large window. At their center was an older man in a lion's-skin jacket with an Astrakhan collar. Standing next to him was the head detective of the police department in Reinahermosa, Manolo Segura.

As they watched the first crate being unloaded, and the men around them left the room for a closer look, Manolo said, in heavily accented English mixed with Spanish, "See. I told you my men would get the shipment here. You don't have enough faith in me, McMasters. It hurts my feelings, because I've come through for you every time. If you really want to get out of the filtering business, and start dealing with antiques, you're going to have to learn to have some trust."

Leone McMasters made no reply as the two of them watched the Gargantua forklift sluggishly bring in a crate. The steel beams holding up the warehouse seemed to bend and groan, as if a giant magnet from within was attracting the infrastructure. For a brief moment the warehouse felt like it was capsizing, until the crate was finally set down by the Gargantua forklift. It felt as if each of the crates held a trapped storm, or an individual star being born, or its own Bermuda Triangle. As they unloaded them, the workers could only guess at what they carried.

When the job was finished, the eighteen-wheelers drove away, and most of the workers were dismissed. The reinforced screen doors were shut and the warehouse was lit up like a hockey rink around the thirteen large crates. A group of men gathered around one of them, along with Manolo Segura and Leone McMasters. Two warehousemen unscrewed the side of a crate using power drills, and eight others held it so it wouldn't fall. When it was removed, the eyes of an extinguished sun god carved on a giant stone were looking right at them, with its mouth almost curled into a rueful smile, like a mobster who'd busted out of jail, expecting to be celebrated by his men.

—

WHEN BELLACOSA FINISHED recounting what had happened to him in the last few days, he left out a very important detail. Perhaps because it was difficult to even accept it had been real. He left out the part about taking the Trufflepig. The way he told it to Paco Herbert and Oswaldo, he left the Trufflepig squealing there in that mock hospital room, afraid they'd hear him if he would have taken it. Bellacosa's mind kept going back to the Trufflepig sitting in his bathtub, with that bag of baby carrots. He was uneasy at first about not telling them, but as he continued with the story the more it sounded like it actually happened that way. Paco Herbert listened attentively and every now and then would jot something in one of his notebooks.

As he spoke, Bellacosa was deeply worried about his brother. Oswaldo looked weaker, more pallid than in the previous encounter they'd had. Bellacosa felt helpless and full of regret he didn't try harder to find him, didn't ask around enough, didn't dig deeper. When Oswaldo moved closer to the flickering flame of the Bavarian candle, his pupils looked heavy as mercury and in the darkness retreated like fish into an abyss. There were times it wasn't clear if Oswaldo was paying attention, and his head would drop as if he was dozing off. Then, slowly, he would nod or ask a question and seem genuinely interested.

When Bellacosa finished his story, Oswaldo said, "All that makes perfect sense to me," as if he'd put the facts together on another plane of thought and confirmed that all the three-dimensional pieces fit.

"So, hold on a minute here," Paco Herbert interrupted. "What they were doing in those labs sounds like they were trying to extract something like a vision from the people they were hooking to the Trufflepig. You said they asked you to remember if you saw any ancient monuments? Let's remember, the Trufflepig is a mirror. It must also be a mirror of the subconscious. Of course. You said the men they were hooking up, most of them were traffickers, right, in the filtering business? I'm sure they were guilty of committing terrible crimes. Which is why they probably suffered and died, like you said about the one with the heart attacks. From the shock of what they'd done in life, when looking at what the Trufflepig reflected in their minds."

Paco paced back and forth in the kitchen, muttering to himself, while Bellacosa thought of something to say to Oswaldo. Suddenly, like a man about to be hanged, Oswaldo sat up and began to plead with Bellacosa, as if they were alone to confide with one another in a monastery. He said, "*Hermano. Hermano*, I'm leaving you. This bridge where you see me. Where I've been living. No man should be left to live on this bridge. I stopped taking the broth, *hermano*. The worm's been growing inside of me. Killing me from inside out, eating me like an apple. Rosita. Rosita del Escalon. She's the only one that can help me now. To finish the ritual. Because my soul can't be reversed now. Look at me. I can't be left in this world much longer. But it's okay. I did my deeds. My family is taken care of and I did my deeds. Manolo. You know, Manolo Segura, he's going to get his death, too. The Phantom Recruits. They put a tail on him. He's trying to become a big shot, get in with the kingpins. They'll get him, brother, you'll see. Slowly, they'll capture the heartless. I'm ready to move on. And never return. I don't want to come back here, brother, to this inferior heaven. Rosita can finish the process now, if you take me to her. Otherwise, I'll be left here on this bridge. And could never rest in peace. My soul will be in turmoil forever. Can you please take me to her? Take me to Rosita, brother?"

Bellacosa, holding his brother's dry hand, promised he would take him to Rosita. Oswaldo lost consciousness and Bellacosa's shoulders trembled with profound sorrow.

Paco Herbert said, "I don't think he's dead. But he will be. He did this last night a few times. And like nothing he comes back to, you'll see. But I think sooner or later he won't come back. That's the first I've heard about the Phantom Recruits from him. You know about them? This is incredible. And what did he mean about the worm? I don't understand."

"There's a worm growing inside of him," Bellacosa explained. "And he's got to get it out every day, or it will eventually kill him. He said he hasn't been doing it. So that's probably what's killing him. This woman he's talking about, I don't know how to find her."

"He kept repeating her name last night. Along with yours. Rosita del Escalon. I checked public records this morning and found her. She lives in this old, tiny town, Los Alfaros. By the Rio Grande. He's your brother, so I'll leave it up to you to decide what to do. But, of course, I'll help."

Bellacosa stared at his brother's flickering shadow against the wall, then hoisted him over his shoulder with surprising ease. It was the first time he'd felt his brother's bones against his bones as a grown man. Paco Herbert opened the door and blew out the Bavarian candles. Bellacosa carried Oswaldo toward the old Jeep as it snowed, and the ceiling of the sky got lower and darker, like the city of MacArthur had been pushed under a table.

An old woman carrying a blue plastic grocery bag saw them and crossed herself.

Bellacosa said to her, "*Buenas noches, señora.*"

Paco Herbert, slightly concerned they'd been seen, said to the woman, "We're journalists."

They spread Oswaldo out in the back seat, then both got in the old Jeep. Bellacosa drove ten miles below the speed limit, at the behest of Paco Herbert, as he fiddled with the needle on the stereo. The cleanest signal was from the public access station, and *The Aria Hour* was on.

"Puccini."

"You know about this kind of music?" Paco Herbert asked.

"Not much. But I know Puccini. Back when we were growing up there was a classical conservatory in Reinahermosa. They shut it down years ago and not many remember it. But I heard a lot of public recitals then, with my mother, as a boy."

"You think your brother would remember?"

"Oswaldo? Maybe. Who knows. The truth is we grew up so different."

"How?"

"I suppose just by different luck. Oswaldo had intellectual sensibilities. He was studious and enjoyed staying in school. I always read things here and there, but learned things mostly by working hard. In the world. The streets. Where am I going now?"

Paco Herbert read the directions aloud off his notebook, then asked, "Do you know where that is?"

"We can find it. This county isn't too complicated a mousetrap. Like the old folks used to say."

Paco Herbert turned his head and in the purple darkness looked at Oswaldo's yellow, tubercular complexion. He winced, as if a hand inside his body was slowly squeezing his heart, threatening to take it. As they drove down Business 83 past Tenth Street, police vehicles were swarmed by the shoulder of the road with their lights on, and bundled-up officers were redirecting traffic. A couple of SUVs had rear-ended, and a garbage truck was on its side in front of them, trash spilled and blowing all over the road.

They drove past, into the town of Palmhurst, then Peñitas, and when they reached the ghost town Los Alfaros Bellacosa struggled to orient himself. Cold winds knocked at the windows like ghosts demanding to get in. Bellacosa recognized the area as being close to the Mexican border and the Rio Grande. They were driving down an unmarked road when suddenly it dead-ended. A bright red steel rail blocked a brushy area, with the shivering bones of a mesquite and some birch trees. The windows in the old Jeep fogged up, the heater going full blast.

Bellacosa began a three-point turn, when off the road, about fifty yards away, the headlights flashed on a small brick shack, its chimney emitting a thick red smoke, like a carpet rolling out toward the sky. Paco Herbert and Bellacosa stared at the feathery snow and the blood-soaked smokestack for almost a minute without saying a word, the Jeep's wipers slapping wildly.

Bellacosa got out and left the old Jeep running, walked toward the brick shack. Paco Herbert thought it would be wise to stay in the vehicle, and looked back at Oswaldo. He no longer held that wince, and was now in deep sleep. For the first time, Paco Herbert took a good look at the piercings around his mouth from the *huarango* thorns. Paco Herbert wondered if he could breathe out of them with his mouth shut, and if it was difficult to drink water. Those human acts, however, no longer seemed to apply to Oswaldo. Paco Herbert saw that Oswaldo was stuck in an interminable limbo, neither in hell nor in holy land. His soul was being tugged and stretched all over by invisible demons.

Paco Herbert reminded himself Oswaldo was once meant to be a counterfeit shrunken head. Only a pure-blooded Aranaña native could be involved in the process, if the shrunken head was to have any street market value. He'd written an article a few years back on the primary syndicates involved, from the kidnappers who found the victims, to the high-society dealers who found private collectors and buyers, who derived an exoticism from having them around, to lean on as conversation pieces and appear cultured. Paco Herbert had never heard of any victim surviving. Usually, if the victim's blood was too European, and it was too late to dye the flesh a darker shade of brown, hired henchmen hopped up on crystal-kind would chop them to pieces and dissolve the remains in barrels of diesel gas. Or they'd simply mass bury them in a secluded area. There was one occasion when a group of unidentified men marched into a busy shopping center and dumped eight thirty-two-gallon garbage bags full of dismembered bodies right by the magazine and newspaper racks. They did it as a warning to all the rival syndicates, to flex their muscles about what they were capable of.

Now that drugs were free game, and the borders were opened for big businesses to cross into each other's countries after the trade agreement, Paco Herbert thought everything had only gotten worse. The main trend now was drugs that made you lose your humanity to the extreme. Super-drugs like crystal-kind were being cooked up, drugs that flared the reptilian part of the brain, that made people take pleasure in being sadistically cruel toward other living things and to themselves.

Bellacosa returned and opened the back door. "This is the place," he said.

Paco Herbert got out and Bellacosa hoisted his brother over his shoulder again. The old woman who'd removed the *huarango* thorns from Oswaldo was holding a lantern and wearing a maroon shawl under the thickening snowfall.

The sky was a bulbous purple obsidian stone, and the snow crunched under their feet. Paco Herbert greeted the old woman. She didn't respond and held the lantern close to Oswaldo's face as he was carried inside the warm brick hut.

The old man with a bald head dotted with liver spots sat warming his gnarled feet at the fireplace. He had a short table by his side with a steaming cup of hot chocolate. Inside the fireplace was a cast-iron urn within the embers. The old man nodded at the men as they walked in, along with the old woman. There was a bed fashioned out of boards resembling a pallet, and the old woman, without saying anything, instructed Bellacosa to set Oswaldo on top of it.

She removed Oswaldo's heel-worn boots, his socks with the toes burned off, and revealed his pallid yellow feet and brown, untrimmed toenails. From a small wooden oval box under the rickety bed she sprinkled a talc between his toes very delicately, like salt over a meal. Then between each toe she placed very short, thyme-like twigs.

The old man set his feet down on the floor and said, "Sit down, please."

There were four chairs around a small, square table in the hut, along with an icebox. A narrow stove sat by the entrance to a dark room with no door that was the only other space in the hut. Paco Herbert noticed the fire's shadows extended well beyond the chimney. They danced around the room, sometimes creeping along the walls and hiding inside dark crevices, eyeballing all of them like children, anxious to reveal a secret.

"Please sit down," the old man repeated.

"Can we help her in something?" Bellacosa asked him.

"That depends. Is one of you family?"

"He is my brother."

"My wife's going to ask for a little of your blood. From the tip of your third finger. Are you afraid of knives, or the sight of blood?"

"I'm not afraid of it. What's going to happen to him? Will he recover?"

The woman turned to face Bellacosa, and her husband read her expression for a silent moment. Nothing was said by either of them. From the waist of her long dress, the old woman pulled out an old brown knife with a dull-looking blade.

The old man said, "I lament to tell you this man was brought to us after he had already passed. My wife, her blood and her kind, are from the old world. Just by looking at his wound she recognized the thorns in the cicatrix pattern sewn around his mouth. She tried to finish it then, but he insisted to put it off when he woke up. The man had unfinished affairs, you see."

In a heartbeat, Rosita took hold of Oswaldo's right wrist, with his palm upward, and she sliced open his middle finger like it was a clove of garlic. Bellacosa jumped closer, startled, and Paco Herbert also moved in.

The old man said, "He has no blood of his own. What

they did to this man. You don't do that to people. They drain all the blood from the stone. First the sheep. Then the wolves. And then the men."

Paco Herbert wrote this expression down in his notebook.

"They take your paradise," the old man continued, "then our dreams of paradise. Then they try to take us, the dreamers."

Rosita, with long metal pincers, fetched the cast-iron urn from the fire and, wearing oven mittens, unscrewed the top while wrapping the urn in a thick wool fabric. Inside the urn was a boiling liquid that hissed like a rattlesnake. She placed the wrapped urn beside Oswaldo's head and grabbed Bellacosa's right hand. Looking into his eyes with the utmost compassion and gratitude, she sliced open his finger like she did to Oswaldo. Bellacosa's finger bled very much, and she guided the trickle into the urn. The four of them watched the blood ebb into the inky, boiling, mirrorlike liquid.

"This needs to be performed," the old man continued, as Rosita removed Oswaldo's coat and his shirt, signaling for Paco Herbert and Bellacosa to take a seat once again. "His soul needs to rest. Right now he lives in none of the seven worlds. He perceives only the darkness of every one of those worlds and is confused about where he belongs."

Rosita placed the urn with the molten liquid, and Bellacosa's blood bubbling along its surface, beside Oswaldo's head. On the mantelpiece over the fireplace was a bushel of branches, shrubs, herbs. She grabbed them and passed them quickly over the flames. A soothing smell like burning orange peels streaked around the room, easing the tension.

Rosita held a meditative stance with her back to everybody. Then, moving like a fencer, she scrubbed Oswaldo's body with the bushel, and in a high-pitched voice delivered a sermon in incomprehensible tongues. It seemed she was reciting a speech, or a prayer, or a one-sided dialogue with Oswaldo. Her face was animated and her voice carried a cursing tone. A grassy shadow-presence floated over Oswaldo's body, and at one point Rosita spit on his bare torso and brutally beat him with the bushel. She stamped her feet and her high voice damned the grassy shadow-presence. Rosita spread the branches and herbs from head to toe over Oswaldo's body, and stood over his head. She placed one hand on his forehead and one over his mouth.

The old man said, "I will be going to bed. She needs to spend all night with him in this way, to sweep his insides. I know it's not very nice, especially with the weather, but I'm going to have to ask you not to spend the night in here. You see, we only have our bedroom in there, where I will sleep. And she has to be here with his body and spirit, on her own. You understand, right, *caballeros*?"

Bellacosa approached his brother as if to say goodbye, but, not wanting to interrupt Rosita's process, he changed his mind and opened the front door. Paco Herbert took a couple of pills from his pocket and swallowed them dry as they walked away from the hut, the ground carpeted in snow. He took the back seat of the old Jeep and Bellacosa sat in the driver's. Both of them were tired. Too much had happened that evening alone. It had finally stopped snowing and the wind was like an invisible iceberg, piercing through the freezing night.

Bellacosa turned the car on for the heater, and the radio was broadcasting news capsules. The anchor was saying, ". . . now that it's arrived safely back on earth. This project, first conceived fifteen years ago, is finally bringing financial relief for the investors of Marswater. All fifty gallons the shuttle *Homeria* brought back were sold within an hour of the craft's landing. You're asking yourself, 'Now, exactly how much is a sixteen-ounce bottle of water extracted from the red planet worth?' The answer is four hundred and eighty thousand dollars, or seventy million cubic pesos."

Bellacosa shut the radio off and muttered, "The silly rich." He looked back at Paco Herbert, expecting him to be writing like a maniac, but he was already dozing. Bellacosa turned the car off, leaned back on his seat, and pretended to sleep until it happened.

THE SUN ROSE like a burning bale of cotton on the horizon, the clouds passed like a herd of eggplant-shaped buffalo, and the snow started to melt. It was dawn, and Bellacosa got out to take a leak, then knocked on the window over Paco Herbert's head to wake him. There was an old bottle of water Bellacosa remembered under the passenger seat. He opened it and used it to wash his hands and splash his face and drink. His neck was sore and Bellacosa groaned as he stretched.

What's happened in this land, Bellacosa thought. *What becomes of your home when so much change leaves it almost unrecognizable? What becomes of our culture and families, our brothers and sisters?*

He looked at his cut middle finger from the night before. It seemed to be healing well, along with the one on his cheek from a couple of days prior.

Bellacosa heard Paco Herbert whistle a birdcall. He walked toward him on the opposite side of the road, a little past the dead end and steel rail, and as he got closer saw there was a huge vertical drop in the land, as long as a football field. Anybody walking here in the dark would just fall to their death, no question. Along the edge of the drop was cement about a meter and a half in width that ran down both horizons, east and west, like a sidewalk for daredevils. They looked down on a whole valley of dead trees like wooden soldiers covered in snow, and the unaffected Rio Grande was down there, too, running with ease all the way from the Rockies in Colorado toward the Gulf of Mexico.

Paco Herbert said, "You know what we're standing on?"

"The wall."

"That's right, we're standing on the border wall. Isn't that crazy? They don't even have a fence up along its edge or anything here. There could be an accident, a person can fall in and die. But check it out. See all the way over there?

Look, way past that little wooded area, past the Rio Grande. It's the first border wall. We're standing on the second one. That's fucking hilarious. So if you're trying to cross from Mexico, the land drops over there, too. See, instead of building a wall that goes upward here, they dug into the ground, and created this cheap walled-in valley where the river is. It's only along the international bridge that the two walls almost touch. Even if you climb down the first border wall successfully over there, and cross the river, how are you gonna make it up this second border wall? It's a ninety-degree climb, straight up. Not even if you were half-cat could you do it. And if you're a person with a gun standing here, and see somebody trying to cross in this little valley between the two border walls, you can pick them off, like the immigrant is a plastic duck at a carnival game. It's not at all against the law. Even if you're not a Border Protector. Any American citizen could do it. A colleague of mine wrote a report, how Arizona gives tax breaks for people killing immigrants trying to come here. Whole families camp out on the edge of the second border wall to shoot the immigrant people. Because this river only runs through Texas, everywhere else there's just open space between the two walls. I saw pictures of kids with their parents posing in front of dead bodies from far away, with everybody smiling and everything, like it's a vacation for them. Like they're standing in front of the Eiffel Tower or something."

Bellacosa started to walk back as the old man was exiting

the hut, surveying the land, and feeling the snow melting into gray mud under his feet. He smiled and clapped his hands as he looked toward the fat-faced sun. "Go on inside," the old man said. "I'm going to check on my little bonsai trees."

Rosita paid them no mind as they entered. She was collecting all the twigs and herbs from Oswaldo's body, and picked the ones between his toes as well. The urn beside his head had been brought to room temperature. Rosita pulled leaves off every branch, threw them into the quieting embers of the fire. There were two leaves floating in the dark, reflecting liquid of the urn. She picked the brown leaf and placed it over Oswaldo's right eye, then the green one over his left. Oswaldo's complexion had changed to a healthier, tanned brown overnight. His tufts of hair were a little thicker, but equally frazzled, and his ribs were protruding noticeably less.

Rosita signaled for Paco Herbert and Bellacosa to stand away. The old man waddled back into the hut, anticipating instructions from Rosita. He knelt above Oswaldo's head and with one hand held open his mouth, with the other the top of his head. Rosita handed the urn to Bellacosa, like it was a chalice with the blood of the Lord, and she bowed to him.

"Pour it carefully into his mouth," the old man said. "Very carefully. Fast, but don't let it spill over him or us."

This seemed cruel to Bellacosa, felt like he'd be drowning him. He didn't want to do it. Paco Herbert watched, looking very beat-up, unshaven, with dark circles around his eyes and unbrushed teeth. Bellacosa looked deeply into the old woman's eyes of black pearl—they were carved very small and didn't have any whites. The old man was getting impatient with his visitors. Bellacosa got down on one knee, and as the old man tilted Oswaldo's head back and held his jaw open, he poured in the dark ruby liquid. Immediately, Oswaldo's body started to shake, his limbs flopped around like trouts on a dry deck, and with a sudden motion he punched Bellacosa, whose body flung backward. The empty urn hit the floor.

The old man let go of Oswaldo and quickly took cover. Everybody gave Oswaldo space as he retched, and a sound gurgled out of his throat like a thousand ravens flapping their wings; like magma shifting inside him, and, with the utmost grace, like a swan flying away from a still lagoon, a dark green worm about two inches thick ejected from Oswaldo's mouth, and quickly crawled out the open door. Bellacosa and Paco Herbert would later have different accounts of its length but ultimately agreed on a minimum of twelve feet.

Bellacosa had been knocked to the ground by Oswaldo's punch, and the worm crawled within reach of him. It was shiny and left a wet trail on the concrete floor like a trickling garden hose had been dragged out. Oswaldo's trembling winded down, and the old man cried, "Give him his space a few minutes. Sometimes there can be more of those things."

Bellacosa got on his feet. The whole right side of his face was throbbing and the cut on his cheek split open. Oswaldo was absolutely still now. The azure morning sunlight shone in, slithered around the walls and over Oswaldo's body. Paco Herbert, motioning to a part of his own face, told Bellacosa, "You're bleeding."

Oswaldo suddenly sat up on the pallet, like an electric marionette that'd been turned on. He looked around the room like an angry soldier, then made intense eye contact with Bellacosa, as if intending to fight him. With unsteady feet, he got up. Bellacosa was quiet, and slightly shocked that his brother was standing on his own. He could see inside Oswaldo's mouth through the punctures from the *huarango* thorns when they came face-to-face. For the first time, Bellacosa recognized Oswaldo in that mean stare of his. His brother's brown eyes were his own, and in them he could see his grandfather taking them to see their first river when they were boys; he saw their mother cooking them dinner, and in her pain humming a slow, mournful melody, preparing a separate dish for Oswaldo, who rarely ate meat; he saw his own pain and the pain of their entire lineage, and from those very eyes he was prepared to accept whatever judgment came. Oswaldo reached into the breast pocket of Bellacosa's jacket. He pulled out the Herzegovina Flor cigarettes, and pinched out the lighter and a cigarette from inside the pack. Oswaldo lit the cigarette and inhaled not like a smoker, but like somebody imitating a smoker.

"*Hermano mio*," Oswaldo said, in a spasm of deep emotion. He dropped the cigarette, then collapsed on the floor, the smoke never having exhaled from his lungs.

Bellacosa got on his knees, ran his hands along Oswaldo's head, face, and felt the cosmic fabric of all their lost people. Oswaldo was dead. The old man urged them to sit back down while he and Rosita wrapped him in a shroud colored a deep violet. The blood on Bellacosa's face dried.

Rosita set Oswaldo in the position of the dead, with his arms crossed, chin up, and ankles locked together. Bellacosa and Paco Herbert carried out Oswaldo, wrapped in the shroud, on the pallet bed: Paco Herbert noticed it must have been made especially for him; the pallet was exactly the length of Oswaldo's body, and they'd even made it so two people could easily lift it.

A pile of potato-sized stones stood by a row of skeleton pecan trees. Rosita signaled them to lower his body. The old man had found a walking stick for himself and tapped it seven times on the hard, frozen ground. Bellacosa felt foolish in thinking they'd have to dig a hole. The air was biting cold and the sun was elastic, the sky wearing the bashful blues.

Rosita was the first to start piling the stones around Oswaldo's body, then on top of it, and between the four of them they had him covered in less than ten minutes. Everyone looked to Bellacosa, as if waiting for a eulogy, but to Bellacosa everything that'd happened had been eulogy enough. He didn't have anything else to add.

People are always saying nothing ever happens until it happens, he thought. *But for me, things have always been happening, from the very beginning. Every week there's a new tragedy to answer to, a new miracle to be grateful for. I'll never understand people who get bored, who claim nothing ever happens to them. Which one of us is doing things wrong?*

When enough silence had gone by, Rosita pulled out a small medicine pouch. She filled one of her fists with cadmium-colored dust, like powdered sky, and threw it over the stones and Oswaldo's shrouded body. The stones crackled as if they'd suddenly turned hot, and a silver smoke started to rise from them like burning sage. Oswaldo's body beneath the rocks caught fire, like it was laced with fuel. The violet shroud turned dark green, then gray as it was eaten up by the flames. A voice in Bellacosa's head said, Hermano, *this is what it comes down to. We grew so apart only to have life bring us together in this way. How many times have we been brothers, my brother? They haven't been enough. We'll be brothers again someday.*

AFTER TWO TOWNS' WORTH of silence on the sunny drive back, Bellacosa had a strange memory and said to Paco Herbert, "When we were boys, me and Oswaldo, they grew nothing but oranges on the other side of the border. Here in the U.S., I mean, and back then obviously we had no Border Protectors. It was much easier to cross back and forth, and around the time it started to get into the cold season, our *mamá* would send me and Oswaldo to pick oranges. It would take us all day, and we'd have to get up early, hitch a ride with the old drunk that drove the *carretón*, picking up trash, who went all the way to the river. Sometimes if we helped him and he wasn't too hungover he wouldn't charge us anything for a ride. We had this method of crossing through an irrigation pipe that ran across the thinnest part of the Rio Grande, by Madero and Anzaldua Park. We each carried two plastic bags, these tough ones that wouldn't tear that we'd get from Doña Teresita at el mercado. Well, I don't know why, maybe it's just a small memory of being a boy, but me and Oswaldo had a game. That the only grapefruits we could pick had to have a blue spot. You understand what I mean now? If you're ever around a grapefruit tree, there's a stage right when they're getting perfectly ripe. In that process nature's painting them from green, to red, to orange. All those colors of jungle and fire—that's what we called green and red-orange. In that process, all these changes are happening to each fruit, and there's always a spot that doesn't exist very long in the rind that is perfectly blue. Like the way the sky is right now. Oranges do this, too."

Bellacosa pictured himself crossing the irrigation pipe not as a boy, but as the grown man he was, carrying the fruit and looking down into the Rio Grande. "We would both fill our bags up with oranges and run back before nightfall to *Mamá*," he continued. "She'd sell them to the fruit stand vendor, or they'd give her credit. We did this maybe seven or eight times growing up, and I remember now that's how we always thought about it. That we were bringing back pieces of fire and jungle and sky to our sweet mother."

EIGHTEEN

AFTER SLEEPING FOR MANY HOURS ON THE LIVING ROOM floor, Paco Herbert awoke to a telephone call. Thinking it to be his editor, Paco Herbert prepared for a confrontation and answered using a cheerful tone.

"Are you Herbert? The cat that writes trafficking for *La Jornada*?"

It was a male voice he didn't recognize. Rather than correcting him, Paco Herbert said, "I write trafficking sometimes, yes."

The voice said he had interesting music he'd like to sell him, and asked if he'd like to perhaps meet.

Paco Herbert said, "Music?" into the receiver and the voice replied, "Yes, music. Rare records. Seventy-eights." Paco Herbert caught on that it was some code phrase. After agreeing, he very mechanically and deliriously jotted down the name of a rendezvous point.

Though Paco Herbert was suspicious, the voice suggested to meet at a public place named Up-Up & Away, the bar with slot machines by the airport, at 7:15 p.m. When he got there Paco Herbert found a disheveled man around his age dressed like he was going on safari, with a pleasant, nonthreatening smile. Unlike the other patrons, he seemed happy to be in MacArthur, Texas, was eloquent and polite, had even taken his hat off. Paco Herbert ordered two milk stouts, and after chatting about their backgrounds and sleeping patterns, the man got very serious.

He complimented Paco's choice of beer, took a long gulp, then said, "I'm a big fan, Mr. Herbert, and very grateful you could meet me here. I would like to share something with you, if you don't mind going on a little drive."

Paco Herbert agreed, and before leaving he finished his beer and went to the restroom, where he took the last orange pill from the tin in his pocket. Only now, it seemed, did he hear the man's name from the introduction moments ago: Angelo.

As they drove away in a Lobo pickup truck, Paco Herbert said to the man behind the wheel, "You're an officer for the Border Protectors. It was you who found Oswaldo Bellacosa, by the edge of the river."

Angelo nodded, confessed he'd personally tailed Paco Herbert the night he picked Oswaldo up outside Bellacosa's shack, and even looked up the number of his sublet apartment and personal information. Somehow Paco Herbert felt relieved by this, and he recounted to Angelo what happened in Oswaldo's final moments with Rosita del Escalon, at times with disbelief.

Paco Herbert realized he left behind his blue notebook at the bar. He couldn't believe it, felt unprofessional and displaced without it.

The Lobo truck pierced through the darkness into Willacy County, the part of South Texas with the lowest light pollution. Paco Herbert felt inwardly exasperated from all the driving and spending so much time inside an automobile—point A always being so far from point B. He wondered how they did it in the past, how anybody could have survived all that horseback riding before the advent of the engine. All the battles fought in Texas seemed appropriate, and made a lot of sense now to Paco Herbert. He wiped sweat from the back of his neck and said to himself, *This is the blood South Texas makes you sweat*, and he wished he had his notebook once again.

They were on an unpaved road surrounded by tall brush, with the headlights gutting open the belly of the night. Against the twilight Paco Herbert saw they were approaching a large rectangular structure, and the Lobo truck stopped just short of it.

Angelo left the truck running and from a toolbox in the back grabbed two industrial halogen flashlights. As Paco Herbert tried to gauge the size of the warehouse in front of them, Angelo handed him a light and asked him to follow.

"Is this building government property?"

"No. This is private land."

"Who owns it?"

"A rich man. Entrepreneur. Leone McMasters. You heard of him? He's the one who first invested in the technology to filter food down here, during the food shortage. You know Hatfield's Supercenters, the chain of stores? For many years his big contract was with them, until the companies had a dispute and falling-out not long ago."

Paco Herbert flashed his light up, down, and all over the rim of the night, as they walked toward a steel door by the side of the building. Angelo opened it with little difficulty and somewhat downheartedly stepped in, as if he was visiting a terminally ill friend.

They left the door open and were inside a big, dusty warehouse—in the darkness, the dust and cobwebs made the walls appear like cardboard. The moldy air was stagnant and thick, and to Paco Herbert it felt like trying to breathe inside an old shoebox. It was impossible not to notice the troughs laid out like long coffins all around them. There were about twenty, each running about a hundred feet, and divided into five sections of four rows.

Remembering Bellacosa's account while looking into the dry soil in the troughs, Paco Herbert was relieved not to recognize the corpses in there as human. Patches of muscles covered in white fur emerged throughout the troughs, shining like polished moonstones with direct light—along certain sections, pleading hooves and jaws with thick, browning teeth cracked through the soil that'd hardened around them like concrete.

When he noticed the fine-pointed spikes swirling out from the limbs of the animal corpses, Paco Herbert said, "What the fuck is going on here?"

"It looks like they were trying to make those horses. With the horns on their head. But they all have their horns growing out of somewhere else. Look at that one, it's coming out of its back. That one out of its ass."

What Paco Herbert thought were weeds were actually shriveled tails and thinned manes off the dead horses' heads and backs. He walked toward a horse in a trough with a spike jutting out of the side of its neck. Its pearl-gray eyeball was open and looked right at Paco Herbert like a snow globe filled with ink. He was grateful its mouth was buried but imagined it was gasping there under the dirt.

"And they just abandoned all this?"

"Looks like a failed project."

"Project by who? McMasters?"

"McMasters."

"Why would he just abandon it?"

"It wasn't making him any money. Clearly. Moved on to something that could. Mr. Herbert, have you ever heard of the Trufflepig? What they call 'the shepherd of dreams'? I'm not kidding when I say they've been filtering them, too. These rich investors like Leone McMasters are trying to perfect filtering these fucking imaginary things."

"Why? What for?"

"Why not?" Angelo laughed. "What he, and people like him, are doing is just privatizing a science. They're doing pretty much what the kingpin Pacheco did, but with brains and the right paperwork."

"But it's against the law to filter other living beings. Why would a person that's already rich like Leone McMasters risk it all just to make more money?"

Angelo threw his arms wide open and his flashlight fluttered like pale bats around the warehouse, as if telling Paco Herbert the answer to the riddle was right in front of them. Standing there, Paco Herbert was aghast. None of the stillborn unicorn corpses in the troughs were decomposing, and he got the feeling of being inside a large, abandoned estate, with old sheets covering up rotting, old furniture crawling with worms. He felt nauseous and Angelo said, "Let's get out of here."

Driving away in the Lobo truck, Paco Herbert took a long look at Angelo and thought to finally bring up something Oswaldo had said: "You're a Phantom Recruit."

"I am," Angelo replied. "Which is why I reached out to you. That warehouse is gonna be discovered and disposed of very soon. I wanted somebody to see it."

"The Border Protectors don't know about it yet? Then how is it that you do?"

"Well. Because for now it's only us Phantom Recruits who know. In the underground. See, it's hard to act on something unless an actual client gets involved, because like with any organization, especially a private one, we have to make money. We have people working covertly for us everywhere. As you can see, huh? You can call us spies if you want, but I see us more like Robin Hoods. People in power are starting to learn the extent of our reach. When big things go missing, the Phantom Recruits can track it down. Remember the sign in Auschwitz I, '*Arbeit macht frei*,' when they stole that a few years ago? We knew who was responsible for the theft before a client even came to us. And with absolutely no violence we acquired the sign and returned it. Three years ago, you remember when the trend with the syndicates was to steal statues of great Mexican figures from all over the country, right out of their town centers? They took them all, Benito Juárez, El Padre Hidalgo, Emiliano Zapata, just to show the world they could do it and get away with it. They did it as a status thing, the kingpins wanting to one-up each other and have the statues displayed in the gardens of their supposedly hidden homes. Well, one time they stole the statue of the composer Juventino Rosas, from this rich old man who had stock in Wall Street. This rich man's father was a failed violinist and the tune he remembered him playing most was 'Sobre las Olas,' the song Juventino Rosas is most remembered for. When we found the statue, it was on the small island of Tinieblas, by Costa Rica. You wouldn't believe it if I told you how we retrieved it. But I'll say this. Because we just got our biggest client yet. You want to guess who this client is? Come on, please take a guess. It's Mexico. The Mexican government has hired us to find, guess what? The Olmec heads. Everything's woven closer than you think, Mr. Herbert. Only it gets hard sometimes to add up. But, whatever the case, it's already happened. We found them. At this moment, the Olmec heads are en route back to where they belong, in southern Mexico. It hasn't been publicized because this is a sensitive issue. Remember the name of the man who owns that lot back there, Mr. Herbert. Leone McMasters."

PACO HERBERT retrieved his notebook from the bar and the following morning fled South Texas. He'd established a reliable connection with an orange-uppers dealer at Baby Grand Central and needed to get away from all that to gain perspective and clearheaded insight into his report. After driving all nine and a half hours straight from MacArthur in a rental car, he checked into a room at the Fifth Crown Motel by the south-side airport in Houston. He'd brought with him his notebooks, his collection of newspaper clippings, and little else. On the second day there he found his narrative thread within the story. There was a coffee shop half a block down called Serve's Up, where he ordered quad-shot tall Americanos, and picked up the habit of paying a couple of extra bucks to smoke Herzegovina Flor cigarettes, which he admitted tasted better. His article was developing an environmental slant; piecing together his research and notes, Paco Herbert noticed everything pointed to grave environmental consequences the filtering syndicates and their underground market had created. Experts who'd been running tests on the changing life spans of wildlife, global warming, and bird migrations all over the world were coming to hazardous conclusions that couldn't continue being ignored.

Thinking back on the unicorns in the troughs, he regretted not having touched their horns, and concluded this must've been some kind of sacrilege. He also wondered how much a rich person would pay to have a living unicorn in their home, even if it only lived for a few weeks.

Paco Herbert sat on a vintage Irvine chair in the motel room and dialed twenty numbers, then eight, then two more into the telephone. When he got patched through to his boss and they'd exchanged quick formalities, Paco Herbert said, "Good news, Cecilia. I finished the story—"

"Wire it to me," she snapped.

"Uh, the wire where I'm staying is out of commission. I'll send it tomorrow."

"Run across the street, and pay whatever it takes to wire it from there."

"Um. I can't. Their wire is out of commission there, too."

"Francisco, that's impossible."

"You'll get it in the morning, Cecilia. Promise you."

Paco Herbert hung up and unhooked the telephone.

There was no replica in the motel room, which he liked, but Paco Herbert started to wonder what else was going on in the world, what he was missing, and if the recovery of the Olmec heads was breaking news yet.

Paco Herbert put on his shoes and left the room, the

evening cold like railroad steel. What had started as a five-thousand-word story about illegal dinners was now much bigger, and he felt a walk around the block for some coffee would do him some good. He remembered the name Leone McMasters, along with the idea of power and complete control. *Once any kind of power is discovered, the thing that follows is the usurping of it. It's what every great tragedy is about*, he said to himself. Paco Herbert didn't know how he was going to do all that writing without the orange uppers, and for a moment regretted leaving South Texas, and his dealer. But he planned on staying up all night and finishing a draft to wire his editor anyway. He had the story worked out in his mind from beginning to end. That's the hardest part, knowing the structure. The easy part is sitting down and actually writing the thing. Paco Herbert even had a working title: "Tears of the Trufflepig," a reference to the unexplained residue the Trufflepig emitted from its eyes.

Under his breath Paco Herbert sang:

> *"Where the bee sucks, there suck I;*
> *In a cowslip's bell I lie;*
> *There I couch when Trufflepigs do cry;*
> *On the bat's back I do friggin' fly;*
> *After summer, merrily,"*

and he chuckled sardonically.

On his way back to the motel room, Paco Herbert took a different route, walked under a loud, busy overpass. It was close to midnight, and the bottom of the overpass was covered in graffiti, with new, spray-painted designs over the old—a cycle among the street artists that probably went back decades. He studied a newly spray-painted image. It resembled a giant Trufflepig and took up the length of the cement embankment that held the overpass. Its body was painted purple, its beak and hooves gold. The scales all over its body were black, and the rendition of its eyes made it appear strung out on the drug crystal-kind. Paco Herbert held his quad-shot Americano cup in silent awe of the design, as cars zoomed by overhead.

NINETEEN

THE MORNING OSWALDO WAS LAID TO REST, CLEAR ACROSS the other side of the Valley, thirteen Olmec heads stood together under one roof for the first time in history. They sat on rubbery slabs on top of large pallets, where the Gargantua forklifts inserted their hooks. The metal screen doors were shut and locked. There was no other merchandise inside Warehouse #8QA.

Aside from four warehousemen, there to assist in prying the shipment open and operating machinery, there were six armed traffickers, each wielding an automatic weapon and a holstered handgun. Leone McMasters was in his lion's-skin coat with the Astrakhan collar. His gray hair was slicked back and he had a perfectly trimmed silver mustache. Manolo Segura, the head detective of Reinahermosa, played with a toothpick in his mouth and paced around with a quiet anxiousness.

The Olmec heads slowly lulled everybody with their hypnotic stare, the stare of time and all the slaughter of the centuries. Nobody present could resist touching the giant monuments, their lips, eyes, sticking their fists up their noses, running their hands along them as if they were a pod of calcified beached whales.

McMasters regretted the failed acquisition of the remaining five Olmec heads, and said to Manolo, "How much do you think they'll go down from their bid? Since the other five heads remain at large?"

"*Ni madres,*" Manolo said. "Damned if they're getting away with lowering their price. What do they think is going on here? This isn't your regular real estate sale. It's not as easy as stealing half the *Titanic* from the ocean floor and placing it on the auction block. Plus, these men are men of business. Pansy collectors. They don't have muscle, and they're not thugs."

"Let's hope you're right on that. Sometimes people like these are the kind of thugs who don't need to muscle anybody. They do what they want and get away with it."

"What are you doing over there?" Manolo yelled angrily at the four warehousemen. They were sitting on old swiveling office chairs close to Olmec head Q, unwrapping sandwiches, opening bags of chips, and uncapping bottled Cokes. One of them, in a defensive, indignant tone, replied, "It's lunchtime for us, *jefe*. They give us one hour."

"*Oiga*, a bunch of fucking lazy Poblanos that work here, right, McMasters? What a bunch of *pi-po-pes* they got here in this place, don't you think? You know what I mean when I say *pi-po-pe*, right? *Pinches poblanos pendejos*. These fucking lazy Indians. And that's because they know how much their heads are worth, if somebody would only chop and shrink them—"

"Enough," McMasters interrupted. "I don't want to listen to your racist chatter. It disgraces the men. They work hard, deserve their lunch, and I don't like it."

Unfazed, the four warehousemen ate their lunch, making the armed traffickers feel jealous and hungry.

"It's so damned cold in this warehouse," McMasters said. "Probably colder in here than it is out there. What do you think, Manolo? Look at them. All these dead kings looking at us, like the way the stars look down at night. We made history here. Well, the Indians made history. And we took it. That's the way of the world, huh? But. I'll say. You know what would be wise? For a person to invest in the production of Olmec heads. People will want them, imitation Olmec heads sitting in their front yards. No, no, listen to me, listen to me. These monuments have come to the attention of the public. Like when they stole the *Mona Lisa* out of Paris all those years ago. If somebody could produce a bunch of Olmec heads and sell them for, say, the price of a new truck, then they'd be in business. I mean, this proves it right here, right? This here proves there's a demand for Olmec heads. Don't you think, gentlemen?"

The armed traffickers, not expecting to be acknowledged, shrugged, then slowly nodded and scratched their heads in agreement. One of them, thinking McMasters was comical, grinned, and asked Manolo, "*Qué dice este güey?*" because neither he nor the other armed traffickers spoke English.

"One day," McMasters added, "we'll even take their pyramids."

Outside, in the mountainous distance, a hallowed mechanical whirring was followed by a siren and spurts of gunshots. In that moment of confusion, the four warehousemen who were on lunch break really moved. Two of them tackled a couple of armed traffickers, took their guns, and shot them in their faces, and the warehouseman who had done the talking jumped into the air like a winged rodent, toward Manolo. In the moment Manolo unholstered his pistol, he got an ice pick right in the head. Bullets resounded inside the warehouse, from the guns of traffickers and the now-armed warehousemen.

McMasters was shocked. Being unarmed and frightened, he hid behind Olmec head 53. There were gunshots firing and ricocheting in a rhythmic pattern. At first, McMasters thought the warehousemen were shooting at him; then it became apparent the person shooting wasn't aiming at anything and was shooting haphazardly around the warehouse. He peeked his head out and saw Manolo down on one knee, like singers of *rancheras* are known to do in the middle of performing a dramatic, sentimental number, only he had an ice pick stabbed in his head. With one hand Manolo was desperately trying to grab the ice pick but seemed unable to reach it, though it was sticking out of his frontal lobe. With his other hand he was shooting the pistol at random, all the while spinning in circles on one knee, his muscles spasming and operating on frantic, ebbing instinct.

Then, echoing throughout the warehouse, the small, grinning warehouseman in plain English yelled out, "Leone McMasters. You are surrounded. We are the Phantom Recruits. We know you're unarmed, old man. Give it up and come out with your hands in the air. We're not here to harm you. You have brought turmoil to our international community and will be brought to justice."

McMasters was staring down the pipeline of consequences. If he could have, he would've burned the warehouse down. If he'd been armed, he would have turned the gun on himself, and that would put an end to everything. He peeked again as bullets shot from Manolo's pistol, and saw him spinning, still unable to reach the ice pick in his head, blood dripping down his face and neck. Soon he'd run out of blood and bullets. One of the shots ricocheted from the ear of Olmec head 24 and came close to McMasters, but it clipped off the nostril of Olmec head 53, the one he was leaning on. Struggling to breathe, as if the air had turned to mud, McMasters stared into the eyes of the Olmec head with the clipped nose, and in that moment the last of Manolo's bullets resounded. McMasters thought to himself something similar must've happened to the disfigured nose of the Sphinx.

TWENTY

THE WORLD AROUND BELLACOSA HAD TURNED ACIDIC, AS if the great blue rind of the atmosphere had peeled back, its smell drying out everyone's tongues. At a loss for what to do, and having just buried his brother, he instinctively wanted to pay tribute to the dead before heading home and dealing with the Trufflepig in his bathtub.

When Bellacosa was a boy, his friend Domingo was struck by a car and killed at ten years old. Domingo was a window washer, working a busy intersection when it happened. At the funeral, Domingo's older sister and mother sang a song that was dear to their family and was Domingo's favorite. It was a song about Mexico that Bellacosa had come to relate to with a terrible sadness that wrung him by his roots, and on the way to Dorita Zepeda Children's Cemetery, he sang some of the lyrics:

"Ya se cayo el arbolito, donde dormía el pavo real
Ahora dormira en el suelo
Porque no hay otro lugar
Ahora dormira en el suelo
Como cualquier animal."

He stopped at Smiling Suns Flower Shop, and, like a somnambulist, entered the store. The sister proprietors were having some kind of disagreement, which they dropped to build a nice flower arrangement for a young lady, like Bellacosa had requested. After a moment, Bellacosa saw they hadn't been arguing, just having a loud discussion about the weather. They were thrilled it had snowed the previous night, but it was bad for the plants, too, they said. The sisters sold him a bouquet with three different colors of roses, and Bellacosa thought about getting coffee and pie, but felt a linger of Catholic guilt, knowing one must always go to a cemetery on an empty stomach.

When he got to the cemetery, he thought of his brother's sons, Luis and Ricardo. They were already young men, enrolled in universities, and their mother had remarried. Bellacosa felt ashamed to think the truth: that Oswaldo's family would get along fine without him. Then he said to himself, *But I am getting by, too. Sometimes barely, but I'm also getting by without my family.*

It took Bellacosa twelve minutes to find her headstone: Yadira Graciela Bellacosa Aguirre. A child who'd been born wise, he thought, *my own child, made out of my own mother, my own wife*, que en paz descansen todas mis bonitas, mis hermosas. He couldn't help but think about his experience with the Trufflepig—and seeing his daughter as if she'd grown to be a teenager and hadn't died when she was still a girl. Bellacosa deeply regretted having buried Yadira at this cemetery, since it was so colorless and gray. They had strict rules about how long flowers and offerings could remain at the gravesides here. He wished they'd buried her where his boyhood friend Domingo was buried, at Cementerio San Felipe in Reinahermosa, which even from the street seemed more like a celebrated memorial-garden than a graveyard. But what did he know of death and burying children when this happened? He was proud he'd had his wife cremated, her ashes scattered all over the shores of South Padre Island, among the dolphins.

Bellacosa thought of a saying: "The undertaker also has mouths to feed."

He set the roses down on Yadira's grave, and felt very in touch with the love he still had for his daughter and his wife. He looked up at the trees, where herons were known to find refuge in the mild South Texas winters of years past. He didn't remember paying attention to those birds before, but now that he never saw them he definitely noticed their absence. Herons or not, his daughter would always be buried here, and he couldn't forgive himself for it.

Strangely, after a moment's silence, instead of feeling sadness, Bellacosa felt a mild comfort for the first time. Thinking about his daughter, he wasn't remembering her suffering, the treatments she'd gone through in her final year, the year that wasted her away. He now had an image of Yadira as a teenager, the way he'd seen her in his dream with the Trufflepig, and he felt grateful.

Bellacosa crossed himself and decided to take a stroll around the yard, not to look at the headstones, but to get a feel for this clear blue day. All the gray with the occasional flowers in the graveyard reminded him of the jagged skyline of Reinahermosa. He could see the crowd of workers and old ladies heading to the market, waiting for the bus that carried them to Colonia Doctores. He could see the mangy scavenger dogs walking confidently out of alleys, the *paleteros*, *eloteros*, and *limosneros*. He saw the young boys playing all the old games during the day, and teenagers kicking a soccer ball in the evenings. From second-story windows daydreaming young girls with braided hair looked down on them. The fences were tall, with broken glass sticking over the mortar, the vehicles passing smoky and loud.

BELLACOSA was in the old Jeep, driving away, thinking about women, and considered visiting his only female friend, Ximena. He was out of touch with modern dating, and didn't enjoy going to bars, or being around the kind of people who hung around those places. The truth was Bellacosa got along fine being alone. When he really missed women he'd talk to his dead wife, which often helped. It was a form of self-therapy he'd discovered worked for him.

He admitted women were the sole reason he enjoyed eating out more than cooking at home. He enjoyed talking to the waitresses, making friendly conversation with them. Rarely did he otherwise get the opportunity to talk to strange young women, without feeling imposing or like a creep. Bellacosa remembered how in society people are taught that anyone can be a creep—women are taught this, especially, from the moment they are born, and with good reason. He blasphemously wondered if it was for the best that his loved ones weren't around all this corruption and degeneration anymore.

Bellacosa realized he was driving back home and didn't want to go back there quite yet, wasn't ready to see what condition the Trufflepig was in. He drove past Will Shuppe Park, where a family was having a birthday celebration with barbecue and balloons, while kids in dark jackets and flannel were flying colorful kites shaped like Quetzalcoatls, and Bellacosa headed downtown.

BABY GRAND CENTRAL was bumbling busy. People ran around buying grains and nuts and beans and fruit, with the frantic disbelief seen in silent films. Bellacosa found an empty spot along the yellow counter of Marselita's. Colleen Rae and Anastasia, the young woman from Detroit, were on staff. He ordered only a cup of coffee and sat out the rush. The two young ladies refilled his coffee as they ran around, and snuck him an eight-ounce glass of mineral water. Bellacosa looked beyond the kitchen in the back, and at the workingmen in suits who ate hurriedly and often tipped lousily. He overheard the waitresses whispering among themselves what was up with the people today, saying something about a leviathan being upset. He wanted to ask what this meant, but they seemed too busy for conversation.

After it died down a bit and the waitresses looked less stressed, Bellacosa asked Anastasia, "Excuse me. Earlier you two were talking about the people today and said something about a leviathan. What did you mean?"

"Oh, yeah. I don't know, people are being weird today. Isn't that right, Colleen? She blames it on the leviathan. Tell him about it."

Colleen Rae set a bus-tub of dirty dishes under the counter and said, "You know, all of us are living inside the leviathan, as the leviathan swims along the sea of the universe. Sometimes the leviathan is happy or good-humored enough to tip well, and other times none of these rude assholes tip a damn red cent, because the leviathan is being temperamental. And you see it everywhere in the world, right away. Working these kinds of jobs, especially here in particular, you get to see what the overall vibe of the world around us is. All these guys that come in here, like those assholes you got into it with the other day, they're corporate over at the Hatfield's Supercenters office building. You know, that big chain you guys have all over down here. We don't have anything like those stores in D.C.—"

"In Detroit either."

"Anyway, those corporate guys make a fuck-ton of money. They even have a cafeteria over there, where they can eat for free, but a lot of them come here anyway. They probably don't even consider it a different business than where they work, they're so self-centered. They tip less than a dollar and leave their change like they're the center of the world. It's bullshit."

A few other men in suits arrived and were attended to. Bellacosa sipped his coffee and watched them. There was something comical about the way these suited men took themselves and their jobs so seriously.

Anastasia passed him by and said, "You sure you don't wanna order anything? It's about to die down real hard here in a bit."

"You know what, sure. I'm having a *tamal veracruzano* today. I've never had it here. Was thinking earlier of the banana leaf used to wrap them, and that smell they carry."

"Okay, all right. I'll put that right in for you."

Moments later, while unwrapping the *tamal*, Bellacosa told himself this little place, Marselita's, from the people employed right down to the food they served, was one of MacArthur's hidden treasures. Though they deserved more attention and nicer clientele, he was glad it wasn't better known.

Without question, the meal satisfied him, and he let the staff of Marselita's know. By that point, Baby Grand Central had died down significantly and the waitresses were more relaxed, folding silverware and restocking the condiment bin. As she was removing his plate Bellacosa asked Anastasia, "What do you ladies do outside of working here? The both of you?"

"Oh, yeah? You're that kind of nosy, huh?" Anastasia smiled. "Well, Colleen Rae here's a musician. And I'm a painter. I actually did the cover for her new record. My parents are Haitian immigrants. They were artists there, before moving to the States. They still are, but not full-time, since they decided to have a family."

"What part of Asia?"

"Asia? No, *Haitian*. From *Haiti*. You seriously believed I said I was Asian? That's the best, I'm gonna tell my mother that one."

"Hey," Colleen Rae cut in, pointing wrapped utensils at Bellacosa, "was it with you that I had that conversation about reading the tarot cards? Remember, I had that book with me about learning the tarot, and you were kind of a jerk. You said I'd only be able to learn the technicalities of the deck if it was handed down to me, from someone who knows. Like how you learn karate or something and you need a sensei. Anyway, after thinking about it and getting to know the cards more and more, I think what you said makes a lot of sense. You said you knew somebody, right? A woman? Can you introduce us? I mean, you think she'll be down for taking me in as a protégé or something? I'd pay her monies for her troubles, of course. Who is she? Do you mind telling me?"

Bellacosa nodded. "She's an old friend."

"That's it?"

"Yes."

"All right, well, can I get her number?"

"If you want. I can take you down to meet her at the end of your shift."

"Really? You don't mind? That'll be great."

"No, I don't mind. If you don't mind riding in a car with an old man."

"You hear that one, Anastasia?"

The waitress from Detroit said, "Whatever, I've seen Colleen Rae leave here with men a lot older than you."

Both waitresses laughed and smiled at Bellacosa. He was confused as to what part of the conversation was the punch line and felt like the butt of their joke. Nevertheless, twenty minutes later, Colleen Rae excused herself and in the ladies' room at Baby Grand Central changed to her street clothes. While Bellacosa waited he sized up the new customer at Marselita's, another man in a suit, this one older and dark-complected. Bellacosa listened to him ordering, and thought he recognized that high, singsong voice. As he leaned closer he saw the man had the face of Tranquilino, the Arananña Indian man living in Calantula County.

Bellacosa made an abrupt move toward him with a greeting gesture and said, "Tranquilino, hello."

The man jerked backward as if about to get robbed. He replied, in perfect English, "Excuse me?"

"I'm the one that wanted the 7900 Rig at your place. In Calantula County."

The man, visibly scared, said, "I'm sorry. You have me confused with somebody else."

Bellacosa thought the suited man was joking. He was the carbon copy of Tranquilino. As Colleen Rae came out of the ladies' room, Bellacosa watched the suited man walk away, with an air that he'd been offended.

Bellacosa, embarrassed and perplexed, apologized to Anastasia for chasing away her customer, and Colleen Rae said, "What was that?"

ON THE WALK to the car Colleen Rae said, "It's funny how powerful images can be. Especially if they've been around for a long time, like a crucifix, or the Statue of Liberty. Even images in the tarot. Social archetypes that you start noticing patterns of, like the Hermit, or the Hanged Man. Those images are so relevant and powerful to us, still to this day. And it's funny, what our ideas of certain images become. Sometimes our idea of them has nothing to do with what they originally meant. A swastika is a perfect example of that, how the party in Germany just stole a symbol that had existed for a long time. And the Hanged Man. I always had the impression that the Hanged Man represented something like a doomed fate, but that's not what the reality is at all. The Hanged Man is a transition, of beginnings and endings. Saying goodbye to one life you knew for another. It's mostly a good omen. But you see some doomed person on a movie or show visit a creepy person and the character draws the Hanged Man in the Celtic Cross spread, and everyone back home thinks, 'Damn, he drew the evil card.' Not so. That's just bad research, and bad writing by the show's writers."

"*También como*. What's his name in English? Janus?"

"Janus? The figure, like with the two faces? Yeah. Changing one's face into another? Oh, no, one face looking to the future, one to the past. Saying goodbye to one thing and hello to another. There must be a middle point in there, too, right? That middle point where you're switching from one face to the next? Must be painful in the middle of the transition there, your face and bones all contorting. But then afterward, you're looking ahead with a better face."

They arrived at a good evening hour, and Ximena was on her porch, having golden pear tea and reading. She chuckled lightly and wrung her hands when Bellacosa's old Jeep pulled into the street. When she saw there was a young woman as well, she yelled, "*Buenas tardes*, come in. Come in, *mijita*, come in."

Colleen Rae had never seen a house in South Texas with so many artifacts and plants, managing to look well maintained and malnourished at once. When she introduced herself she noticed Ximena's different-colored eyes. One was pearly gray and the other a dark blue, and her auburn hair carried a long white streak down her left side.

There was an extra cup on her tray and Ximena poured some tea for Colleen Rae. Bellacosa greeted Ximena and excused himself to the restroom. After using it he walked to Ximena's tidy and rustic kitchen, like it was his own.

On the sill above the dish rack Bellacosa saw five ceramic cups, all with dry coffee grounds. They were the cups Bellacosa had drunk from at different points and were arranged chronologically. The one on the far left had a fine line growing from the center of the cup, toward the lip, and with each consequent cup the line became more and more chaotic, until the final one on the right, which was like the seismograph of a small earthquake. Bellacosa ran the hot water and washed each one of those cups as best he could, arranged them carefully on the rack, and dried his hands with a small green towel hanging on the oven handle.

Bellacosa decided he was going to cook dinner, and while Colleen Rae and Ximena got to know one another he drove not to Hatfield's Supercenter, but to Corner Mart. He picked up four carrots, two potatoes, a stalk of celery, a red onion, jalapeño, garlic, and a pound and a half of beef chunks. He cooked *caldo de res* the way his mother used to make, but added potatoes because that's what Lupita would have liked. Ximena demonstrated to Colleen Rae a few of the lesser-known tarot spreads and explained their uses. Bellacosa left the stew simmering and smoked a Herzegovina Flor standing on the sidewalk in the darkening evening, as loud ranchero music blared somewhere down the block.

Though he'd been chopping, running to the market, and making noise in the kitchen, both Ximena and Colleen Rae were surprised when the smell of the *caldo de res* wafted in the air around them. Bellacosa announced dinner was ready.

Colleen Rae shuffled her tarot deck and put it away. Ximena helped set the table and grabbed soup bowls with the appropriate cutlery. She set gingham towels next to the silverware, and each of them ladled their own bowl. The ladies were very complimentary and thankful for Bellacosa's meal, and he felt grateful, too, saying it was nothing. The three of them had dinner and spoke very little. Candlesticks were lit in the middle of the table, erect as majordomos.

Bellacosa insisted on washing the dishes, but the three of them took care of the cleanup together. The conversation between the two women was waning, and everybody became aware of the late hour. Ximena exclaimed what a nice surprise it had been that they dropped by, and reminded Colleen Rae she could visit anytime for another talk. She thanked Bellacosa for the dinner once again, and he kissed Ximena's hand and thanked her for always being hospitable. Ximena and Colleen Rae exchanged numbers, and then she and Bellacosa rode off in the old Jeep.

"Wow," Colleen Rae said, "what an intense, wonderful woman. Thank you so much for doing this for me."

Bellacosa grinned and said, "It's not a problem. If I didn't go to Marselita's and visit Ximena I'd probably never talk to wonderful women."

Colleen Rae wasn't put off by this comment, and when they got to her apartment she thanked Bellacosa again and gave him a kiss on the cheek. He felt like a vulnerable, shy boy and slightly blushed, telling her he'd see her again someday.

BELLACOSA PARKED along his street in north MacArthur, and as he opened the door to his shack felt something kicking inside his chest—he was ready now to deal with the Trufflepig. When he walked in, he half expected the bathroom to be filled with the animal's piss and shit. The Trufflepig was on the towel in the tub, just the way he'd left it, only the carrots were all gone. The water was untouched, and Bellacosa sat on the seat of the toilet.

"Pinche Huixtepeltinicopatl. Pinche animal cola pelona," he said to the Trufflepig, and considered that it was just another dumb creature of the earth. Yet he couldn't help feeling attached to the thing, and he petted it as if it were a pet dog. Clear residue leaked out from the Trufflepig's eyes and Bellacosa said, "Why are you crying, huh? You're such a gentle little thing to be crying," and it wagged its stumpy tail. He petted the Trufflepig, thinking about his brother, and said, "*Ay, hermanito.* My poor little brother."

Now that he was home, his mind and body gave in to being tired. Bellacosa decided not to do anything until the morning. He shut the door to the restroom, leaving the Trufflepig in there, and fell asleep on his bed, unable to believe it had snowed in South Texas the night before.

HE DIDN'T REMEMBER his dreams, but he awoke with a clear image in his mind's eye of the sea. It was calm, with many different shades of kerosene-blue, and for the first time the idea of the sea didn't strike him as romantic, but chaotic and unforgiving, even in its most placid state.

Bellacosa took a shit with the Trufflepig watching from the bathtub and chuckled, deciding the creature was, in its own way, quite lovable. He took the Trufflepig back into the living room and then bathed, shaving off his graying mustache of over ten years.

He sat in front of the Trufflepig in the living room and felt the creature was really making eye contact with him. Bellacosa thought he understood what it intended by its gaze, and went over the things he'd seen over the past ten days. He felt very much in touch with his entire life now, felt that all the bad things and the good things had accumulated into something bigger, something towering and looming over all of life since the beginning of time. Looking into the eyes of the Trufflepig, he saw his daughter, his wife, his entire family, and then the Mexican and American people. And crouching behind all of them was the native Aranaña tribe, always moving toward a singular prophecy.

Bellacosa grabbed the Trufflepig and walked outside. He put the creature in the passenger seat of the old Jeep, buckled it in. Bellacosa drove northwest, toward the Ballí Desert. On his way there he shifted from the oldies station to the rock, then *conjunto*, country, and as he approached the desert found the talk radio station, where the host said, "I am King Solomon, I am the King of Israel," in a very life-affirming manner. Bellacosa turned up the volume as the host continued: "This is the new model among young, ambitious professionals, which has been dubbed as Power Mantra Now. It began in meditative circles in New York City and Seattle, where young professionals would choose a historical figure, and take on the power their name and imagery derives. For instance, John Rathers, in North Carolina, evoking the ex-president, when he looks in the mirror each morning repeats, 'I am Teddy Roosevelt, I built the Panama Canal,' and the feeling gives him a breath of confidence that carries over to the office. Another believer in the practice is Delilah Affront, from New Port, Michigan, who before a business meeting repeats, "'I am a strong woman, I am Eva Perón—'"

He shifted the dial. The folk station was airing music from Hawaii, and Bellacosa cranked it up even more, looked down on the Trufflepig, winked at it, and petted its head. When the tune ended he shifted the station again, and a news anchor said, "The arraignment is scheduled for next week. The American president also approved a Border Protectors convoy to escort the thirteen stolen Olmec heads, along with the Mexican Marines, to their rightful locations. Although both governments deny internal knowledge of the thefts, they agreed to conduct a joint investigation on the matter. Meanwhile—"

TWO HOURS LATER, Bellacosa arrived at the edge of the Ballí Desert, the land many people claimed God had yet to finish. Looking at the gold, glittered sand and blurry horizon, Bellacosa was sure that not only was the land finished, but God had already destroyed it many times over. That's why the Aranaña disappeared, carrying the Trufflepigs they'd saved from their collective dream of the fiery Huixtepeltinico volcano—they escaped one destruction only to enter another.

Bellacosa left the old Jeep unlocked at the edge of the road and pocketed the keys. Carrying his Trufflepig, like the Aranaña people did so long ago, he pounded his chest with one fist and said, "I am Esteban Bellacosa. I am the King of Egypt," and walked into the gushing neck of the Ballí Desert.

ACKNOWLEDGMENTS

The first draft of *Tears of the Trufflepig* was written between October 6, 2014, and January 6, 2015, on an Olivetti Underwood Lettera 32. I am grateful to the Alfredo Cisneros Del Moral Foundation for their generous 2014 award, which helped immensely during the execution of this project. Thank you to Sandra Cisneros and Roland G. Mazuca, and thank you to Gregg Barrios and Ben Olguín, for nominating me. Special thanks also to John Phillip Santos.

Much love to my mother, who is no longer with us but whose presence is always a guiding force; love to my father, down in South Texas, and to my sisters and extended family across all borders.

This project wouldn't have been possible without the artists and friends who sustained me psychologically for many years, so thank you to Elva Baca, Fred Garcia, Jim Mendiola. Thank you to Chris "XPPR5dash9" H. for teaching me klezmer; to Palfloat, Rert Gallery, and all of Night Viking. Thanks to my brothas, Angel and Elias, and Carlito Vestweber.

Thanks to Joe B. III, Becky G., and the booksellers of Malvern Books, past and present.

Texas-Czech: Bohemian-Moravian Bands 1929–1959 was a great inspiration, particularly "Circling Pigeons Waltz" by John R. Baca's Orchestra, along with "La Carta" by Violeta Parra and "La Noche de Mi Mal" by Chavela Vargas.

This book wouldn't be in your hands without the vision and insight of Soumeya B. Roberts, for finding this query (scribbled, smudged, and torn, fluttering in a vast wasteland) and believing in it with such dedication, and also for helping figure out the riddle of it.

Majorly grateful for Jackson Howard really clicking with this story and taking a chance as my editor—what an incredible process it's all been. Grateful for Emily Bell, Sean McDonald, Abby Kagan, Na Kim, Logan Hill, Chloe Texier-Rose, and everybody working at the MCD × FSG Originals laboratory.

And thank you, forever, to Taisia K.